Prior to being developed
for the Cutting Edge series,
Stained was short-listed for
the Sanlam Award for Youth
Literature in South Africa.
Author Joanne Hichens lives in
Cape Town, South Africa, where
she writes mainly crime fiction
and short stories.

IN THE SAME SERIES

Bone Song
SHERRYL CLARK

Breaking Dawn
DONNA SHELTON

Don't Even Think It
HELEN ORME

Gun Dog
PETER LANCETT

Marty's Diary
FRANCES CROSS

Seeing Red
PETER LANCETT

See You on the Backlot
THOMAS NEALEIGH

The Finer Points of Becoming Machine
EMILY ANDREWS

The Only Brother
CAIAS WARD

The Questions Within
TERESA SCHAEFFER

Stained

JOANNE HICHENS

Stained
JOANNE HICHENS

Series Editor: Peter Lancett

Published by Ransom Publishing Ltd.
51 Southgate Street, Winchester, Hampshire SO23 9EH, UK
www.ransom.co.uk

ISBN 978 184167 715 6

First published in 2009
Copyright © 2009 Ransom Publishing Ltd.
Cover by Flame Design, Cape Town, South Africa

For my daughter Jessica,
with love

stain: v.1 mark or discolour with something that is not easily removed. **2** damage (someone's or something's reputation). **3** colour with a penetrative dye or chemical. n. **1** stubborn discoloured patch or dirty mark. **2** a thing that damages a reputation. **3** a dye or chemical used to colour materials.

South African Concise Oxford Dictionary

CHAPTER 1
So you like babies?

Crystal September is opening up to me like she never has before. Crystal is mostly like barbed wire these days. Keep out. Touch and I'll cut. She didn't used to be this way. This is since she left school to have a baby.

'They talk about getting pregnant like it's AIDS or something. Put the fear of the Lord into you about having a baby,' Crystal says, 'but motherhood grows on you, really.' She seems content right now. The two of us sip tea at the table in her mother's kitchen. Ricardo, propped in his pram, babbles his contribution to the conversation.

'You want to know what motherhood is like, Grace? I'll tell you, on the good days it's not so bad.' Crystal leans forward and plants a loud kiss on Ricardo's forehead.

'What about the bad days?' This is what I want to know. Gory details please.

'You know what my philosophy is, Grace? Don't tell people your troubles. Don't tell people anything much at all. If they ask, lie. Forget the bad days.'

'There must be something you can say about how tough it is, being a mother and all?'

'No one is interested in hearing troubles.'

'There must be someone you can talk to about the bad days.' I encourage Crystal, hoping she'll describe shitty nappies, or the trials of breastfeeding, or at least confirm what a hassle it is trying to lose the extra weight. Anything. I have a school project to write.

'If you tell people the truth, they turn away. Forget about the bad days, Grace. Ricardo is here now. So what can I do about it?'

Shardonnay, Crystal's sister, slams the front door right then, calls *Hey* as she comes through and dumps her rucksack under the kitchen counter, then skips out into the passage.

'Hey, Shardonnay, what does anybody know about anything?' Crystal yells at her sister's back as Shardonnay runs up the stairs to her room. 'Shardonnay, I'm talking to you.' Darkness clouds Crystal's face, her mouth tightens. 'Shardonnay, for one, doesn't understand.' Crystal looks at me as if I do, so I nod my head, hoping she'll at last give up the juicy bits.

Crystal is sunshine and storm. Her eyes are sapphire blue, but when the darkness takes her mind, her eyes turn black as night. This is the best we've done for a long time and I don't want to say the wrong thing right now and piss her off. My notebook is open on the grimy table. It's cold in this kitchen. There is no sun here. Only the smell of damp. I tear a page from my notebook, and wedge the folded paper under one leg of the table to keep it still. I'm waiting.

Crystal doesn't have to tell me how difficult it was in the first few weeks when Ricardo had colic, crying for hours every evening before he fell exhausted to sleep. Martha, my foster mother, and I heard him from our side of the wall. Poor little bugger, screeching his lungs raw.

Crystal sighs, as if this interview on pregnancy and motherhood is now hard to bear. She gets up and mixes the formula with boiling water from the kettle. She reads aloud instructions from the label on the tin of *Promil* milk powder.

'Six scoops *Promil* to two hundred millilitres water. Put some of this practical stuff into your project, Grace. Help girls who have babies.'

Crystal absent-mindedly hands the baby his bottle. I snatch it away from his grubby, gripping hands and his open mouth like a baby bird's, and Ricardo wails.

'Hey, Crystal, it's too hot!' Plain common sense warns me the baby will burn.

'Ooooh, sorry little son,' Crystal says. 'Good thing Grace is here. I'm not thinking straight.'

She coos over Ricardo, distracts him with a yellow plastic spoon, making it fly around in front of him like a budgie on the loose. His smile stretches into dimples, a family trait shared by Crystal and Shardonnay. He extends his chubby arms and squeals as she lets him grab one of her fingers. He keeps smiling and she says, 'See, Grace? It's not so bad.'

Ricardo looks at me and I pull my mouth skew and he laughs.

'He's the cutest thing,' I croon, and fall right in love with Ricardo. Right then and there, I fall in love with this baby all over again, the same way I do every time I see him.

'Don't get too excited, Grace. He smiles at everybody. Life is hilarious when you hardly born. He doesn't know anything about the real world, does he?'

I risk another of my observation-type questions. 'You're a teen mom. You had to leave school. It must be hard. You know, nearly done with school to being a full-time mother?'

'Isn't that the truth.'

So far Crystal hasn't lost her temper and she doesn't seem to mind talking but still I hesitate before I ask, 'What about Keegan? Does he help?'

'You kidding, right, Grace? Keegan Arnold tells me it's not his baby. I'm not going to fight and struggle in court or anything like that. If he doesn't want to be part of Ricardo's life that suits me fine.'

She walks over to the window and crosses her arms in front of her chest, hugging her body as she looks out into the back yard and the patch of sun there. It's like she's holding herself together.

'D'you need help sometimes?' I ask.

'You volunteering, Grace?'

'Why not?'

'I can always do with an extra pair of hands. Sure, come over and look out for Ricardo when you want.'

'I'm good with babies.'

It's true, I am. I like babies. It's an instinct, I suppose, to take care of creatures that are helpless. I hide my face behind my hands again and then I open my fingers and show Ricardo I'm still there. Peekaboo! He laughs. Two tiny half-moon teeth white as porcelain glisten on his lower gums.

'It's tough now with Benita working

at the old people's home and Shardonnay studying for finals,' Crystal says, then she shouts up the stairs 'or singing those damn pop songs all the time.' She turns her voice down to a reasonable volume. 'You can take him off my hands after school sometimes.'

Crystal yells again, to deaf ears. 'Isn't that right Shardonnay? No time for your little nephew. Too busy with your head in the clouds up there.'

To me Crystal says, 'See what I mean? I can't count on her. Shardonnay doesn't hear a thing.'

'Hey, I hear you, I hear you, Crystal.' Shardonnay crosses the threshold into the kitchen. 'Tell you what, let's go to the *vlei*, Grace. We'll take Ricardo with us. How's that?' Shardonnay looks in my direction, beckons silently. And Crystal shrugs an okay. I get the feeling she's more than happy for us to take Ricardo to the park.

'So, Crystal, can I quote you for my life skills project then?'

'Write what you want, Grace.' Crystal turns away from the three of us, distracted by the budgie chirping in his cage on the counter. 'Wayne's bloody pride and joy,' she murmurs, checking out the budgie from her stepfather's project at Pollsmoor Prison. 'Can you believe hard-core inmates save injured birds and sell them to the public?' Crystal says, running her fingers along the bars of the cage.

'The project's a success, isn't it?' I ask.

'Who would hurt a budgie in the first place, that's what I want to know. And those men in prison, they've murdered somebody. Why would they care a damn about saving a stupid bird?'

Shardonnay and I lift the pram down the steps in front. We leave Crystal brewing in the kitchen. We walk on the pavement along the highway. The highway, Prince George's Drive, separates the rich from the poor like a line drawn. On our side are council houses and duplexes and block on block of dreary council flats. Beyond that is shackland, stretching for miles, made up of thousands of one-room structures of wood and corrugated iron, covered in plastic to keep out the rain when it comes. People in them waiting for a proper roof over their heads. Hardly any green on this side of the highway. No trees, no grass. On the mountain are the mansions with gardens and views of the sea.

We walk past a length of wall painted with Disney characters. Maybe someone reckoned this would brighten the place up or stop the gangsters spraying their tags all over. If you keep going this way, after a long walk you'll get to the dunes and the sea. If you head in the opposite direction, then you'll hit Cape Town. Only an hour by train to a different world, to skyscrapers and tourists, where the sun sets late in the evening, where there's money and opportunity and people are moving on up.

At the park, we go for the swings meant for little kids, not us. We squeeze our bums into hollow tyres and swing back and forth, our school shoes scraping in the depressions at our feet. Just dirt. Just grey. The weather long ago stripped the colours from the roundabout, the jungle gym, the seesaw. Kids hardly play here in case there's gangsters about. But you can't stop having a life just because you might get shot by a stray bullet.

Today it's warm out, with this unseasonal wind, the *berg* wind, like heavy breath. The summer is close, though this wind will bring rain.

Shardonnay's hair is tied in a ponytail and pulled back sleek against her skull. When she wears it loose, it falls to her shoulders in silky layers and frames her face. Not like mine, kinky and dark from the brown side of my family. You notice her cheekbones as smooth as polished apples, and the dimples under them, and the cat-green eyes shining at you from a complexion like amber. Her tunic is way shorter than regulation length and her socks are rolled at her ankles. Even after a long day of boredom and stress at Capricorn High she smells like mandarin and peppermint, or magnolia, or forest fern. She smells like the fancy shower gels she spends money on. Apart from that, her skin glows honey-gold, storing the sun in it. I understand why the boys want to be close to her.

Ricardo has fallen asleep. His bottle hangs from his mouth. Eyelashes rest on plump baby cheeks. I want to reach over and stroke his face, but I know better. Let sleeping babies lie. We're quiet for a bit, then Shardonnay starts on her favourite subject: Ramon Hill.

'He's so hot,' she sighs. 'I've never felt like this about a guy.'

I've heard this before but I don't say anything, me being a good listener and all, as Shardonnay says I am.

Ramon is hot, she's right. He's tall and taut, his hair straight and black, kept off his face by a cowlick. He's the coolest guy in the school, but his middle name starts with a Capital T for trouble. I know that. But I don't say it. Ramon, with his new silver *Citi Golf* that his father bought him for his eighteenth birthday. Ramon with his skew tie and his shirt hanging loose from his longs, the white of the shirt contrasting against cappuccino arms. And on top of all that, straight white teeth in a wide smile. An all round heart-stopper. Red-hot like fire. Unpredictable. No wonder so many girls are in love with him.

'His mouth is so soft,' Shardonnay says. 'I know he loves me by the way he kisses me. Gentle, warm. I can kiss him for hours.'

'Doesn't he want something more?'

'They all want that,' she laughs and twists herself in the swing. 'We clubbing Friday night. You should come, Grace, break out a bit.'

'Martha would say no, I bet.'

'The evil foster mother spoiling your chance for fun? Easy, Grace. Just don't ask her. Don't tell her a thing.'

'I'll think about it.' I put an end to what would otherwise be Shardonnay trying to convince me how I'm missing out. We talk about this and that, Ricardo being no trouble at all, asleep the whole time in his pram.

Shardonnay runs to the slide and slips to earth. She hangs upside down from the ladder on the jungle gym, her knees hooked over the top rung, her hair coming loose from the hairgrips on either side of her middle parting. She's flashing white panties sprinkled with red hearts, and laughs when I say she's immodest.

'Get a life, Grace.'

Sure, that's my problem. I like babies, I do my homework, I'm neat and tidy and I'm responsible. I don't have a life.

Back home, the duplex smells of Cobra Wax. Martha's been busy. She calls me from the yard. She's planted pansies in a pair of old hiking boots. Peace in the home spills from the top of a pot shaped as a head, the matted plant is green hair. A ceramic frog smiles from under geraniums in the bed alongside the vibracrete wall that is the border between our duplex and the September's – Crystal and Shardonnay and their mother Benita, and Wayne their stepfather. Martha's on about the spring coming, and attracting sugarbirds to the birdbath she bought on sale at Garden City, then she says, 'Will you sweep the yard once I've planted the new creeper?'

'Sure, Martha.' The 'Stardust' pink azalea – that's what the label says – has left a trail of soil where she's dragged it across the paving stones. Martha's pampered Maltese mutt is lying in his basket in the sun. He blinks at me the same way Martha does sometimes, as if she can't quite make out what I'm about.

Martha is earth. Solid. Stable. She wears kaftans of swirling florals, in greens, oranges and browns. Her thinning bob is tinted auburn, with low-lights she calls them, streaks bleached to tangerine. I'm relieved I don't share her genetic material. She's a lump of lard. She's given up on losing the rolls of blubber. She blames her thyroid problem.

Apart from trying to get her garden to grow, there is another area of priority – as Martha puts it – in her life. And this is me.

My name is Grace. A Christian name chosen for me by my foster mother, Martha, to show that God has bestowed his mercy and his blessing on me. I was left. But I was found. And I am loved.

CHAPTER 2

I want to be a star!

Tuesday morning Martha calls outside my bedroom.

'Hurry up, Grace, it's nearly seven.'

I look sideways at my clock radio, useless on the dresser if I don't set the alarm the night before. I've overslept.

I'm dressed for school and brushing my teeth. Accidentally, I spit a streak of toothpaste on my blazer as I'm rinsing. Even after I've wiped it, there's a faint mark on the lapel. I rub harder but it's still there. So what? I throw the cloth on the floor. The hem is coming loose at the side of my tunic.

I could sew it up using Martha's emergency kit in the bathroom cabinet. On most days that's what I'd do, fix it. But I leave that, too. Today I will not live up to my reputation – neat, tidy, responsible.

'Here, at least have an apple,' Martha says when I tell her I don't have time for breakfast.

Please! I'm not a kid any more. I want to yell, *don't treat me like a child*, but I bite my lip, hard, till I taste blood.

'I've packed your lunch. Have a nice day!' She waves and blows me a kiss the same way she did when she dropped me off at Meadowlands when I was a little girl. Still putting treats in my lunchbox. Still putting notes on my pillow to be read at bedtime. *I love you. You are special, Sugar-shoes, Sweet-toes, Cupcake.* Still blowing me kisses, like I'm still going to pre-school.

Education, education, education. Martha's voice is in my head. *That's the only thing that'll take you out of this life. I don't own a house. I don't have shares or money to leave you. There's no inheritance, Grace. You'll have to make your own way.* And believe me, I want to make my way.

Today at school, I can't concentrate, and admittedly I don't try too hard. I'm wondering about Shardonnay and why the *skinner* behind her back doesn't bother her; all those whispers and cell phone messages and the rumours spreading around the school. She's immune to gossip about herself.

At break, Hazel Hendricks spits *Teef* at Shardonnay as she walks past Sha and me sitting on the bench. As if Shardonnay hasn't been called a bitch before.

'You quicker than the MacDonald's Drive-thru,' Raquelle Rogers adds, just quiet enough so that the guys standing down the drag, with their hands in their pants and grins on their faces, don't hear. 'You think you can be a star? You haven't got what it takes. Your claim to fame is you a slut, that's all. See what the guys are doing? They checking out your tits, Shardonnay September, on their cell phones. Showing yourself like that, for the whole wide world to see.'

'You just jealous.' Shardonnay shrugs off the insults as the girls walk away.

'That Hazel is a bitch is all,' Sha says. 'She and Raquelle been giving me a hard time since I made it so far in *Pop Idols* last year. That picture's a bit of cleavage that's all.' She turns and looks me right in the eye. 'Just watch me, Grace. I'm gonna be a star. I'm gonna make it this time. They just pissed off they didn't even make it through the first round. One judge said Raquelle's screech was like nails against a blackboard.' Sha shakes her head as her eyes follow the girls walking across the quad. 'Look at them, their own tunics couldn't get any higher. Who do they think they kidding? They after Ramon, I tell you, always giving him looks like you wouldn't believe, hey, Grace.'

And sitting there next to her, feeling the warmth of her, I know it's true – that the girls are jealous. Because all the boys want Sha. Shardonnay is the prize.

In maths Mr Saayman tells Clint he's retarded. *How you made grade eleven is a miracle*, he shouts. He calls Theo a redface.

If I had the guts I'd stand up to the jerk. I'd tell him he's supposed to be an example to us. He's the teacher and what are we learning? He's not supposed to insult us. But hey, I'm not going to rock the boat. I won't waste my energy.

In Life Skills, Mrs Williams says, 'Don't use slang or swear in your essays. Express your ideas clearly. Take an interest in the world around you. You *can* make a difference.' She hands back our essays, titled *Ten Years of Democracy*. She marks in green, says it's healthier. She explained once she's never liked red. Where she comes from in Mitchell's Plein there's too

many stains on the pavements – the spilled
blood of children involved in gangs and
selling sex and drugs, and stopping those
stray bullets. *Mind you don't end up that
way*, she says. *Pay attention. Work hard
in school and make something of your life.*
She talks about Mitchell's Plein like it's
another country, not ten minutes by taxi
along Prince George's Drive.

'How's your project on teen pregnancy
going?' Mrs Williams asks me on my way out
the door. She looks at me as if she knows she
can count on *me*, at least, to hand work in
on time. I tell her I'm still doing research.

The bell rings and we're out of there.
She calls after us, 'Don't leave it till the last
minute, people.'

Shardonnay's eyes are closed. Her face
is relaxed. Her soft mouth smiling. She's
humming to the tunes in her head, both of
us waiting for Miss Hugo in the music room.
And when Miss Hugo comes, me, I just

hang out there. Sitting, leaning against the wall, I tilt my head and look up, away from Shardonnay's face that glows like she's in heaven. I look at blotches on the ceiling, stains the colour of mauve hydrangeas, from the winter leaks. Each year another flower forms on the ceiling of the music room of Capricorn Senior. The frame around a print of some composer or other, sitting at his piano with his head bowed, is warped from the rising damp. And paint flakes off the walls too, collecting on the navy carpet. What's the handyman done? He's put burglar bars on the windows to stop the gangsters from trashing the place worse than the weather.

I listen to Shardonnay breathe life into a classic *Norah Jones*, her voice as breathless and wistful and jazzy as Norah herself. She lifts her arms and spins around, she's that pleased to be singing. Born to sing, just like the words say to anyone who comes along.

'I'm going to try out for *Idols* again, Miss Hugo. How else am I going to get away from Prince George's Drive?'

Miss Hugo laughs. 'You can do your audition for *Idols* whenever you want. You've got the voice. You'll go far. But enough for today.'

Shardonnay is for real about wanting to be a star. Forever listening to the latest pop tunes and singing in break and humming in class. Practising, preparing for the next competition.

When the teacher leaves, Sha says, 'If Charlize Theron from Benoni can do it, then I can do it. Why can't it happen to Shardonnay September from Muizenberg? I'm choosing *Hip Hop* for my dress when I collect my award at the Grammies, after I cut my first record. Yes, Grace, I see myself on stage, the crowd going wild! Hearts and souls will fall in love with Shardonnay September!' she laughs, happy for now, those cat-eyes lit like she's been switched on.

I have my dream too. But then I feel a sting on my arm and look closer to see a flea jump away, disappearing into the worn pile of the carpet. A flea on my skin doesn't bother me. It's a reality check that's all.

On the way home, Shardonnay says, 'Just watch, Grace. When I win *Idols*, I'll be going places.'

'Where d'you have in mind, Sha?'

'I'm gonna see those big white letters that spell out HOLLYWOOD. I'll go to LA, get into showbiz.'

Martha's got this calendar called Great Destinations, hanging on the back of the bathroom door. She got it from a travel agency. There's all these glossy pics of great places you can travel to. Ancient Greece! Magical Mexico! Sunny Bahamas! I'll take any of those places, thank you very much. Me and my backpack.

I say, 'You go ahead and take Hollywood by storm, Sha. I'll settle for the laid-back life.'

'You? Never, Grace. You gonna change the world. But me, I wanna be a star.

Who wouldn't want to be? Hey, did you know Charlize Theron's mother shot her dad in front of her when she was fourteen?'

'Everybody knows that.'

'I guess she still thinks about it. I wonder what he did, to get shot like that by his own wife?'

'Get the latest *YOU* and read all about family murder!'

'Seriously, Grace, men that get killed by their wives, they must be pretty twisted. They get what they deserve.'

In her room, Sha turns up the music, stands on her bed. Shakes her hair loose. Satin ballet shoes hang from a hook in the wall behind her, alongside a photo of Shardonnay in a tutu and angel wings, taken when her daddy was still alive. On the opposite wall, the one she faces now, is a framed commendation presented to her father when he was a cop, and a collage of ten thousand eyes – the fans of Sha's dreams.

'You know how long it took me to cut out all those eyes? A bloody long time,' she says. Eyes that stare and worship.

She belts out some pop, thrusts her pelvis, the bell-bottoms she's changed into just about falling off her hips. It's pretty good if you're into karaoke. But there's a richness to Shardonnay's voice and a confidence about the way she sings into the shampoo bottle that makes you listen. She could be the real thing.

Before the song is over, Wayne, her stepfather, bangs on her door. 'Turn the goddamned racket off.'

Sha jumps off the bed. 'Shit, I didn't know he was home,' she whispers.

CHAPTER 3
Party girl

Martha has fed me, clothed me, kissed grazed knees, paid school fees, schlepped me to Sunday school and church, for as long as I can remember. *An education, Grace, is all I can give you*. That's her mantra. Plus a dose of God on the side. I'm sick of it.

Friday night I lie to her.

Ramon Hill, extra-hot in black denims and a black Diesel shirt and his midnight hair sleek and shining, picks us up round the corner from Sha's and mine, then gets Freddy Martin at his flat. They stop at the abandoned container that used to be a satellite police station, on the corner of

Prince George's and Faure. Freddy rushes in and out for the hits of *tik. Tik-tik,* Freddy says, is the sound of the crystals as they pop around in the light bulb before you pull in the smoke and get high.

'This, Ramon, is good stuff,' Freddy says, waving a fistful of straws of the crystal meth at Ramon and then at us, me and Shardonnay sitting in the back. 'I got extra to chase away the headaches on Monday. And if you fat and want a good figure, this is the drug for you ladies, but I see you don't have that problem.'

His eyes linger on *my* shape, Sha being definitely Out Of Bounds. Freddy's curls are gelled springs on top of his head. I don't ever want to touch Freddy, with his leer, and his pimples between the pinpricks of stubble on his neck.

Ramon parks the *Citi Golf* right outside Liquid Dreams. Before I get out of the car, I say to Shardonnay, 'Martha would kill me if she knew I was here.'

'Hey, you feeling guilty, Grace?'

'A bit.' But it's more than that. Freddy, with his wet mouth, gives me the *grills*, the creeps.

'But she won't know you here, hey, will she? Unless you tell her.'

'She wouldn't like it, that's all.'

Inside the club Shardonnay smiles over her drink at me. 'Hey, Grace, good thing she didn't check you out in those clothes.'

'She'd freak out.'

'You look twenty-one in that crossover top. And *stunn-ing*, girl. You got your alibi, Grace. She thinks you going to a movie right? If she gives you shit or whatever, tell her what a brilliant *fliek* it was. Long too. And how you went for coffee afterwards to discuss the ins and outs. She'll be impressed! Tell her to call your friends. We'll vouch for you. Ha, ha!'

'Don't they ever check ID?' I ask. Twins who live down the road from the duplex with their single-parent mother gyrate on the dance floor. 'Those girls can't be older than fourteen.' The twins specialise in pelvic thrusts and jerks that get attention, their belly rings glinting in the light. 'They shouldn't be here,' I say, shaking my head.

'What else is there to do on an effing Friday night?' Sha says.

'It's not right.'

'Hey, you joking, right? Get a life, Grace. Chill, you starting to work on my nerves. Just school school school with you. Look, you can do what you want. You sixteen. Martha's not even your real mother. Don't take this trip so seriously, Gracie.'

That's me. I admit it. I'm serious. I do well at school. I'm leadership material. An example to the younger girls. Right. Sure. Sitting here in the deep muck of Liquid Dreams.

'Cheers.' I clink with Shardonnay, the two of us huddled in a dingy booth, me sipping sweet *Brutal Fruit*, Sha taking deep hits from her bottle. The hot-pink satin of the short skirt hugs my hips and bum, but hardly covers my thighs. I cross my legs and the skin-tight micro-mini creeps higher. Freddy fixates on a bare stretch of my flesh, but moves off as soon as some client calls his name – I'm relieved – to do business out of sight.

Ramon is back briefly from wherever, and puts his hand on my shoulder. It's like he touches me and I'm burning. 'Grace, relax. Enjoy yourself.' He sits next to me. His thigh brushing against my leg is an electric shock.

Ramon tilts his chin at Shardonnay and she jumps and follows him to a corner of the dance floor where I watch them get close. Sha's hips melt into his heat.

So it's me at the table on my own. The décor is black walls, black plastic seats. Tables with black tops. A stream of takers at the smokes machine. The DJ in his glass box, earphones on, eyes shut, does the squeaky thing with the vinyl. Nothing liquid about this club, apart from the booze.

Hard-house assaults my eardrums. *Doef, doef, doef,* the mindless never-ending sameness of the dance tracks. The constant beat is as close to me as my heart beat. Merging, taking me over. Smoke spirals at my eyes. The air is dense with warm breath and the smell of sweat and Impulse, and Hugo, and DKNY. I'm dizzy. Ready to explode. I need fresh air. I settle for a sip, hold the bottle to my mouth and drink what's left.

Ramon and Shardonnay grind into each other, and graunch right there on the dance floor, the lights washing over them, moving back and forth, fragmenting their solid bodies.

What happens is the beat – not to mention the *Brutal* booze – gets in my blood. Neat and tidy Grace disappears. I am warm and loose. Shardonnay pulls me to the dance floor. I dance with Shardonnay. She thrusts her hips close to mine. Ramon stays near. Freddy comes back from wherever he disappeared to, and pulls me to him and kisses my neck. Someone calls him away. He tells me, 'Later Babe.'

Justin Timberlake. Ramon grimaces when the music slows down, change of pace type thing. No one likes to like pop. Not in the clubs anyway. Shardonnay belting it out in her bedroom is a different story. But we keep on dancing to *Black Eyed Peas*, to words that tell you there's a problem out there in the world. We keep moving no matter what, to this true song, about people addicted to everything that'll hurt them.

Ramon brings another cooler to me on the dance floor. Fingertips touch. I feel the sizzle. Then – *doef, doef, doef,* back to the dance staples, the music is a headache, back to the beat, beat, beat.

Bummer is, I can't blot out Martha's worried eyes, Martha hovering there in the background. Martha biting her lower lip as her hand reaches to move a damp curl off my forehead. Her likeness is imprinted. I shake my head, but I can't get rid of her.

Fuck you Martha. Watch this. I'm free.

I'm breaking out. I'm doing something nobody would dream 'good' Grace would do. I'm dancing, I'm sexy, swaying, pumping, grinding, going with the flow.

But then Freddy comes near. He grips my hand, pulls me to him. His tongue is wet, probing, hard in my mouth. He says, 'Too bad I can't stay. Business first, Grace, before pleasure. I'll get to know you better next time, Babe.' And suddenly I'm paying attention. I'm wiping my mouth, thinking *no way, this will never happen.* Me and Freddy will never be an item, not at Capricorn High, not here in Liquid Dreams.

I breathe a sigh of relief as I watch him leave out the door, into the black night, and the sensible Grace clutches the neck of her bottle close and takes it slow.

Way after one, Ramon stops the car outside Sha's duplex. I swear I see the curtain move at Martha's window. I bet she's been waiting up all this time.

I go quickly to my bedroom, and I watch them from my window. I spy on Shardonnay and Ramon kissing at her door. His hand moves under her Lycra tube, at her breasts. When they're done deep-throating, Ramon roars off, a flash of silver in the *Citi Golf*. He leaves Sha struggling with the key under the flickering street light, but finally she's in.

I go straight to the bathroom. I pull off my clothes and stuff them in a plastic packet. They stink of ciggies and sweat. I brush my teeth. Rinse my face. My hair reeks of smoke too. In my bra and panties, I walk past Martha's room, past the strip of light under her door.

'That you, Grace?' she calls, her voice a sleepy croak.

'Hi, Martha,' I whisper. Who else could

it be? 'Yes, it's me. I know I'm late. We stayed for coffee after the movie.'

'I'm glad you're home.'

She's turned the bedside light on in my room. There's a mint cream on my pillow, and a note to me, in Martha's best calligraphy that she learned at adult education:

I love you.

You don't need me as much, but when you do, if you do, I'll be there for you.

Martha.

Suddenly I'm glad I lied to her. I try to sleep, but I can't. My mouth is dry. I go to the kitchen for cold water. On the fridge is a print of two tiny hands. My hands. Painted and pressed to the paper when I was just a kid. Martha's kept all this stuff I made when I was small. On a shelf is a clay crocodile, a papier-mâché bowl, a jar decorated with strips of wrapping paper. All this useless, childish trash she's kept.

Back in my bedroom, I rip Martha's note in half. I'm bleary eyed and reckon I could fall asleep before my head hits the pillow, but I have an urge to look at my real mother. I slide the photograph from under my mattress. I touch the face of the dark-skinned woman in the photo. She's standing on the beach, her feet sinking into the sand, her flimsy sundress blown between her thighs by the sea breeze. She's smiling for the photographer, his shadow at her side. Her sandals are placed neatly alongside one another, on her beach mat of straw. My mother had to be as young and pretty as the woman in this picture. My mother is not a mountain of flesh with varicose veins. In my mind, my real mother is fresh and young.

Unless she's made enquiries about me there's no way I'm ever going to find her. Martha knows the date my mother left me, wrapped up, cared for, clean and fed, at Cape Town station. But that's all she knows. Sometimes I wonder if the truth is ugly. Like it wasn't worth my mother's while to hang on to me. That I was found thrown away in a bin, crying because of the pain of hunger. That my mother dumped me because she didn't want me, not because – as Martha says – she wanted a better life for me. I put this version of my mother in the mental *outbox*.

The pretty photograph goes back in the cardboard box at the top of my wardrobe, along with the others.

Of course she loved me.

I light a match, set fire to Martha's note. The halves burn close to my fingertips, then to ash in the metal bin. I lie down. Some drunk sings in the street. A loose gate bangs in the wind. Cars rev, some guys dice on the highway. There's a crack, like a backfire, or a gun. My head settles into the slight spin. I'm dreaming of Ramon. I dream of his lips parting, his teeth glinting in the light, and the smell of him, hot and musky.

CHAPTER 4

The places I want to visit…

I could have been born anywhere, but I tell people Cape Town. If you say something often enough then it's true. Martha's always wanted me to call her Mom, but I don't. It's like that would be true then, and she's *not* my mother. If she could read my mind she'd have a stroke this second. She'd repeat the list of everything she's done for me over the years. Yadda yadda yadda, *fed you, clothed you, kissed your skinned knees.*

My biological mother loved me, I know it. I like to think she loved me so much, she gave me up because she had dreams for me. She couldn't afford to give me what she wanted. Even the basics she couldn't give me. From the cupboard I take out the threadbare baby blanket she'd wrapped me in, and think myself lucky that she made the sacrifice of giving me up. I was found tucked under a bench on an arrivals platform. Did I come from Beaufort West? Or the Karoo? She could have brought me from any number of hopeless *dorpies* – dull one-horse towns, with names like *Droerivier, Vergenoeg, Bittereinde* – dotted along inland routes in the SA map book. Dry River, Far Enough, Bitter End. Or – preferably – she brought me from a breezy coastal stop, from Pearly Beach, the Stand or Gordon's Bay.

So I'm lying there the next morning, warm, curled under the duvet, the baby blanket drawn under my chin. I'm wondering about the truth of where I was born – Was it in a state hospital some place? Are there records? – when Martha knocks for the second time, 'Grace, are you going to make it to the pet shop?'

I flash to Melvyn Green waiting for me behind the desk, tapping against the edge of the counter with a rawhide dog twist. *You're late. What is this job worth to you?* Mumbling as he sorts hooves, pigs' ears, catnip. *Youth of today, don't take anything seriously.*

If I don't go I'll never hear the end of it from Martha, let alone Melvyn Green. *I trust you on the till, Grace, I trust you with the creatures, Grace.*

Melvyn Green looks like a creature himself, a cross between a fish and a hamster, with his bulging eyes and protruding teeth. Why couldn't I at least have a good-looking boss? Someone to sweat over in slow times.

It's as if the real Grace is trying to get loose here, trying to rip off the label attached to her chest. The responsible one. The good example. The girl you can count on. I reckon I've been making up all my life for being left at the station.

I suck in a deep breath. Stretch into my length, arms above my head, forcing the energy to flow into stiff muscles, and will myself upright. It doesn't work. I stay horizontal under the duvet, dark blue with stars on it, and I'm wishing it was still night and I was in my dreams. With Ramon.

'You'll be late,' Martha trills, trying desperately not to nag, but nagging all the same. I'm Grace Hunt. Hunted. Worn down. Harassed. I want to shout through the door, *Fuck off, Martha. I'm tired. I was up late last night. I'm not going in today. For once I'm not going in. Screw this Saturday job.*

I sit up, swing my legs over the edge of the bed. My feet touch the carpet. Actually, I feel fine. Steady. The couple of coolers I had the night before hardly did a thing to me. I wonder about Shardonnay and Ramon and Freddy. I wonder how they handle the action Friday, Saturday, Sunday nights? I cup my hand at my mouth, blow into the cave and smell my breath of stale booze.

There's time for a quick shower. I wash the smoke from my hair.

Martha nags again. 'You having breakfast?'

Always on about bloody breakfast, even on the weekend she goes on about cereal and fruit being a good start. *Most important meal of the day, Grace. Your carbohydrate gives you energy, keeps you going, and fruit is full of vitamins* – not that she ever eats any – *you can eat as many apples, naartjies, pears as you like!*

'OK, Martha,' I call. 'I'm up, I'm dressed, I'm coming,' I let her know so she'll shut up.

At the table, Martha peers at me over the cereal box. Blinking. Waiting. Stroking the mutt in her lap. She wants information. I know she won't press me but she wants to know all the same. She has this way of raising her pencilled eyebrows and tilting her head slightly to one side, asking a body language question: *When will you come clean and tell me?*

My spoon bounces against the porcelain cereal bowl, the clink, scrape, slurp of breakfast punctuates the silence. She can't take the wait any longer.

'How was your night out? Didn't we say home before midnight?'

There's no ranting and raving but there's an edge to her voice.

'Nothing to tell, Martha. Saw a movie. Talked. That's about it.'

'How did you sleep?'

'Like a baby.' This part is true. When I eventually *got* to sleep.

She sighs. 'Pass me the sugar.'

She's diabetic. She wants me to care, say something like *No Martha, here's the Canderel instead.* I pass her the sugar. Dainty cubes in a bowl she keeps for me. Pale pink and green and blue. *Have six lumps, Martha. Send your insulin haywire.*

I stand and smooth down my Mr Price hipsters. *I don't have to tell you a thing, Martha.*

'What's happening to you? I worry about you,' Martha says.

Overprotective. Ruining my life. *Screw you, Martha.* I run out the door, past Crystal and Ricardo, mother and baby outside the flat, catching the early sun. Crystal is sitting on the steps writing in her notebook. When she sees me looking she slides the small notebook with the black cover quickly into the pram, alongside Ricardo. She scowls, as if she's been caught out. As if I haven't noticed before that she scribbles in there, trying to keep the writing a secret.

From The Journal of Crystal September

I went out yesterday. To the clinic. Even with the baby, men still notice me. It's my smile. Always has been. Me and Shardonnay with Daddy's dimples. Which was all Daddy left us apart from a whole lot of pain. And he wasn't even killed in the line of duty. No, a button spider got him. His arm swelled up like a rugby ball. At the hospital they cleaned out the poison but it was too late.

I put Ricardo in the pram. I strapped him in tight, and pushed the bottle in his mouth. He loves his bottle. He never says no to his bottle. It was hot out, with the Berg wind. I felt the sun on my back as I pushed him first along the highway, then round the circle and up Atlantic Road towards the clinic. There was a man there at the steps, on his way to the library with his pile of books. But as soon as I smiled, he put the books down right there on the steps and helped me carry Ricardo up. What a nice looking man too. With a nice car. And a nice wife waiting for him in the passenger seat.

I held my head a little higher. Pushed my burden in through the doors. And when I was done at the clinic, I pushed Ricardo past the school. Keegan Arnold. Letisha. Zelda. All of them finished with school. Getting on with their lives.

At home, Ricardo was asleep already. I kissed Ricardo on his eyes, his baby flesh *so warm and soft through my lips. I know I love him. Sometimes, in small moments alone with him, I know I love my child. My flesh and blood. None of this is his fault. He didn't ask to be born. But here he is, isn't he? So pretty when he's sleeping.*

I stroked his cheek, like cool velvet, and wheeled him to the kitchen and covered him with a blanket. The blanket Grace from next door gave me at the baby shower. Yellow and white crocheted treble stitches. Worn and soft. From when Martha made it for Grace when she was a baby. Grace didn't want it any more, she said. That Grace, though, is starting to get on my nerves asking all these questions about what it's like to be a mother.

As if I could ever tell her.

I must say though, the baby shower is a nice memory. From the others I got a rattle, a frame decorated with teddies. Nappies, baby shampoo, cream. And all the necessaries like Fissan paste for his rash and Dr Martin's colic mixture. Martha gave the baby a silver moneybox. Of course it's not real silver. It's silver plate, and no way can I save anything to put in there.

At the baby shower we ate samoosas, chicken pies, rooti, milk tart, doughnuts. Letisha said to me, 'At least you don't have to write exams now, girlfriend, you lucky!'

This is my life now.

Ricardo is my life.

I catch a taxi to the Blue Route Mall. At Animals R Us I clean the hamsters' cages. Wipe the fish tanks. Kids come in and smear sticky fingers against the glass I've just cleaned. A little boy pleads to hold a bunny. *Or a guinea pig, please!* It's against policy. Melvyn tells me that once he let a kid hold a dwarf hamster, and the kid squeezed the hammie so tight its eyes popped right out of its head. At the end of my shift, I pocket a miniature rawhide bone for Martha's mutt.

Stained

I make a stop at Music City. Put on earphones and listen to *Staind*. Off-centre stuff. About kids screaming messages to parents they just don't get.

CHAPTER 5

Rollercoaster ride

Back at the duplex, Ramon's *Citi Golf* is parked in the street. He's with Sha. Not me. This is reality. Not some stupid dream.

The mutt gets all excited at the treat, wagging his backside and scampering out to the yard. He collapses in a lavender bush in the sun, chews the bone there. Next door, Crystal is hanging the brights on the line. Ricardo's small clothes. And Shardonnay's purple dress that she got on lay-bye at Truworths for last year's *Pop Idols* audition.

Shardonnay's come in now, and calls over the wall, 'Come with us to the carnival, OK Grace? Meet you in front.'

The carnival is a community effort to raise funds for charity, so Martha doesn't give me a hard time about going. If the vibes had a voice though, I'd be hearing: *Why are you hanging out with this group? When will you be home? At least tell me that. What about your school work?*

Stuff the schoolwork, Martha.

So I set off with Shardonnay and Ramon and Crystal and Ricardo to the carnival in Wynberg. Ramon stops to pick up Freddy. He sits in front, thank God. Us girls and Ricardo squeeze into the back.

We wander around, part of a crush of all ages, along dirt paths between stalls selling sweets and baby clothes and second-hand books. There's chances to win stuffed animals and junk, playing pop the balloon and guess the number of jelly beans in the jar. It's all good. At the Greek stall a group of kids dances to traditional bouzouki. Ramon downs an Ouzo. 'Why not try something new?' he says, his breath smells like liquorice. We move along past stalls of a host of nations, past India, China, France, USA, Zambia, past Holland where Styrofoam shapes have been cut to recreate a Dutch street.

Being here reminds me of Martha's calendar. All those places I want to go.

The furthest I've been is Montague Springs in the off-season, when Martha has the sulphur baths all to herself and floats around and orders cocktails with little umbrellas in them. Martha buoyed by the minerals and salts and her good spirits at being on holiday.

The guys stop for a hot dog. Sha and me say *no thanks*. Even though my mouth is watering for the spicy sausage with onions and tomato, cool chicks don't scoff in front of the guys. We sit on the grass in front of the stage and listen to the latest *Pop Stars* group, and our stomachs' rumbling. My gut is churning. I'm watching Ramon eat. The crisp skin of the sausage pops. I want to lick off the fat dribbling down Ramon's chin.

'Hey, can you believe this bunch won? There's hardly a good voice in the lot,' Shardonnay moans. 'Look at their moves, hey, there's no natural rhythm. They sing so off, I can't believe it. Singing the same old song they got famous for. I tell you Grace, I can do better.'

Crystal asks if I mind watching Ricardo. 'I'm gonna wander around a bit. Seeing as you all watching the band.'

'Go, Crystal, I'll look after him,' I offer. 'He has his bottle and his blanket. He has me. Don't worry about him.'

She hardly looks back.

Ramon and Freddy pull out a couple of beers from under their jackets, sneaked out of the beer tent. Everybody is having a good time. Mothers, babies, fathers, toddlers, kids and carefree teenagers.

When Crystal comes back, we go to the rides. Ramon watches Ricardo. Me and Shardonnay and Crystal scream on the rides, like kids, letting rip.

On the Octopus, I shriek, my stomach somersaults. This crazy person is me, Grace Hunt out of control, doing as she pleases. In the Cage I stretch my arms above my head. The G-force pulls me back against the wire mesh. I keep my eyes open. I don't scream. I don't have to. I'm loving the freedom. I want to go again and again.

Down side is, Freddy wants to ride along. Sweaty Freddy with his pimples and his slicked-back hair and his pockets full of packets. In the ticket queue Freddy squeezes my hips. 'C'mon,' he points to the Big Wheel, 'we'll scope out the neighbourhood from up there.' But Sha calls me to look after Ricardo. I shrug and run off.

The last ride we do is the Spook Train. Freddy shunts Sha off her seat and sits right next to me before I can make an excuse. In the dark tunnel Freddy puts his arm around me, cops a feel of my breast. This is way worse than any ghosts and shit that's supposed to scare us. He whispers

'You should spend your bucks on the real high. These rides cost more than a straw of *tik* you can buy at Liquid Dreams. And for you I'll give it to you free.' He nuzzles my neck, his stink breath in my ear, asks *do you want to suck my cock?* I pretend I don't hear.

I hear Martha in my head. *You're special, you don't ever have to do anything you don't want to do.*

We're home by ten. Even Crystal had a good time.

Martha says 'Grace, the family service starts at half past nine tomorrow. You can sleep in a bit.'

I'm supposed to feel excited, right? About one of those services that go on forever, with kids running up and down the aisles and Father Adams joking about bringing them into the fold young, and how outside of God's house is a welcome mat for all. Maids and Madams and babies welcome.

From The Journal of Crystal September

The first thing to do is you have to find out if you pregnant. I paid sixty-two rand for a pregnancy test from the chemist. Foolproof, the chemist said. I did it early in the morning, before anyone else was up. I wanted to do it that night, but I waited for morning. I followed the instructions like I knew I should. Peed on the strip and waited to see if the blue lines would show. Which they did. Then I knew for sure I was pregnant.

I sat on the wicker laundry bin in the bathroom for a long time staring at those parallel stripes, till Shardonnay banged on the door and said, what you doing in there, Crystal, you so selfish, you always hogging the bathroom, hurry up, I'm late for school!

I knew soon I wouldn't be going to school any more.

I pushed the baby out just like the nurses told me. Shardonnay was there. And Benita and Wayne, in the passage, waiting for the news of whether it was a girl or a boy.

The next day I brought Ricardo home.

Yesterday when I went to the clinic with Ricardo I waited a long time. The way it is, you wait your turn in the queue for baby-weighing and the shots. There are so many people queuing. Mothers with their babies smothered in blankets. People for HIV tests and pap smears.

There's a box outside Sister's door where you put your baby's clinic card, and then you wait for Sister to take that card from the box and call your name.

You wait, watching other mothers cooing and giggling over their babies. Pulling out their breasts to feed them.

The only empty seat was next to an old man who stared at his broken shoes. I wanted to be sick smelling the red wine on him. On the other side, a large woman, as black as night, with cellulite dripping from her arms, kept sneezing. I wanted to get out of there, but at last it was Ricardo's turn. I had to undress him and sit him on the scale. His fingers flexed, like a starfish, as I let his hand go. His mouth stretched in rage, poor baby, at sitting naked on the cold scoop. The nurse's aide said, he's gaining well, no worries here, as she pencilled in his weight on the card. Ricardo clung to me, wet eyes, his nose running. The nurse handed me a paper towel. Now dress him and wait to see Sister, she said.

It was Sister's tea break. I sat opposite Sister's open door, watching her eat her sandwich, biting neat semicircles into the bread, and chewing slowly. She was reading a You *magazine. I breathed deeply. Stayed calm. When what I wanted to do was grab that sandwich and stuff it down her throat. Sister brushed crumbs from her desk. Washed her hands at the small basin in her room. All this I could see, like slow motion.*

I got up for my turn, but it was someone else's card she took from the box. Not my child's card. I waited two hours. I hate the way Sister looks at me when I go in her room. I can see it in her eyes, that disapproving look she reserves for the young mothers.

She asked how it was going. Alright, I said. No moans now, Sister said. At least you've got your boy. Like Ricardo was a handbag or something, an accessory I'd wanted. She gave me a bottle of StoPain *for his cold.*

Hold him tight now, Sister said. She squirted polio drops into his mouth. Now roll up his vest, she said, as he cried at the horrible taste of the drops. Roll up his vest way up to the top of his arm, she said. Hold him close to your body and grip his elbow. Then Sister jabbed the needle in his arm and he screamed blue murder and dug his fingers into my flesh. Like a burr.

Finally I'm alone. Old Mr Campbell from across the way has kicked his lab-cross out the flat, right into the street. The poor thing is whimpering on his front *stoep* now. Scratching at the door, wanting to get in.

I get the portable CD Martha gave me for my sixteenth, plug in the earphones, and turn up the volume so I don't hear the dog whining, so I don't have to know how damn sad that dog is.

I listen to all these songs about the same thing; so much hurt, and pain, and how hard love is. Who needs it? Any kind of love. We all want it though, don't we?

I touch myself between my legs, lightly, then pull my hand away, like I've touched a hotplate. Guilty all of a sudden, my fingers burning, guilty that I'm poaching Ramon for my dreams. Because that's what I'm doing, imagining me and Ramon together; his arms around my waist, his fringe falling across his forehead, his hot breath on my neck, holding *me*, Grace Hunt, not Shardonnay September.

The neighborhood is quiet. Even Mr Campbell's dog is taking a sleep down there, finally let back in to his tattered basket in the yard. My eyes close.

But I feel Freddy's arm tight around me. Suffocating. He won't let go. I can't breathe.

I wake with a start. I recite the Lord's Prayer. I promise to pay attention to the Gospel. I promise to sing with all my heart in choir practice. I promise to focus on the positive. Pay attention to my school work like Martha begs me to. *Your education Grace, it's all you have. Education will take you places you never dreamed you could go.*

I promise to stay out of clubs, to leave Shardonnay and her angry sister alone. To pay attention to my own life.

CHAPTER 6

Send down your blessing…

Maybe it's not a bad idea to get on my knees and wipe the slate clean, after clubbing and raving at the carnival and perving about Ramon. Not that I'm religious or anything. Church is my concession to Martha, my long-term foster mom. I'm in the choir, too. I don't mind church, actually. The architecture is comforting, and whatever God is, I like to think there's something more to the world than we see.

I get up, brush my teeth, wash my face. Back in my room I look in the full-length mirror and study myself, trying to be objective. Trying to see myself the way the boys see me. Those blazing eyes travelling the length of a girl's body, undressing her right in the school quad, working greedy eyes up and down and nodding their heads – or not, depending on what they see. I'm not too shabby. Sha's right, my stomach is flat enough for a belly ring. I wonder for the millionth time about my parents. Which of them was other than white? Had to be one, or both, to account for the tone of my skin, like milky coffee. Half dressed, I reach up for the box of photos and find another likeness of my mother.

This could be her, this really could. A young woman in her bathing suit running into the waves. Same proportions as me. Full hips, same small waist. My strong point if I'm analysing my figure. Can only guess about her hair, tucked into a cap.

I remember when I was twelve, Martha said, 'You're not going to iron your hair. Tough, but you're not going to do it.' Martha was against me buying one of those hair straighteners. 'You'll ruin it if you iron it. You'll dry it out and burn it and I won't let you.'

What does *she* know about ethnic hair? With that blow-dried bob of hers? So once in a while I get to have my hair done professionally, which costs Martha, but she's doing it because she wants to. She said so. Now I love the Salon. I say thank you and I accept her gift. Next time I'll go for braids that cost a bomb.

I put the old photograph back in the box. Push the box to the back of the cupboard.

Rely on yourself, Grace. This is your life, whoever your mother is or isn't. Get on with your own life. But I can't help looking at a small photograph I've propped up against the mirror; a pretty woman on a swing in some lush garden where the bougainvillea in the background is a bright purple. The lighting is fresh morning, gentle sun filters through the leaves, the blooms so translucent they look as if they're made of tissue paper. I know I have to stop doing this. It doesn't do me any good. No way a girl like this could be my mother. I pluck the pic off the mirror, thinking I'll crush it and toss it in the bin, but I snap it into my purse and put the purse in my bag, along with lipstick, ciggies and collection money for the children's home. Father Adams saves for the kids whose mothers died of AIDS and left them to fend for themselves, and the ones like me whose mothers basically dumped them.

I finish dressing. I grin at the mirror. I've got decent teeth, white and strong. After all these years of Martha nagging me to brush and floss and her 'no sweets' policy, though I'd find the evidence of her own vice hidden behind the pillows on her *Lazee Boy* – the wrappers of chocolates and sweets she'd scoff at night after she sent me to bed. Before she was diagnosed with diabetes.

I'm lucky I haven't had too many pimples. My face is smooth brown. I think I'll do. I'm OK. Through the eyes of the boys, and my own, and what else matters?

All the same, I'm not Shardonnay. Not even close.

When the boys see Shardonnay they fall in lust. It's like you can see the boys stop whatever they're doing when she walks past. They look at her and they forget about what's happening. They don't make rude comments about what's in her panties like they do with some of the other girls. You can see the boys' glistening eyes follow Shardonnay. The boys want to kiss Shardonnay in secret places. The boys *want* Shardonnay.

'Grace...' Martha's knocking on my door. 'I promised Crystal a lift to church. Go on over and hurry her up.'

There's the waft of fresh baking. I catch Martha licking icing off a spoon.

The September's kitchen is cold, even as summer draws near. It's as if the sun never filters through the yellowed lace curtains, like it's given up trying to get light into their lives. The olive green counters are dirty. My soles are tacky on the sheen of grease on the patterned linoleum. Ricardo gurgles in his playpen in the corner. He's shaking a bunch of mixing spoons.

Crystal is painting her nails in the kitchen. One hand with silver-pink nails is spread now over the lip of the chair.

'Good morning Mr September,' I greet Wayne, all trussed up in his Sunday suit, coming in from the lounge with his coffee mug. Church TV is on in the background.

'Hello, Grace. I hear you've been helping out with the baby.'

'Just a couple of times. He's so sweet.'

'We'll see you around more often then.' He smiles, his gapped tooth smile, his eyes a sharp, cold blue, like ice.

'So Crystal, are you coming with us, me and Martha?' I ask.

'Thanks, Grace, but I don't need a lift. Mommy is going to church after all. And so is Wayne.' She looks across the room at her stepfather. 'I'll ride with them.'

'You can drive us there, Crystal,' Wayne

says. 'Can't let all those hours of lessons go to waste. All that time I spent teaching you. You're my investment.'

I remember the lessons came to a halt when Crystal accidentally knocked over a dog in the road, a half-breed stray ending up as road kill. She still hasn't got her licence. There's a giant red letter L on the back of Wayne's *Mazda*.

'Well then, I'll see you at church.' On my way out I ask, 'What about Shardonnay, is she coming?'

Crystal shoots a bullet-look at Wayne. Would be lethal if looks could kill. I wonder what nastiness is happening here.

'Never mind Shardonnay,' he says. 'She's staying home to look after Ricardo. Give her big sister a break. It's tough looking after a young one. Our gift from God.'

I'm wondering if it's still an issue that the 'little bastard', as I've heard Benita call him, doesn't have a father who'll stand up for him. Or is it Benita's dead baby that still haunts their house?

'Don't complain that you never go anywhere, Crystal,' Benita says. 'You say Ricardo ties you down, but look at you, out last night, and today too.'

'Mommy, we went to the community carnival yesterday and this is church,' Crystal says, nervously twisting a button at the bottom of her tailored jacket.

'So what you painting your nails for? And all that make-up? Who you trying to impress?' Benita snaps. 'It's God's house. D'you have to look like a whore in it? I hope it's not the priest you've got your eye on, you little slut.' Benita's mouth is a red slash, like a crossed out wrong answer.

I see the wine glass, on the kitchen table, the rim waxy with the stain of her shade, a deep crimson, and the empty bottle in the sink. The glass reminds me of the wedding and everybody sloshed and the DJ playing all those old numbers. Benita smooching and sucking in everyone with that slash of hers, at the reception at the Scout Hall. Trestle tables laden with a three-course meal – tomato soup, roast chicken, jelly and ice cream. Benita dancing cheek to cheek with her new husband, while her two girls fluttered handfuls of rose petals on the bride and all around.

But that was a long time ago. I'm out the door by this stage, not wanting to stick around to hear them bickering.

I remember that Wayne and Benita were married two years when she found out she was pregnant. She'd just had a fortieth birthday bash. Rented the Tech Football club and called it a combined birthday/baby shower. Her nursing friends clubbed together and bought the Triple-X baby pram. A superior make with canopy to shield baby in rain and sun, with carryall for the shopping underneath the padded seat, extra comfort for baby. I know this because Ricardo now has this pram for himself and the info is all written there on the stuck-on label on the back. In the third trimester the gynaecologist told Benita the baby was in trouble. A week later her baby was dead.

Then she packed away the pram along with the rest of the gifts. She spent a month in bed. Wayne started staying out later. Benita took on night duty at the old age home. The doctors said don't try again. They told her she was lucky to survive, that she too could be dead. Something about raised blood pressure, a mal-formed placenta. Something no one ever talks about.

It's all part of God's plan – Martha talking rubbish, offering her brand of comfort along with veggie soup, stew, pies.

Martha is waiting outside for me in the car.

'You're so quiet, Grace,' Martha says on the way to church.

'Don't feel like talking, that's all.' I'm thinking about how a few months after

Benita's baby died, Crystal got herself knocked up by Keegan Arnold. But he said no way, he didn't want Crystal's baby pinned on him.

We inch along Main Road in heavy traffic. The whole world and his brother heading to the church or the beach or wherever they're going. The sea is deep turquoise, the swells are big. There are surfers out, doing their worship in the ocean.

'Is something bothering you, Grace?'

I don't answer.

Martha tries again. 'Sweetheart, we used to talk more than we do. I know you're growing up, you've got your own life, but sometimes I feel excluded. Please, I want to be part of your life.'

She's irritating me with her baby names and lecture, and doesn't back off, so I say 'There's something I've been thinking about for a long time.'

'Well, what is it?'

'I want to meet my biological mother.'

We drive in silence, stop, start, till she turns left into the parking lot opposite the church. She parks the *Toyota* and sits there with her hands on the wheel, not saying anything. Not even looking at me. Then she leans back into her seat and folds her podgy hands in her lap.

'Grace, this wasn't what I expected,' she says, 'though I knew the day would come.'

'Is it a problem for you?'

'You know how difficult it would be to trace her. Practically impossible.'

'Martha, why are you so negative about this?'

'I'm realistic. I don't want you hurt, that's all.' Her tone is so gentle it gets my back up right then and there.

'We'll be late.' I get out of the car, clutching my bag, wanting a cigarette, blinking super-fast so the tears pooling behind my eyeballs, waiting to spill over, will stop. I could use a big swig of communion wine right about now. I do not want red swollen eyes in church.

I run ahead of Martha. She calls after me, 'We'll talk after the service.' So good about it all. So supportive. So keen to talk things through. *Fuck you, Martha and your hypocrite Mother Mary manner.*

In the ladies' toilet I brush rouge on my cheeks and re-touch the soft shade of coral on my lips. A hint of gold hair mascara glitters on my hairline, a reminder of the carnival. I fix my breasts in the low cut T-shirt. My eyes are fine.

Ramon sits next to me in the choir pews. He joined the choir this year on account of his father being appointed Deacon. Father Adams needed some tenor voices in the choir and Ramon's father volunteered him. Ramon has to work for the new car and the designer duds – Diesel, Nike, Timberland. He has to show what an upstanding young man he is, the heir to his dad's empire, the clothes shop where his father sells cheap copies of all this designer stuff. My heart beats. No way could Ramon know he's the real reason I come to church. Does anyone see the throbbing at my throat? His long legs spread out in front of him in black denims. He's wearing a smart jacket. His tie is straight. His shirt sleeves buttoned at the wrists. He has long fingers with neat nails. The kind of hands, spread out on his knees, you want to have touching you. I glance furtively at his face. God is a joker – why else did he give Ramon such long eyelashes?

The service starts. I don't listen to what Father Adams is on about. All I can concentrate on is the heat of Ramon's leg against mine. On the other side of Ramon there's Hazel Hendricks, her fingernails stroking the length of his thigh as if she was alone with him, not sitting in a packed church. My leg tingles with pins and needles, but I don't want him to think

I even notice that his leg is touching mine, so I keep still. When we stand for Hymn 369 his arm brushes against mine and I think – what is happening, girl? You need a boy like this like you need a hole in the head.

I concentrate on the clarity of my voice and the tune and the words:

O God in heaven whose loving plan

Ordained us for our parents care

In the congregation Crystal and her family and other families from the neighbourhood, all in their Sunday best, sing their hearts out about love and respect for one another:

And from the time our life began

The shelter of a home to share

Martha's jowls quiver. Her bob lies limp on her scalp and pale neck. She wipes the sweat from her forehead with a hanky she

embroidered herself, with daisies and a bee
on it.

Our father on the homes we love

Send down your blessing from above.

Then we pray:

Almighty God, in penitence we confess *and
with sore knees* that we have sinned against
you through our own fault in thoughts *dirty,
about Ramon,* in word and deed *touching
myself* and in what we have left undone *bed,
homework, my life coming undone...* Make
our hearts clean, Oh Lord, and renew a right
spirit within us *me in particular.*

Ramon and the Septembers, and me and
Martha, wait in turn to smile and shake
hands with Father Adams as we file out of
church.

I overhear the fisherman in front of me.
'Come look in the back of the truck. For
you Father, there's something special. The
freshest of yellowtail.'

My mood too, is lifted. I'm not sure if it's the clean slate Father Adams — and let's not forget God — assured me is mine, or if it's the smell of Ramon today, lingering in my imagination, of soap, fresh and clean.

I shake my head to get Ramon out of there. I catch up to Crystal walking up the path to the hall, Benita and Wayne following behind. My mouth waters for a slice of the milk tart Martha baked this morning.

'Crystal, if you not into milk tart, try the caramel cake. Martha's special recipe,' I say but Crystal is in another world. 'Crystal? You there?'

'I'm not really hungry.' Crystal picks at the crushed nuts on the brownie on her plate. Who can blame her being upset, with Keegan there on the other side of the table, barely acknowledging any of us.

Keegan, a catch once, had lost his spine. His bones, his brain and flesh turned to mush when he turned his back on Crystal and the baby.

Shardonnay told me, when Wayne and Benita went knocking at his door – Wayne fierce with his gold tooth and warder's uniform, his baton in his hand slapping his palm the way Shardonnay told it to me – Keegan cowered alongside his mother. He said, 'I swear I never touched Crystal in that way.'

'Keegan has a future,' his mother said. 'My son is going to Technikon or university. No way can he look after a wife and child. Crystal must have an abortion.'

Wayne said, 'It is against God's Law to kill the baby. We need a baby in the house. If it isn't going to be Benita's, it may as well be Crystal's.'

And that's how it was decided.

Send down your blessing...

From The Journal
of Crystal September

Wayne said he'd teach me to drive. I reversed between the orange pylons that were set up in the parking lot near the beach. I knocked one over, then another. Then we drove in the road. It wasn't my fault I hit that dog. Wayne wouldn't let me stop. The poor dog fell at the side. Keep driving, he said, people should take better care of their pets, though I think this one was a stray. On the highway his hand brushed against my thigh. He said drive to Tokai Forest. He gave me directions.

At the Forest there were only a few cars, being a Monday morning. I saw a woman striding along a dirt path with her head down, three Alsatians pulling at their leads. She disappeared around a bend. She could set those powerful dogs on any man who dared threaten her. She would be safe.

It was supposed to be better when Mommy married Wayne.

Mommy said, he's got a good job with the prison services, a stable job, plus medical aid and a pension. He'll give us things we can't afford. He's a generous man. I'm a good-looking lady, why shouldn't I remarry?

I miss Daddy, I said.

I know you do. I'm getting married again so you and your sister can have a father.

Mommy didn't fall pregnant for a long time. What did the doctor say? He said she was suffering from perimenopause. Her body was drying up before her time. No son for Wayne. But then Mommy did fall pregnant. It was a miracle, and Wayne was happy and so was Mommy.

Then she lost the baby. It just fell out in a messy pile on the bathroom floor, Mommy yelling for me to help her, as she clutched at her stomach.

Wayne said, What God giveth, he taketh away.

What are you going to do, Crystal? Letisha Abrahams kept asking when I told her I was pregnant.

I have to have the baby. What else can I do?

You can have an abortion.

Wayne put his foot down. An abortion is out of the question, he said. I am the head of this family. I will not allow a baby to be murdered.

I put on weight. I 'blossomed', people said. I got fat, that's what.

Mommy, I'm scared, I said to Benita. I don't know how to look after a baby.

Don't look at me, girl. Get away from me, Benita said and pulled her arm from my 'grasp', as she called it, and shook me off like I didn't matter. You got yourself into this mess, she said. You sleep around this is what happens. Don't touch me. You've made your bed.

The birth hurt like hell. But you get over these things, don't you? There's no time to dwell on that sort of pain. The worst was the baby sucked my nipples till they cracked. Like, I'm sorry to say, he was sucking the life right out of me.

Keegan Arnold called me a slut and a whore. He wouldn't take a pregnant girl to the end of year farewell. I sat at home that night, with the baby, while the others wore their designer dresses they'd been saving for their whole lives. They got a picture of themselves, all bright and shiny and smiling about their future, in the People's Post.

I saw Keegan today, in church.

He wouldn't greet me. He couldn't even look at me.

CHAPTER 7
Are you satisfied?

I'm with the two of them, Crystal and Shardonnay, at each other's throats after church.

'What, you saved this for me, Shardonnay? You said you'd look after him.'

'Well, I did, didn't I?'

'Can't you even change a nappy? How long has he been in this dirty nappy?'

'Maybe he just made it, Crystal. Saved it for his mother. I didn't know he crapped in his damned nappy!'

'Lost your sense of smell have you?'

Ricardo sits on the grimy floor, tears and snot stream down his face and no one is making a move to get him.

'Pick him up, Crystal,' Shardonnay orders.

'Why should I?' Crystal doesn't move.

'He's your baby. That's why.'

'You said you'd look after him.'

'Crystal, why should I look after your baby now you home, hey?'

'You won't put yourself out for me in any way. I can't count on you.'

'I'm not the one who got herself pregnant.'

Crystal lunges at Shardonnay.

'Temper, temper,' Shardonnay teases as she sidesteps behind the table.

'Don't you go calling me a *ho*, Shardonnay, as if I don't know what's going on at school. Where d'you get the money for the trinkets you buy? Clips and nail polish? That suede jacket with the fringe? The leather pants? What about that fancy Nokia? Texting all the time to your fucking boyfriend.' Crystal is on a roll. 'I saw Ramon today at church, by the way, talking to Hazel from around the corner. Chatting her up. I saw him yesterday in her street, just around the block from here, making eyes at her. Staring at her with those brown eyes of his like she meant something to him, as if he didn't have a steady girl. And today in church, I swear, he put his hand right on her thigh.'

'You lying, Crystal. Just because I've had it being the babysitter.'

'You think Ramon cares about you, Shardonnay? You wrong. The only one Ramon cares about is Ramon. Even at church he can't keep his hands to himself.'

Then Crystal starts on me.

'And you, Grace? What you looking at? You think you can judge me? You and your pathetic school project, carrying a bag of maize meal tied to your stomach for a day or two. You think you know anything? Grace, you want to know what it's like?' Crystal has Ricardo at arm's length, the nappy hanging down almost to the little guy's knees. Full. Stinking. She sits him on the kitchen table. Ricardo screams hysterically as she pulls herself away. 'He's all yours!'

I'm worried that he'll roll over, do a Humpty Dumpty smash to the floor. The sisters are so worked up they can't think of his safety. I jump to the table and lift him off.

'I'm taking him upstairs. You two calm down and I'll sort him out. What did this baby ever do to the two of you?' I shake my head, pissed off that the sisters can't seem to put anyone but themselves first.

In Crystal's room I lie Ricardo on the plastic covered foam with the sides that stop him from rolling off. I pop the studs on the soiled *Babygro*, wet where pee has seeped through, and pull his sausage legs out of the suit. He's quietened down now that he has attention. The Velcro fasteners on the disposable are easy to open. I clean his bum with a baby wipe, all the time holding my breath against the stench, and I slip a fresh nappy under him. His bum is red with rash and in some places the skin is badly chaffed. I wince for him as I smear on *Fissan* paste, secure the nappy and dress him in fresh tracksuit pants and a tiny T-shirt.

'There, there, you snuggly-bear. Better now.'

I pick him up and cuddle him and take him downstairs to the kitchen where Shardonnay has her head in her hands and Crystal looks like she's been crying.

'Crystal, he's all cleaned up,' I say. 'Please, take him, he wants his mommy.'

She hardly holds him. Just takes him from me and props him against a pillow in his pram and stuffs a dummy in his mouth.

'There. Are you satisfied?' She glares at him, as if she expects an explanation. 'You always want something don't you?'

I'm still trying to fix things. 'How about I take Ricardo for a walk?'

Crystal doesn't answer, just slumps into a chair at the table.

'Crystal, go and relax,' I say. 'Watch TV or something.'

'Wayne is already in there with his beers,' she says, a resigned tone to her voice.

I keep trying: 'Shardonnay, come with me to the flea market, it's lovely out.'

'Lovely is out of this house,' Sha says and walks off. She comes back moments later stuffing notes in the front pocket of her jeans. I strap Ricardo into the pram and quickly shake up a juice bottle.

In the street, Shardonnay aims a kick at Mr Campbell's lab-cross sunning himself on the pavement.

'Shardonnay, what's got into you?'

'Don't look at me like that, Grace. He was in our way. He can't spread himself on the pavement like that, licking his balls. That's all he does, that bloody dog.'

***From The Journal
of Crystal September***

Letisha Abrahams and Zelda Africa came to the kitchen door just now. Letisha in pink North Stars, and her legs and butt poured into sequined jeans. The halter-top tied behind Letisha's neck embroidered with the word Gorgeous. *Making the most of the warm weather to show herself off. She came right in and sat herself down at the table. C'mon Crystal, she said, come out with us girl. Sitting at home all day is no life.*

I have a kid now. Everything is different.

Wow, you lost your weight, hey, Zelda said. Crystal, you looking good girlfriend.

Still can't get into my jeans, I said.

Come out with us, Crystal. We'll go to the flea market, too. We'll buy all sorts of cheapies. Get us some ice cream. An outing will do you good. C'mon, girl, no excuses now.

I can't, I said. I told you before, Letisha, I can't waste my money on rubbish. And finally she and Zelda left.

I waved as they walked back to the highway. Letisha, and Zelda the fashion plate, wearing her high top boots in red patent leather in this heat, with laces criss-crossing her shins, and a mini clinging for dear life on her pelvis. A stretch of brown thigh in between, an invitation for trouble, doesn't she know? Those plans to finish at Tech will change if she doesn't watch out.

I am trapped in this house, with the crusty dishes and the sound of the rugby from the TV. I want to rush out the door, fly down the street with my arms waving above my head, screaming. Then maybe people will say, what's wrong with Crystal September?

I am resting on my bed upstairs. I stare at the ceiling. I can leave my body if I focus hard enough. I look back at myself from up there. Sometimes I can see I'm holding the heart-shaped cushion that Keegan gave me when I thought he loved me. And I see my journal near me. The things I write here are for my eyes only.

I remember the day at the ice rink. The lights glimmering, pale blue, pink, yellow reflections in slick stretches of ice.

I pretended I couldn't skate well. I stumbled, and held on to Keegan's arm as he pulled me along the ice at the edge of the rink. Trust me, he said. I won't let you fall. That was love; me and Keegan slip-sliding, gliding, my nipples hard and showing from the chill. I knew it would be icy. But it didn't matter. The colder the better. I'd counted on

Keegan noticing my body. I wanted Keegan to want me.

My teeth were chattering, and he pulled me closer, at the side of the rink, and rubbed my goose-pimpled flesh to get the blood circulating, then he gave me his jacket. He bundled me in his fancy suede jacket, and I saw Letisha Abraham's jaw drop, wide-eyed and envious that I, Crystal September, had scored the rich boy. The boy in the neighborhood who was going places.

He's a catch, Letisha said. Crystal, you worked your magic on him, you and those high cheekbones, and those dimples of yours. What boy can resist? Girl, you and your sister are blessed with good looks.

But I know that Shardonnay is the star, the brighter one.

In one of those dark nooks and crannies around the rink, Keegan kissed me. I closed my eyes and lost myself in the softness, and after the kiss I nuzzled into his neck. He laughed, said, Crystal, you know you have a block of ice there on your face instead of a nose! I tasted his skin, his neck, nibbled at the warm flesh I wanted more of, my body tingling the whole time, coming alive.

Outside, late afternoon already, I had to shield my eyes from the light it was so bright. Keegan took his jacket back. My mother will kill me if I don't get home with my stuff, he said. I should have known then he had no guts.

Ricardo faces me in his pram. Chubby fingers clutch the bottle.

'Hey, prop him up a little, Sha, so he can drink properly.'

Thinking of my project, I ask: 'Did Crystal breastfeed?'

'You serious? She hated every second. Maybe she did it for three weeks, but she couldn't wait to put him on the bottle. Sometimes I think she really hates him.'

'Look at him Sha, he's so cute. Nobody could hate the little guy.'

'If you into babies, I guess he's sweet.'

'Hell, Shardonnay, what is it with you and Crystal?'

'I don't know,' she sighs. 'Crystal says he's a ball and chain. She's too young to be a mother. She takes her frustrations out on us.'

We walk along Prince George's Drive, past prostitutes and a car wreck from last weekend, past signs that promise beach access developments for the millionaires. We walk past the shipping container used as a meeting place where Freddy gets his drugs from, and see the twins from the nightclub popping in there, as if they're off to Girl Guides or something. We cross the circle when there's a gap in the traffic. Nearly at the beach I ask Shardonnay if she's calmed down.

'It's what Crystal said about Ramon that got me so furious. That he's into Hazel, that he's flirting with her, touching that bitch.' She shivered. 'Crystal knows which buttons to push.'

Ricardo smiles. Those pearly teeth sparkling against the bubble-gum-pink gums. He tilts his head to the side and I swear he checks me out like he knows me. I stroke his cheek and he grabs hold of my index finger, with these fingers of his like cocktail sausages, that wrap around mine.

He's charming me with his sideways grin. The game is on now. We're both smiling. I peer at him again under the canopy of the same pram Benita's friends bought for her baby that died. Soon we're both laughing. Even Shardonnay is thawing out and putting her issues with Crystal on the backburner. And she can't help smiling at Ricardo's mirth, Ricardo giggling and gurgling as if the two of us pulling faces is the funniest thing he's ever seen.

Shardonnay and me chat about stuff.

'You know, I love Ramon. He would never let me down. I'm so totally into him. I'm true to Ramon no matter what anyone says. You think I don't know what they say? I know what they say,' she spills her guts.

She asks what I think about Freddy. Before I get to answer *not a helluva lot*, Ricardo's empty bottle drops onto the pavement. He's fallen asleep. I pick up the bottle and wipe sand off the grimy teat. He might want a sip later.

Shardonnay says, 'There's perks, going out with a guy like Freddy.'

She can say what she wants about him. Freddy is the kind of guy that'll have you dropping out of school, or dead, before you know what hit you.

We cross the main road and turn right towards the outdoor market, busy as usual on a Sunday. The stalls there selling food and produce and clothing and junk. Whatever you want you'll find.

At her favourite stall, chock with hair accessories and jewellery, Shardonnay picks out a pair of diamante earrings in the shape of hearts, holds them to her lobes and I agree they're worth the price. She chooses them and another pair, gold tassels that glitter in the sun as she jiggles them, and pays with a crisp hundred rand note. With the change, Shardonnay buys a lipstick the same metallic shade as the boob-tube sheath with the chain-link belt she'd bought just a few days ago.

At a book stall there's a stack of worn Mills and Boon romances, and thrillers and sci-fi. I'm not interested in the paperbacks. I make a beeline for the stall I always go to, run by a pensioner who collects 'curiosities' he says. On his table is a tray of battered brass door-handles; there's porcelain and glassware; even a mannequin's head with a wig on it; old broaches and watches and frames and photographs.

I find the shoebox of old postcards and black and white photographs and I flip through them. There are photographs of couples on the beach and strolling in the street, holiday snaps of families posing in front of the Muizenberg bathing boxes. There's a posed wedding photograph where a coy looking couple gaze at each other with love in their eyes. I wonder why the picture is here and not framed, hanging on a wall in a family home somewhere.

I see a photograph of a young woman, a teenager really, showing off a brushed silk evening dress, dark fuchsia contrasting against her skin like milk. She's caught in a laugh, holding up one side of the full skirt as she poses. She is angelic with the lighting shining from behind, a halo of moonshine around her smiling face so full of life, full of faith in the future, so full of promise. I pay two rand for the snapshot.

You're not doing this again are you? The voice in my head talking. *It's a game. A dream. The mother fantasy. When are you going to stop this? You're building up quite a collection.*

But what if this woman is my mother? What if I could track her down from this one photograph? Wouldn't that be something?

Shardonnay looks over my shoulder and says, 'What do you want that old pic for? It's not worth anything. You can't do anything with it.'

'I like the off-the-shoulder dress. Maybe I'll get something made up like it for the school dance.'

'Getting fashion conscious now with the dance coming up are you?'

'Why not?' I gaze down at the picture. 'Look at her. She's got a sense of style at least.'

I don't tell Sha that the girl in the picture has gleaming teeth, like mine.

All the while, Ricardo sleeps, his head drooping to one side. I buy him a stuffed dog on a gold string for two rand and hang it from the canopy on the pram. Sha buys him a bucket and spade. We walk down the road towards the beach, where we sit with our backs against a low cement wall, protected from the warm wind, the pram on the path behind us. Blue sky, white sand, warm wind, a feathering of cloud on the horizon. We watch the even sets of waves out there, and the surfers.

Ricardo is awake. I put him on the beach. For a fleeting second I see myself on this same spot with Martha, years ago, cracking girl-toes out from under a heap of sand after she'd buried my feet. I fill Ricardo's new bucket with sand, pat it down flat and turn it out. He smiles and claps his hands at the castle. I make another. I plant an ice lolly stick into one. Sha decorates the other with cigarette butts she picks up there near her feet, and beer bottle caps.

Back at the duplex Crystal pulls the plastic bag from Shardonnay.

'Here, let me see that.'

'Give it back.'

'I asked you where does your money come from, Shardonnay, for all this stuff?'

And then Crystal turns on me. 'Give that back,' I shout, when Crystal pulls out the photograph from my packet. I try to grab it back from her, but she waves it over my head.

'Another possible pic of your mother? Don't you get it, Grace? She's never coming back for you. Left you in some filthy toilets. Not even on the front steps of the church. She's never coming to get you. And a pretty white girl like this, how could she ever possibly be connected to you?'

And I regret the day I ever told Crystal my fantasy.

'You know Crystal, you don't know how lucky you are to have Ricardo.'

'You can start an album of mother maybes,' she's saying now. Heat rises right up my throat and I flush as her bitterness taints the truth. She throws the photograph and the packet down and I wonder why any of us bother with her. I quickly put the photograph in my bag.

I leave Ricardo in the pram, with Crystal. I've done my good deed and this is what I get for it. Shardonnay and I head up the stairs to Sha's room, and I'm saying 'What is it with Crystal? Why does she have to lash out like that?'

'Don't mind Crystal,' Sha says. 'She's in a mood is all.'

'You're telling me. I thought she'd be OK by now.'

Shardonnay just shakes her head. 'Is that what you do, collect pictures of girls you think may have given birth to you?'

'Don't you ask me what I do, Sha. I won't ask you what's going on at school.'

The subject is closed. We play pop tunes. Shardonnay practises her *Stacie Orrico*, moves on to belting out *Beyoncé*, singing about how she can cope with being dumped by any guy, how tough she is, and how strong.

I wonder, when will Shardonnay confront Ramon? There's no way she'll let what Crystal said go. About Ramon and Hazel, and Ramon hanging out on Scarboro Street in the first place when it's further away from his house than Shardonnay's place.

Back home in the kitchen, Martha is buttering sweet potatoes, the steam rising from the cross section. I'm salivating at the smell of roast chicken. Carrots and peas are in a pot, ready to be steamed. I get cutlery from the drawer to lay the table. Then I go to my room.

I draw the curtain aside. I see Benita leaving the house next door. She's in her nurse's uniform, the name of the old people's home emblazoned on the back, her cross to bear. Hardly a moment later Wayne arrives in his *Mazda*, back from Pollsmoor and his budgie project. I spy Shardonnay leave with Tashreeq Arendse – his arm over her bare shoulders, her body all smooth curves in that silver sheath she's wearing – in a shiny red *BMW*. The two of them are laughing.

So now I'm sure the shit has hit the fan with Ramon.

So much for Couple of the Year.

I smile a small smile to myself and settle down on my bed, listening to songs about love. And I flutter my fingers across my belly.

A little while later Martha opens the door.

'I knocked but you've got those earphones on your head again. I've been calling you. Didn't you hear a thing?'

'That's the whole point, isn't it?'

'Well, come and eat now,' she clucks, a real mother hen.

Martha's world is governed by food. Fulfilment is feeding people. Feeding me. But all I can think about during the meal is Ramon and Grace, like in my dreams.

From The Journal of Crystal September

I tempted Ricardo with mashed fruit. He pushed it out with his tongue and shook his head. He'd had too much of a good time at the beach. They spoiled his appetite with the ice cream. I scooped up the drips and pushed the food back into his mouth with the back of the spoon. Then he squealed and spat some at me and I knew this was it – he wouldn't take any more. So I ate his food myself. Apple sauce. Tasty. He wanted the spoon to play with, so I gave it to him. I swear he threw it down on purpose. The spoon clattered to the ground. My nerves were already frazzled, and Ricardo not eating his food just made things worse, so I yelled at him. You tired, you going down now!

I pulled him kicking and screaming from the highchair. I held him tight as he struggled and his face turned red with his screams for that spoon. I know he didn't mean to, but he bit me. On the arm, as I struggled with him. And he wouldn't open those jaws of his and let my skin go till I flicked him on his ear. And again. And I pinched him. At the top of his thigh. And then he really cried, silver tears streaking his cheeks, Ricardo looking at me like he couldn't believe I'd hurt him.

I felt bad but it was nothing, really. And when he was done crying, and I carried him upstairs, he was so tired he fell asleep right away in my arms. I held him a while, stroked my hand across his soft skin. His eyelashes curved against plump cheeks, rosy from the heat of lying close against my breast. His ear had folded the wrong way against my arm. I lifted his head and straightened that delicate shell-shaped ear.

I stroked him, my small animal. I felt the shape of his skull that was larger than most, the doctor said when he was born.

Room for his brains. He'll go far, the doctor said. I wondered how he would ever hold up his head on such a scrawny neck.

I felt the softness of his dark hair, growing at last.

Ah, sweetie, I do love you after all. When you are asleep. When there is no one else in the house. It's when you wake up, and your eyes contrast against the brown of your skin that I feel differently about you. Those pale blue eyes like ice, always with me, following me. It's those eyes that turn me cold.

CHAPTER 8
Talking about sex

I run down Seaview to Capricorn High, and get there as the bell rings. Most kids are inside already, and then there are the boys doing business on the field. The teachers pretend they don't exist. Teachers are supposed to be in positions of authority. They're supposed to run things. Fact of life: teachers turn a blind eye to business that goes on in the quad and on the edges of the school. They turn a blind eye to Freddy and his pals and their *skelm* business. They're afraid that if they do something about it, their own kids – who might or might not go to this junk heap of a school – will probably end up dead in a drive-by shooting on a Saturday afternoon.

I throw my books into my desk just in time to file into assembly. Fifteen minutes later, all one-thousand-two-hundred odd of us are packed in the school hall, waiting to hear a celebrity talk to us about sex. He's chatting on stage to the principal. There's a red ribbon pinned to his T-shirt. So many ribbons these days, tough to keep track of which colour coordinates with which cause. But everybody knows red is for AIDS. The principal introduces the celeb. We pay attention because he's famous. He's an entertainer and he's funny. He talks about AIDS and how you have to use a condom to protect yourself and how us girls must insist on the guy using a condom. Some of the younger kids giggle. *Ja, go ahead, laugh*, he says, *but listen too.* He's not shy. He says sex isn't a secret any more. If you think sex is a secret, then that's what'll get you into trouble. Knowledge is power. Know the consequences of unprotected intercourse. You can get pregnant. You can get crabs and sores and warts and some of it you can cure and some of it − like herpes blisters − are with you for the rest of your life, there on the walls of your vagina or oozing pus on your penis. And crabs will crawl around and drive you mad with the itching. You can get HIV/AIDS. Why take the risk?

'You know,' he tells us, 'some girls think if they keep their eyes closed when they have sex they won't get pregnant.'

That gets laughs, but there are girls in that hall whose eyes are about to pop out. These are the girls who don't know anything. He tells us it's our right to protect ourselves. That's what it's all about. Living a life without HIV and AIDS. The only way to learn is to talk about it.

'If you wash your vagina with *Dettol* and vinegar, that won't stop you from getting pregnant either,' he jokes. Then he comes over all serious and the whole hall is quiet and he says, 'If you don't look out for yourselves, if you have sex and you don't use a condom, what you can look forward to in your future is pneumonia and tuberculosis and Kaposi's sarcoma. You have to know what you're getting into. You can do anything with your life in this young democracy. You can be a teacher, a pilot, a doctor. If you work hard, you can be whatever you like. But if you make one mistake, then you can die before your twenty-first birthday.'

His talk takes us to break. I sit on one end of a wooden bench and open my lunch-box. Silver-paper parcels packed there; wrapped biscuits, dried mango, a cold chicken pie and cherry tomatoes. Martha has packed chopped pineapple pieces in a tiny Tupperware, and a toothpick to eat them with.

'I don't have to prepare lunch for you, but I enjoy doing it.' Martha smiled this morning, handing over my lunch-box which I grabbed before she kicked up a fuss.

'See you later, Martha.'

'Are you coming straight home?' she asked, but I pretended I didn't hear her. Wanting to know my every move. Faking it as my mother. The church glow has worn off. I don't have a mother. Martha is as irritating as a stone in my shoe.

I'm sitting close enough to Raquelle Rogers and Hazel Hendricks now, the two of them on the next bench, to hear their conversation about dance dresses and corsages and about which boys will escort them. *Older men*, they say, *who've left school and are doing important things with their lives.* Like waiting tables, and working at the *Engen* filling petrol tanks and cleaning windscreens. *Ja*, right.

Shardonnay is in the tuck shop line waiting for her polony sandwich and coke. She gets back, Hazel and Raquelle on the bench shooting her dirty looks till Hazel can't help herself and says, 'You went out with Tashreeq Arendse last night, isn't that so, Shardonnay September? You one of those sluts the man in the hall was talking about, spreading diseases? What, you just gone and dumped Ramon, is that it? Well, we not complaining about that!'

They get up, laughing, and leave. So I put it out there in a hushed tone. 'Shardonnay, there are rumours going around.'

'About what? Be specific.'

'You know what I'm talking about. Crystal said it. You're not exactly short of cash these days.'

'So what. I told you I don't care what these *slette* say about me. Grace, you promised you wouldn't bug me about any of it.'

'Just be careful, that's all.'

'What do you mean?'

'Crystal's not happy sitting at home with Ricardo. You don't want to get pregnant, or worse.'

'Grace, who d'you think you are now, the school counsellor? Your imagination running wild about my private life? I got the message from that TV celeb in there, I don't need it from you.'

She shrugs off this conversation, gets up and tosses her hair over her shoulder and her junk food in the bin. And I'm alone again, me and my toothpick and my triangles of pineapple, thinking mostly that school sucks. I should keep my mouth shut. Again I'm on the outside. On the fringe. Some kid called me off-centre once. I think that best describes me.

After break I yawn my way through science and technology. In English, Mrs Williams says *Grace, get yourself a glass of water.* I'm grateful to get out of the classroom for a few minutes. In the cloakroom I drink from the tap and splash myself awake. I dry my face with toilet paper. The mirror is in pieces. Smashed by the half-brick used as a doorstop? Who knows? So I don't bother to check myself out. I help myself from the box of condoms supplied by the Department of Health. I don't need them, but they're free.

Call it the wrong place at the wrong time, but as I leave the loo, with my condoms in my pocket, Shardonnay comes out of the guys' toilet diagonally across the passage. I lift my hand, about to call her, when Tashreeq comes out following her,

Tashreeq straightening his uniform, his pants and his shirt, as if all he was doing in there was taking a leak. Shardonnay turns back and whispers to him.

Sha's lips are moist; they look swollen, plumped up as though she's had Botox injected like the women in *Extreme Makeovers* who can hardly move their mouths. Problem is, Ramon comes down the corridor from the other direction and he sees Shardonnay and Tashreeq in the last moment of a clinch. He stops in his tracks, watching as Tashreeq disappears into a classroom down the passage.

Ramon catches up with Shardonnay. 'Where the hell have you been?' he yanks her arm.

'None of your business,' she says.

He raises his hand as if he's going to hit her.

She yells, 'Go ahead, go ahead if that's what you want to do, hey, Ramon. Then explain to me what you were doing with what's her name around the corner, and why your hands were, in broad daylight, all over her, that bitch Hazel, at effing *church*. You think I wouldn't hear all about it?'

He just looks at her. There is big trouble in Paradise.

Ramon turns away, walks off shaking his head. 'You nothing but a slut, Shardonnay.' He looks back at her. 'What was I doing with you anyway? You think I don't know about you and Tashreeq? Everybody knows what happened last night. Now this.'

Shardonnay backtracks past me, as if I wasn't there, into the girls' cloakroom. I follow her and wait for her to finish puking in the toilet.

'Shardonnay, are you OK?'

'Leave me alone, Grace.'

'Shit, what's going on?'

'Don't make this into a big deal.'

'Shardonnay, it is a big deal.'

'Don't act like a loser, Grace.'

She looks at me blankly, as if she really doesn't click what I'm on about. 'What the hell are you playing psychologist on me for? As if you'd understand.' There's weariness in her voice and she's looking at the fragments of her face in the shattered mirror, her mouth a distorted, jagged line.

'Girls are jealous, that's all. Jealous of Ramon. Jealous that men find me attractive. Ramon loves me. We'll sort it out. The rumours are no big deal. And why shouldn't I make a little something on the side?'

'Is that what you're doing?'

'*Transactional sex*. That's what it is. See, it even has a name. Tashreeq is just business.'

'It's prostitution, Shardonnay.'

'Don't be naïve, Grace. Doing this I get nice clothes, stuff I need. And I don't go all the way.'

I can't believe what I'm hearing, that blowing guys regularly in the toilets for bucks isn't something that's going to affect her for the rest of her life.

'Jesus, Shardonnay. You can pick up infections. How can you *do* this?'

'If you think I'm the only one, you wrong. It's not as if none of the other girls are doing it. Wearing make-up to school and coming back to class from wherever with most of it smeared off. I make more on the side than the others, that's part of the reason for the hassles.'

Shardonnay rinses her face with the trickle of water from the tap. She straightens her hair, then closes her eyes to the bits and pieces of her broken image.

'Shardonnay,' I say quietly, 'do your buttons up right.' As if I'm trying to fix her. Make her look right again.

I leave her there, in this other place she's gone to in her head, her fingers gently stroking the hollow at the front of her neck, as if she's forgotten I'm there with her.

I'm on the fringe. Alone again.

After school I go over to the Septembers to ask Crystal some practical info. The kitchen door is open so I go in. I know if I hear *Days of Our Lives*, or *Isidingo*, then Benita is home. Rugby, cricket, bowling, then Wayne is in the lounge with his beers and smokes, every so often clearing his throat with his rasping cough. Now no one is in the lounge. The TV is off. A saucer overflows with *stompies*. Ash spilt on the coffee table. An over-turned beer bottle dribbles from the mouth.

'Anybody home?' I call. I go upstairs, peek into the open door of Benita and Wayne's bedroom where the queen-sized bed with the pink satin headboard takes up most of the floor space. The bed is a tangle of sheets and blankets. Benita and Wayne both gone. 'Crystal, are you home?'

'She's in the yard,' Shardonnay calls from her room, so I look in. Shardonnay is curled up in bed.

'Had a rough day, Sha?'

She puts on the music. The CD player pumps out lyrics about being bruised and confused. I sit next to her, on the bed, page through an old *Seventeen* while Shardonnay starts singing softly.

To Sha life is a pop song. All the pain and sadness of the world is sorted out in the songs. She knows the words to all these songs by heart. Her voice aches with longing. I should give Shardonnay the benefit of the doubt. Ramon hurt her. She hurt him back. Who am I to judge?

So I forget about Crystal, comfortable on Sha's bed as I am, paging through mags. A pile of ancient *Cosmopolitans* and *Fairlady* magazines. We're like on the same wavelength again, checking out the fashions and giggling at how styles have changed, though the models are as skinny as the girls like praying mantises in the latest glossies.

'Me and Ramon patched things up,' she tells me in a quiet moment. 'I phoned him. Told him he's the one I love. I couldn't get through the day without making up with him. Crystal was talking rubbish about Hazel in the church. He never laid a finger on her. I'm the one Ramon wants to be with. He can't live without me.'

I keep my mouth shut. There's an awkward moment as if Shardonnay wants me to agree with her. Sure, who am I to judge, but the truth is the truth. She loads *Dido* in the CD. More love gone wrong. Then there's a thin cry from the room next door.

'Do you hear the baby, Shardonnay?'

'That's Ricardo alright,' she sighs.

His whimpering escalates to a full throttle scream. Nought to one hundred in like two seconds. Shardonnay shouts from her bed, 'What about the baby, Crystal?' She bangs against the flimsy DIY partition.

I get up off the bed and go to Crystal's room. There's Ricardo lying in his cot, one hand clutching the bars, the other at empty air. He sobs like he knows he has to put up a fuss to get any attention. His face is filthy, his hands too, as if he's been playing in the dirt in their yard. I scoop him up. I get tissues from my rucksack and wipe his face.

Crystal shouts from the bottom of the stairs: 'I'm telling you I can't stand it any more.' She comes in from the back yard carrying the yellow washing basket.

'He's your baby, Crystal,' Shardonnay yells.

'And someone else's. Don't you ever forget that. D'you think I made him by myself?'

'You have to look out for him.'

Crystal shakes her head. 'He looks just like his father.' The bitterness of her tone silences me and Shardonnay. Ricardo whimpers on my hip. He's seen his mother and he wants her. She stands there and suddenly shrieks at the baby, 'Shut up, shut up,' so loudly the entire street probably jumps.

Ricardo freezes with fear and clings to me and after she disappears down the stairs, I say to Shardonnay, 'Your sister is in a bad way.'

Ricardo's wail is a rope of pain, trying to lasso his mother as she leaves right out the front door.

'It's OK, Ricardo.' Shardonnay strokes his cheek and pats his back trying to comfort him. I rock the little guy back and forth till he's quiet.

'We should talk to Benita or call Social Welfare or something,' I say. 'Crystal's really not coping.'

'She'll get over it,' Shardonnay says. 'She needs time to get used to having him around.'

'Sure, but how much time? Ricardo is sitting, playing, he'll be talking one of these days.'

'Hey, Ricardo, it's not your fault you were born. You not to blame,' Shardonnay croons, wiping the tears dripping from his chin with the back of her hand. We change his nappy on Crystal's bed. Dress him in a clean stripy T-shirt and shorts. 'You feeling better now, *boytjie*?' Sha says.

In the kitchen the dishes from the night before, caked with gravy and strings of Smash, are stacked in the sink. There's a wet slipper in the basin, a smell of damp, flies buzzing against the closed window.

'Here, hold him.' I pass Ricardo to Shardonnay. I move the slipper to a piece of newspaper on the floor and I wash the bottle. I do the dishes too. I wait for the kettle to boil. There's milk powder left in the tin on the counter, with simple instructions on the tin, pictures even. I mix the formula, give the bottle a good shake and wait for it to cool. Ricardo finally gets his fingers around the bottle, sucks and sucks and in a minute the milk is gone. He's calm now, in Shardonnay's arms. I make another bottle for the greedy guts, he's that hungry.

From The Journal
of Crystal September

Ricardo giggled a stream as light as bubbles as he watched the washing on the line, blowing this way and that. He liked the sheet especially, whipping in the wind. When the gust died down, he gurgled, like he was getting ready for the next bout when the wind would lift the sheet and send it billowing skyward again. I made sure the pegs held the sheet tight. I took down the dry washing, folding shirts and pants and towels. Slowly the pile of washing grew in the basket. If I spend time folding Wayne's shirts and Benita's uniforms, they are never as creased later, and they're easier to iron.

It happened when I turned my back. He did it when I bent down to pick up the pegs that had spilled from the Tupperware on to the cement. I picked up the pegs then turned towards Ricardo.

What are you doing? I yelled at Ricardo. Stop right now! But he didn't listen. He kept on laughing and throwing dirt from a plastic flowerpot onto the clean pile of washing. Onto Wayne's shirts.

I pulled the pot from his hand and threw it across the yard. I don't know how he got it. Look what you've done! Bad boy, bad boy, I screamed, fire in my throat, choking the oxygen out of me. I looked at the stains on the washing. I don't have eyes in the back of my head. I can't do a thing with him around. What do people expect of me? And I was that upset I hit him on the arm then. Hard. A loud smack that left my fingers sore. I didn't care about the welts my fingers left. I felt pleased when he wailed. Something in me felt satisfied.

I'm sorry now that I smacked him. But I must say, when I first saw the marks on his flesh, I felt that he had deserved it.

And his crying. I felt like he was shedding the tears I should be crying.

I picked him up. He hung from my neck. Wet streaks on his dirty cheeks. I stopped to look at myself in the mirror in the passage. The radio was on in the kitchen. I stood listening to that old song Teen Angel *crackling on Classic Tracks, all about the boys in the neighborhood loving you if they could. I looked at the photograph in the silver frame, of me and Shardonnay in our pretty dresses at the wedding, of Benita and Wayne holding hands after all those promises they made to each other.*

Ricardo calmed down. I put him in the pen where he couldn't cause trouble. I gave him some things he couldn't break. Mixing spoons. A battered stainless steel teapot. He banged the lid open and closed.

I soaked the soiled shirts in a bucket. Then scraped and stacked the dishes from the night before, but before I could even run the water for the dishes Ricardo trapped his finger under the lid of the teapot and started crying. There's always something. I picked him up. Heavy bastard. Marched with him upstairs, dumped him in his cot. Where you must stay till I'm done, I said. But he wouldn't stop crying, his body shaking, his hands clutching at those bars as if he was a prisoner trying to get free.

I made the beds in the other rooms. Heard a plane overhead. Thought about Shardonnay and Grace talking about going places. I want to go places too, but where will I ever go? How will I ever get away?

In the yard again, I hung the things I had to rewash. I could see Martha's washing in her yard, and washing in the yard beyond that and beyond that and beyond that, like looking in trick mirrors where you see the same image to eternity. I stumbled sideways, I don't know why, straight into a broken plastic chair and scratched my calf *on the sharp edge of the plastic. I felt better watching the blood as it ran quickly down, staining the fleece of my slipper.*

Later I cleaned the mess away. I wiped off the dried blood and rinsed the slipper under the cold tap.

It was quiet upstairs. Ricardo had finally cried himself to sleep.

'Been next door, have you?' Martha asks.

'Yup,' I say.

'I heard raised voices.'

'Nothing new there really,' I shrug.

She changes tack. 'I picked up some samples of fabric you may be interested in for your dress, in the fuchsia you like.'

'You know I'm not into that sort of thing.'

'Just a thought, Grace. We can go shopping if you like. You're a pretty girl. The dance is a chance to show yourself off a little.'

We decide that she will make the dress. She has all my measurements. Is there anything she doesn't know about me? I agree to do this to keep Martha out of my hair. All I see is Freddy offering me a corsage at the front door, he and Ramon waiting in the chariot to escort me and Sha to the dance where Freddy will sneak in drugs and booze and want to fuck me on the school field afterwards. I may have other plans.

There's a plain omelette for supper, and fruit salad. Today, Martha tells me, is the birth of the Blessed Virgin Mary. Weekdays of Lent, and the self-denial that goes with it, have been good for Martha's diet. She's eaten less, fewer lethal chocolate éclairs, custard slices, jam doughnuts that she sneaks from Shoprite. She asks about my homework.

'All under control.'

'How's the report on teenage pregnancy going?'

'Fine. Hanging out at Shardonnay's is my research.'

She hesitates before she splutters: 'Grace, as far as looking for your mother goes, you could start by speaking to Father Adams. He may have some ideas. He could give you some advice on how you could go about tracing your mother. Or call the Parent Centre if you'd rather do that.'

'Thanks, Martha,' I say softly, taken aback by her encouragement.

'I'll try to help you in whatever way I can.' She places her knife and fork side by side on the empty plate in front of her, joins her hands in her lap, as if in prayer, trying to regain her matter-of-fact composure. 'The way will be shown on the way.' As if the church has all the answers.

CHAPTER 9
Yes, Mommy

'How was that talk at school?' Martha asks, before we clear up.

I try to be pleasant. 'He has a good message. Use condoms. Don't get AIDS.'

'When I was your age it was a different life.'

'You went to a convent, Martha. There weren't any boys to distract you,' I joke.

'I rode my bike in the neighbourhood streets. I walked to the corner café on my own where they sold sweets not drugs. I never even used swear words.'

Stop Martha, I want to say, *it's OK, I understand. Times have changed.* But I sit on my hands as she lectures on.

'When I was your age we didn't have to worry about HIV and AIDS and read about rape and have briefings at school on how to have safe sex and not get pregnant – ' yadda yadda yadda.

She's out of breath. Those hands of hers red and cracked from all her hand wringing and just plain ageing, though she's not even fifty.

And before she gets going full speed ahead, I squash her distress. 'Don't worry Martha, I'll look after myself. I won't do anything stupid.'

'What about staying out as late as you did on the weekend? I don't know what's happening to you, Grace.'

'So you waited up did you?' Yawn.

'Sweetheart, you know I did.'

She starts on about how Shardonnay is not a good influence. 'She's nearly finished school. You're a year younger. It's a different world.' Martha's on a roll. 'What happened to the decent girls in your own class? That Bianca and Tracey? I don't like the crowd Shardonnay hangs out with. She's too wild, Grace. The family too, doesn't seem to be coping with the baby.'

'Don't freak out, Martha.'

'I pray you're not getting caught up in their problems.' Yadda yadda yadda. 'Just know you can count on me,' she goes on and on, 'that's important to me, you can trust me, that's what family is for. Share with me, tell me whatever you want to even if it's hard for me to understand.'

Her jowls shake. She means well but I can feel my eyes glazing over.

I'm transported to the quad. I see the boys' lust after Shardonnay, hungry eyes linger as she walks past. The girls turn catty, sharpen their claws, growl at her back, wanting to scratch out her eyes.

'Grace, are you listening to me?' Martha says.

'Sure, Martha. I'm tired. Tough day. I'll be careful, I promise.' I'm desperate to get her off my back. 'I know I can come to you.' She doesn't have a clue when to call it a day and she's not done yet.

'Grace, it's a dodgy crowd. I don't trust those older boys.' From bad to worse. Making a lot of noise about how we should talk, how I should go to her with my problems, but really, Martha's the one wanting to do the talking. I want to yell, *don't you get it, Martha, there's more to life than school and church.* She keeps on and on, '…and your body is priceless, Grace. *You* decide when you want to share yourself.'

'Martha, I won't do anything pathetic. I want to have a bit of fun that's all. Besides, Sha's our neighbour. I can't ignore her. You the one who encouraged me to help out over there in the first place, remember?'

'That doesn't mean going out all hours of the night and getting mixed up in their problems.'

'Martha, stay out of my business!' I can see she doesn't like this one bit. I've been keeping cool, trying to *communicate*, but suddenly I've had it. She's been stringing together all these pearls of wisdom that I'm not interested in wearing like a noose around my neck. I'll do anything to shut her up and before I can stop myself – and maybe I don't want to – I say the words always in the back of my mind: 'Stop pretending to be my mother!'

She's close to tears, her jaw and double chins trembling.

'Well go to bed then,' she sighs, nearly crying.

Yes, Mommy.

In my room I lie on top of the duvet. Earphones cutting off reality. But even *Staind* can't block out Martha from my mind, Martha fingering her plastic beads, blinking, pushing her orange hair off her face, going at me with that mouth of hers. *Don't drink and drive, don't be a passenger in a drunk's car.* Yadda yadda yadda. *These days it only takes one beer to show up on a Breathalyzer test. Make sure you've got airtime. Phone me if you need me. I'm only a text away.* Going on and on.

Shut up, Martha!

Even the rain when it comes, a relief from the oppressive heat, and clattering against the tin roof, doesn't drown out Martha's voice. I turn up the volume, to obliterate her nagging, always telling me what to do, what not to do. *Screw you!* I'll do what I want with my life.

Nothing spectacular happens during the rest of the week. It rains for days. I keep clear of everyone.

Shardonnay calls one night. 'Freddy's coming along, Grace. To the after-party on Saturday. You said you liked him, didn't you?'

Did I? The hairs stand to attention on my arms. 'He's OK,' I lie.

'So, you coming to the after-party Saturday night or what?'

Part of what I feel is it's my duty in some way to keep my eye on Shardonnay. Friendly obligation. But there's something secret about her, something exciting, compelling. Something I want for me too. And there's Ramon.

The voice says leave well alone. Martha has a point. I know that Freddy is scum. And Ramon is trouble. I need a boy like Ramon like I need a hole in the head. But I say, 'At Liquid Dreams? Sure, I'll be there.' After all, I can do what I like.

'Cool then, Grace. You'll be Freddy's date for the dance then,' Sha says.

I say nothing. Any luck the first-class prick will disappear as usual to the toilets the way he always does, to take care of business.

'Goodnight, Sha.'

I get back to my school project. The responsible me is revived, for no particular reason. In the genes from whichever side. I must have had a father too. I sort through my notes on teenage pregnancy. I jot down statistics from the Welfare brochure I picked up at the clinic:

Twenty-five per cent of South African girls aged fifteen to nineteen are HIV-positive.

One in four girls under the age of sixteen has a first baby.

One in two street children is a prostitute.

Two out of three marriages end in divorce.

Later in the week I get a late-night text from Sha:

Wat u doing?

Just lying here going 2 bed. U?

Cum play outside.

Not 2nite. 2 late.

I watch as Sha and a dark shape skip along the pavement, down the road towards the park and are gone. From the window I see that the moon is a perfect circle. The night is alive. The gate bangs in the wind. Martha's bamboo chimes rattle in the yard. There is a laugh, a whoop from somewhere; the beat of a boom box, the rumble of a skateboard on the pavement under my window. It's nearly midnight. I turn on the light and pick up a pen and my notebook and I write.

My real mother is soft smiles. She is sand

castles and the secret moon shining in my room. She is sweet breath on my cheek at night. A warm hand on mine. Martha tells me *chew with your mouth closed, do your homework, remember your manners*. Yadda yadda yadda. Treating me like I can't have a mind of my own.

I turn on my side and close my eyes again, against the shadows lengthening with the head lights of a passing car, and Ramon comes to me in my dreams.

Early Saturday morning I catch a taxi to the Blue Route. That wind has started up again, the *berg* wind, whipping up plastic packets and dust and scrap in the streets, the wind that drives everybody crazy.

'Glad to see you, Grace,' Melvyn says, chomping on his seed bar with his hamster teeth.

I clean the cages where budgies, canaries and diamond doves are cooped. You can't hold them. You can't pet them. You can't touch them. I don't much like birds, but I pity them in this limited environment. I sweep the bottom of the finch aviary, replenish the water, pour fresh seed into two dishes. Ring up a few sales of dog food, gold fish, hamster sawdust.

Animal Welfare arrives later in the morning.

'You have too many rats in the cages. Sell them by the end of the month or get rid of them,' they order Melvyn and he agrees he'll do that.

A working mother on her way to an office job, in a tailored business suit the colour of Melvyn's African Grey parrot, comes in carrying a cage. Her nose tweaks at the smell of the shop. She asks: 'Is the owner interested in buying rats?'

Melvyn says, 'People don't have a clue,' as the woman in her heels and dangly earrings leaves with her cage of baby rats so tiny they're see-through.

A do-gooder brings in a mangy cat and kittens in a cardboard box.

'Please, do something,' she begs.

'We can't take them here.' Melvyn holds up his hands in resignation. 'We've just had Animal Welfare round saying there's too many rats in the cages. There's no place for kittens. Try the Animal Welfare, or SPCA, or the vet.'

No one takes babies too seriously. Rats, kittens, the human kind. Maybe it all seems like a good idea at the time.

After my shift, I try out some hot CDs at Music City but I don't spend money there. I use part of my day's wage at Clicks, for MUM, Colgate, and a present for Martha. A guilt purchase.

In the afternoon, I walk to the market and head back to the old man's stall. The trestle table is packed with more second-hand paraphernalia, bits and pieces of junk he's collected during the week. Boxes heavy with belt buckles, tools, vases, pottery mugs, porcelain figurines. Little Bo Peep and Miss Muffet I recognise from *Mother Goose,* read to me by Martha, repeated over and over till I could recite the rhymes myself.

There it is. The box of old prints.

I rifle through black and white images of people who'd be so much older than these captured memories, who would most likely be dead all these years later. I run my fingers along the scalloped edges of a postcard, soft, yellowed, of St James beach. If the picture was taken now of the strip of bright bathing boxes, graffiti and gang tags would have to be edited out.

I like the quality of some of the old photos; some of them hand-painted, the subtle touch of rose on cheeks and lips, the hint of blonde or brown on a permanent wave. I find the photograph I'd noticed the time before: a woman with her profile to the camera, sitting with her daughter on the beach. The mother is smiling, enchanted by the little girl burying her mother's feet in the sand.

I buy a porcelain teddy bear clutching a soccer ball, for little Ricardo's shelf. I'll keep it for his first birthday, a decoration for his corner of Crystal's room. The old man wraps it in tissue paper.

At home Martha appreciates the potpourri sachet I give her, but she's still upset about what I said to her. But I can't help it if what I said is true. She's not my mother. End of story.

Martha sits at the table, the sewing machine in front of her, the lift to her chin a sign of wounded pride and hurt. She reminds me, the ingrate, to do my chores.

Martha finishes sewing the fuchsia dress in the same style as the girl in the picture I showed her, fleetingly. She's pricked her fingers on pins and bent her back at the sewing machine. That dull whirr of the machine the only communication from her for days.

I go to my room. I take the small creased photograph of the young woman on the swing out of my purse and look at it. I rummage in my bag for the photo of the teenager in her evening dress. There must be someone out there I truly belong to. I stash them both in a side-pocket of my bag.

Next door, someone slams a door.

Ricardo is crying.

I haven't seen Shardonnay or Crystal all week.

I lie on my bed listening to *Evanescence*, *Linkin Park*, *Fifty Cent*. Angry, rebellious stuff that puts into words the way I feel. The world better not mess with me.

From The Journal of Crystal September

There, there, better now. I stroked his head. You're OK now.

A little accident, I told Benita. Nothing to worry about. Ricardo was on my hip while I was frying sausage for Wayne's lunch, I told her. I know I shouldn't have had him on me. But he was restless. Always wanting attention. It happened after that. I had already switched the hotplate off when he kicked out at it, that's what happened. The hotplate burned his heel, just there on the edge. I could see the skin was bubbled, peeling off. It's a little burn. Nothing much. I ran his foot under cold water for a long time. Babies have to learn, don't they? He'll never come near the stove again.

Will you, Ricardo?

CHAPTER 10

Home sweet home...

I decide to give Ricardo's present to Crystal this afternoon, and I bought a scented soap for her at the market, a thanks for helping with my project.

The front door is ajar. The TV's blaring. The rugby commentary is so loud I can hear we are not winning. I go inside and call Crystal from the passage. She doesn't answer. I call again, *are you upstairs*? This time I hear a muffled *OK, I'm coming*, from behind the door of her room. I peer into the lounge, where Castle cans and spilt crisps cover the coffee table. The room stinks of cigarette smoke and the acrid smell of burned plastic – it looks like one of Wayne's smokes has melted a hole in the couch cushion. I go through to the kitchen to wait for Crystal. Wayne comes from the toilet where he's pissed out all that beer I bet, sprinkling the seat for the sisters to clean. He hardly bats an eye at me in his hurry to get back to the game.

At least the table and counters are clean. The dishes are done for a change. I wait for Crystal so that we can have tea together, if she's in a decent mood. A broken window clangs against burglar bars. I notice the chipped tiles above the sink. Counters scored with knife cuts. Magnets on the fridge door, a pineapple and an elephant. The number to call for emergencies: 10111.

That's when I see the budgie lying on his side at the bottom of the cage.

I slide the cage along the counter from the shadowed corner, lift open the gate, gently stroke the bird's feathers. The body is already hard, an opaque eye stares at nothing.

'Crystal, come see this,' I whisper as she crosses into the kitchen. First she puts Ricardo in his pen. In the lounge Wayne is screaming at the Springboks, calls them useless, *what the fuck are you boys doing, call yourselves a team*, he screams, his feet on the coffee table no doubt, knocking back more booze.

He won't hear me over the din but I talk softly anyway. 'The budgie is dead.'

'Stupid bird,' Crystal says. 'What did it have to go and die for?'

'Hey, shit man, Crystal,' Shardonnay says, coming in from outside, standing alongside me and Crystal staring at the cage. 'What's wrong with the damned budgie?'

An edge of anxiety creeps into Crystal's voice: 'Are you sure Wayne's bird is dead, Grace?' She stands there, pulling at the zipper on her tracksuit top.

'He's going to be *woes*,' Shardonnay warns. 'He's always on about the budgie project. How great it is for the prisoners. I'm telling you, he's going to be upset.'

And in that moment Benita arrives home. 'Is there a tea party happening here?' she says. 'What about helping me with these bags? Hey girls, you just going to stand there staring, or can you get up off your arses and help me?'

'Mommy...' Crystal starts, but Benita bulldozes right over her. Hasn't been home five seconds and Benita's losing it.

'I've raised two sluts,' Benita says, her lips disappearing into her mouth. 'Good for bloody nothing. You, Crystal, getting yourself pregnant at seventeen, writing your exams in a back room at the school. Do you know how you've humiliated me? Well do you?'

'Ma, stop, you just in a bad mood.' Shardonnay tries to soothe her mother's temper, but Benita is consumed, on fire. She's spontaneously combusting right there in front of my eyes.

'As for you Shardonnay, you think I'm a fool? You think I don't know what you doing with the boys? Is this what I'm working my fingers to the bones for, and Wayne too? For you girls to waste your lives like this?'

Wayne yells from the lounge, 'Keep it down in there, I can't concentrate on the rugby, the lot of you bitches bickering. We've got neighbours. D'you want them to know all our business?' He turns up the volume on the TV. I am not feeling good about what's happening, but I don't move. I wish this was a soapie I was watching so I could change the channel or, better still, switch off.

Benita can't stop. She lowers her voice but there's a vicious tone to it.

'I don't want to involve Wayne, but I will. He can get you girls to see sense. You never too old for a beating. You girls, full of lies and deceit; maybe it's time to thrash it all out of you.'

They shut up with the threat of Wayne and his belt looming over them, fear like an electricity charge between them. They face Benita shooting out her rounds. Ratatatatatat. Benita's blame as rapid as automatic fire – *you you you... it's all your fault things aren't better around here. No wonder Wayne drinks, no wonder he comes home late. I'm sick of you two. He has to support you and what do you do? Waste yourselves on gangsters at school. To think he treats you as if you were his own flesh and blood, you two. What for? You don't even lift a finger to bring in the groceries!*

It's as if I'm not there. Or as if she needs me as her audience, as if Benita needs me to hear that her girls are no good, rotten to the core, and that it has *nothing* to do with her.

'I've done my best for you two. I remarried so you'd have a father. I thought it would do some good after your daddy died. And look how you two ended up. What a disappointment.'

Benita shakes her head. Dumps the bags on the table. She's done. Team building exercise over. Ha ha. She's halfway out the kitchen when she turns back. Lays her palms flat on the table. She's not done yet with her hurtful words.

'You and your fancy ways, Shardonnay. You think you better than the lot of us. Let me tell you, you not. Shut up about *Idols*. You didn't make it the last competition, you think you can make it now? I'm sick of hearing those pop songs through the walls. And you Crystal, what d'you do at home most of the day? Nothing. Your stepfather and I work to put clothes on your back. You think I'm cleaning up old people's vomit and emptying bedpans for fun? Thank God I'm on night duty. I can get away from you two. All I ask is a little help, that's all.'

'I need help, too,' Crystal mutters.

'Don't be cheeky to me, girl,' Benita warns.

Sha knows her place, but Crystal blurts out, 'Benita, can't you see Wayne's bird is dead?' Like a full stop to all of this.

Benita looks at the cage on the counter. Suddenly Benita lunges across the table at Crystal. She slaps her daughter's cheek, her own face puce, the gash of her mouth pulled tight.

'Get out of my sight, just get out of this room,' Benita shrieks. Crystal and Shardonnay run, scared little girls, from the kitchen up the stairs to their rooms.

'Do you see what I have to put up with?' Benita yells at me and I hang my head and move to where Ricardo, forgotten in the fray, is whimpering from fright in his playpen.

His crying is just a background noise to the real soundtrack. Benita storms into the narrow passage. There's a nasty crack, the shattering of glass, maybe an ornament smashing on the tiles. Then there's just the TV and Wayne whooping it up. Someone's scored a try and I'm thinking it must be the Springboks 'cause Wayne is yelling *Yes Yes Yes, what a beauty*, and not bothering about the drama in his own house. I pick up Ricardo and cradle him against my shoulder. He hides his arms between my chest and his body and soon his tears stop.

A framed photograph covered in shards of glass is lying in the middle of the passage floor. A photograph of the four of them, Wayne and Benita, Crystal and Shardonnay, on Benita and Wayne's wedding day a few years back. Benita is flushed and smiling in her off-white meringue, all frills and puffed sleeves. The sisters dressed in replicas of Benita's gown are like two brides themselves, right down to the veils floating behind them in the breeze and dainty bouquets of the prettiest miniature roses in their hands.

Back in the kitchen I find the dummy coated in grease at the bottom of the dirty sink. Martha's voice in my head says, *the dishes aren't done till the sink is scrubbed.*

'Sweetie-pie, Ricardo,' I croon and put him in the high chair. He's not too happy about leaving my arms but I'm keeping my eye on him. He sucks his dummy. 'I'm here. I'm not going anywhere.'

I know it's tough for Crystal, with Shardonnay finishing school and out most of the time. Crystal sitting alone with the baby. First dealing with the colic and now with constant demands of carrying and comforting, and behind the scenes the stench of the *Sterinappi* bucket, the grimy *Babygros*, the sleepless nights.

'Ricardo, you're not one of those dream babies that sleeps through the night are you?' He looks at me and I stretch my tongue onto the tip of my nose and go cross-eyed. I get a smile, finally, and then he giggles and bounces up and down in his high chair. Sunshine and tears is what he is. Like his mama.

A few minutes later Benita comes downstairs, dressed for work in her uniform washed and pressed by Crystal, her bag slung over her shoulder. The logo embroidered on the back of the blue fabric of her jacket is the same bright yellow as the budgie.

'Sorry, Grace, I don't know what gets into me sometimes. Raising a family is hard work, let me tell you.'

And she's gone, the door slamming after her. She won't be back till morning.

I turn back to Ricardo banging a fork on the high chair. I rinse the dummy he dropped while he was laughing at my eyes rolling around, and plug it in his mouth. I swap the fork he'd managed to grab for a spoon, before he takes his eye out.

Crystal comes in the kitchen then. Her cheek is red, and her eyes look sore from crying. She slumps into a chair.

'It's a full-time job, having a baby,' I say. 'Little guy is needy.'

'You don't want to know,' Crystal says.

'Here, I bought this for you.' I give her the pressies. 'That's what I came over for.'

'Means a lot to me, Grace.' She sniffs at the rosemary scent of the soap. 'You know, all Benita wanted was her baby. I think she's angry that I had one instead of her. She's never got over that miscarriage. Her chances of having another child are zero and she can't forgive me.'

She unpacks the bags as she talks, stacks the groceries in the cupboard. Crisps and a Castle six-pack for Wayne and *biltong*, and white bread, sugar, flour, headache tablets. You'd need headache tablets if all you ate and drank was crisps and beer, if all you did was shout.

Ricardo watches her, then squeals and stretches his arms out to Crystal. For once she acts like a mother. She picks him up and cuddles him. His head settles sideways onto her shoulder. He snuggles into the warmth of her neck and chest. The three of us have a moment of peace sitting there in the kitchen at the table, and I believe there's hope for the two of them after all.

I sweep up the glass in the passage, twist out the shards left in the frame and resurrect the photograph on the chest of drawers.

The budgie, under soft bright feathers, is hard and so small. I wrap him in a tissue from the rainbow pack, courtesy of Martha, and tuck him into the front pocket of my rucksack.

'Going so soon?' Crystal asks.

'I've got chores. Sweep the yard. Water the plants. Martha gets stroppy if I don't do them.' I roll my eyes. 'But hey, why don't you visit later? Martha's been baking again.'

'So you can pick my brains more about what it's like having a baby?'

'She's made chocolate cake with caramel-fudge icing. Just looks to me like you could use a break.'

Even as I'm going out of the door, Crystal is throwing a dishcloth over the birdcage. Wayne is at the fridge, pulling the tab off the next beer, glugging it down like that beer is water.

In the street, Shardonnay and Ramon

are at it. Ramon's hands are all over Sha, wrapping around her, then exploring under her shirt right there in plain view. The dream couple so into each other, as if nothing sinful had happened to separate them. So close that you'd swear nothing evil could creep between them.

From The Journal
of Crystal September

After Grace left I tidied a bit. Pushed the cage back into the corner. Emptied the ashtrays. Wayne's mess. Picked up the cans off the lounge floor.

In the kitchen I started packing away the clean dishes. I took the knife from the drying rack. I wiped water from the blade of the paring knife. I turned to Ricardo. And for no good reason – maybe it was the thumping sound of the spoon against the high chair that I couldn't stand – I licked Ricardo's arm with the blade. That plump soft upper arm. I couldn't help it, I swear. It happened so quickly.

His sudden tears with the sting of the cut scared me as I watched the blood bead from a thin red line. There, there, Ricardo, don't take on so. It's hardly a scratch. It'll be better soon.

I sponged the split skin with cotton wool soaked in Dettol. *Ricardo screamed louder with the sting of antiseptic than he had with the stroke of the blade, just a score at his skin, really, so it couldn't have been that sore. But he wailed. His gaping mouth a black hole. I could see right to the back of his throat. I could do nothing to comfort him other than tell him I'm sorry, I'm sorry, I don't know what got into me. How could I have done this thing to you?*

Ricardo sobbed as I held him over my shoulder. I rubbed his back till he sobbed in odd gasps. Don't worry, baby, it's over now. Please don't take on so, Ricardo. I hid the cut under a plaster from the kit in the drawer. There, that looks pretty, I said. I patted the plaster in place. A very small hurt. Nothing to worry about. You'll see, everything will come right.

I'm in Martha's garden. I make a little hole in the flowerbed next to the wall. Near the final resting place of our tabby cat that died last year. It's a regular pet cemetery. I put daisies and lavender in the grave and cover the bird with earth. The Maltese mutt looks at me, blinking. I throw him a dog treat. I put a rock on the grave in case the mutt has any ideas of digging up the bird.

To dust you shall return.

Crystal brings Ricardo over a little while later.

'Poor baby, did he hurt himself?' Martha's hand hovers over the Mickey Mouse plaster on Ricardo's arm.

'That's nothing. A little scrape. Happened after you left, Grace. You know how boys are, always getting cuts and bruises.'

Martha's voice is soft and warm in the lounge, like sunshine. She brings tea and cake. She says, 'Crystal, you're capable of taking good care of the baby. There's a lot of love in you. It'll get better. Bring the little boy over to our house more often. Come and visit with me. I get lonely during the day when Grace's not around.'

'How will it ever get better?' Crystal wants to know. 'He's here for life.'

'He won't always be as demanding. Isn't he cute?' Martha croons and holds him on her mountains of flesh and tickles him under the chin as if he is a kitten. 'Just give yourself time, Crystal. Have you spoken to the sisters at the clinic? They're very nice. Maybe it's postnatal depression. Have you spoken to your mother?'

Crystal picks up Ricardo.

'I have to go.'

I walk with Crystal and Ricardo to the street.

Crystal says, 'Your mother is nice.'

'She's not my mother.'

I wash the tea things. I break a cup. By accident. Or is it?

CHAPTER 11
On the run

Saturday night. The school hall is decorated with cardboard waves and palm trees. The theme is *On the Beach*. There's a DJ. There are parents and teachers watching. The dance is OK. I know that everyone is just pretending; acting like this is the highlight. But it's the after-party everyone is waiting for. Boys in rented suits and cummerbunds, girls in evening dresses, just waiting to strip and change. To get away from the school hall and into Liquid Dreams. I've told Martha Freddy will bring me home from the after party. I'll be late. *He's a nice boy. Don't worry, Martha.*

Liquid Dreams is pumping. Girls gyrate, sweat gleaming on exposed bellies and on breasts plumped up by push-up bras beneath skimpy tops and strappy dresses. Sweat shines on the boys too, on arms with muscles popping like tennis balls.

I'm watching from a booth at the side of the dance floor. The house stuff pounds so loud it's like the beat is in there, in my head, *doef, doef, doef.* It's past two. I'm whacked. But I'm with Shardonnay and Ramon.

I don't admit this to anyone and sometimes I have a hard time believing it myself, but I want some cool guy to worship me like Ramon does with Sha. I want him to put his arms around me and settle his hands at the small of my back like he loves me. But I don't want Freddy drooling near me. Thank God that Freddy, as predicted, sets up in the passage near the toilets at the back of the club, where he spends the night dishing out whatever is in those plastic bags in his pockets – the pills and straws of *tik.*

To Ramon I'm invisible. He knows my name but he doesn't really see me. Tonight he says, *Hey, Grace*, when he picks us up at the duplex for the dance at Capricorn High, but that's as far as it ever goes. No *how are you, what music d'you like, what are your hobbies?* None of that kind of interest.

I don't know if he really sees Shardonnay either. His glassy eyes fixate on her breasts and her flat stomach with the blue stone on her belly ring flashing, and he slides his hand down her back, resting it there on the bare skin between her skirt and top. He *feels* Shardonnay. But I don't think he sees her, really *sees* her. Not *ever*, if you know what I'm saying. So I watch Shardonnay and I watch Ramon, and I'm thinking what I always think about him. A guy like this is trouble. You need a guy like this like you need a hole in the head.

I sit in the booth and watch the staccato dancing, the way the strobe lights break up the movement into single frames. I watch for a long time before I get up, strangling my bottle at the neck, and join Shardonnay and Ramon and dance for the hell of it.

The DJ is doing his thing there in his box, mixing tunes and sending up the pulse rate. High-energy night.

It's like the techno is in your blood and in the walls and in the floor, like every arm and leg in the place belongs to you. As long as there's beat and flashing lights you can dance on forever. Till you need another drink.

Back at the table, Freddy passes Shardonnay a tiny blue pill. He does it in front of everyone, like it's no big deal.

'Hey, Grace,' he says, 'how about one for you? It'll relax you, make you feel tiptop.'

'Maybe some other time, Freddy.'

'You should try it, Gracie, you'll like it. C'mon, girl, what you waiting for?'

And I sigh with relief as some client distracts him back to business.

Maybe that's what scares me suddenly – that I'll try it and what if I like it? That I'll take drugs and sway to this house trash, stoned out my mind and end up pregnant like Crystal or, worse, dead like that girl from school, raped and killed last year on an empty plot she was crossing as a short cut to get home after a late night.

My eyes are on Ramon again. Good to be Bad. All the foolish girls in love with Ramon. Like the boys are in love with Shardonnay.

Later, Shardonnay staggers around and disappears. It doesn't look right. I wonder if it's the drugs or if it's the *Brutal Fruit* she's knocking back like cola. I'm still on an early one, a sense of self-preservation having kicked in – the curse of the responsible.

A while later I check the toilets. There's Shardonnay, her back against the wall in the dingy passage, Tashreeq Arendse giving her a good go, screwing her, Ramon standing right there, smoking, drugged-up, watching. 'What you looking at, Grace? Friends share.' I can't believe it.

Then Freddy is at my side, saying, 'How about *we* get it together, Grace?' Freddy staring at me, licking his lips. 'Let's *dance*, Grace, if you know what I mean.' My tongue is a dry carpet, my palms sweaty, my heart running a marathon. I'm short of breath. I want to be sick. No thanks.

I tell Freddy, 'I really have to pee.'

In the ladies, there are girls writing their names in lipstick on the mirror, totally out of it, falling all over each other. Reality check.

Freddy the creep is waiting for me outside the swing door. Shardonnay and Tashreeq and Ramon are gone.

'You ready for me now?' Freddy says and clutches at his pants. 'You ready for the real me?' He grins. 'I'm gonna work myself into your good *graces*,' he says, as if this play on my name will impress me. Jesus, doesn't that knock the beat right out of my head. I don't want to be forced to beg him to use one of the free condoms in my bag.

I get back to being one hundred per cent Grace. I want to be cool about this. I tell Freddy, 'You're cute. But let's dance first.'

He pushes up against me, pumps my breasts. All the time my heart is racing. I'm praying *get me out of here, please.* Then some kid comes and tells Freddy he's desperate for a hit of this or that. Freddy the main man tells me, 'I'll see you later.' I smile at him, circle my index finger at the top of my cleavage, like I'm really going to be around when he comes looking.

Shardonnay swaying out of control on the dance floor scares me. Ramon's hands are all over her, touching her, and then he leaves and some other guy comes up and gropes her too, and I wonder what's going on here? Who's next in line? I'm not waiting any longer for something worse to happen.

It often does. It's in the papers. It's out there in the mornings on the lampposts. Posters announcing *teenage girl raped by three men in a taxi*, or *child missing*, or – I can see it now – *hard lessons in lust at local night club*. I won't end up one of those victims. Shardonnay won't be one of those girls either. But Ramon isn't going to get us home safe any time soon. Anyone can see that.

Shardonnay is falling about on the edge of the dance floor, so at least I don't have to push through a mass of hot bodies to get to her. I'm thankful there's no sign of Freddy with his bloodshot eyes.

'C'mon Shardonnay, we have to go.'

'Hey, get out of my way Grace,' she yells above the music.

'C'mon Sha, it's late.'

'I'm not coming,' she says. 'I'm staying with Ramon.'

'You have to come home with me, Sha. Please.' I take her arm and pull her from the mass of kids. She drops her bottle. We get out of there. When I look back some cleaner in overalls is mopping up the mess, and there is Freddy eye-balling me, scowling, pushing towards me and Sha, the both of us already at the door.

I take my chances with the shadows, the wind howling now, the sounds of the night like a hundred girls screaming. I run into the road, drag Sha behind me, the sweeping light from passing cars showing the way.

'Why you doing this to me, Grace?' Sha slurs, moaning now, but she's walking, keeping up.

Nearly home. Still on Prince George's. Me and Sha in our tight and sexy after-party clothes. Sha's skirt is torn and dirty. We pass a couple of prostitutes. A couple of dogs bark. Cars go by, cruising for a bit of tail is how guys describe it.

But Sha is falling all over the place. Sha is slowing down. Sha won't move. She says 'Leave me, I can't go on.' She's pissed and drugged. She won't go on. So what do I do? I find my cell phone in my bag.

I call Martha. *Come fetch me. Please.* And tell her where. Taking her up on what she promised she'd do if there was alcohol flowing too freely, especially through *my* veins.

Another car drives past. I cross myself. The car keeps going. Doesn't slow down. Doesn't stop. Then Ramon's silver *Citi Golf* comes down the highway and pulls up alongside us. It's Freddy, talking out of the open window. 'What you doing in the street? Get in bitches,' and he's out of the car with that mean look in his eye.

And then Martha arrives in the beat-up *Toyota* of hers. I never thought I'd be happy to see her, but I am as she tells Freddy to *push off* like she's not afraid of him, and we get into her car. And Freddy's shouting at us, 'Shardonnay, what's Ramon gonna say about his girl leaving his side without a word?' As if Ramon would care. 'And you Grace Hunt, you bitch, you had your chance!'

'I'm glad you called me, Grace,' Martha says, our eyes locking in the rear-view mirror.

'I never sleep a wink before you get back. You know that. It's not that I don't trust you. I'm afraid of the vermin around, preying on vulnerable young girls, waiting to get them drunk and have their way with them.'

You mean *rape them* Martha. Right there in the school, or in the clubs, or on the pavement, or in their cars; throw them out on the streets when they're done using them.

Shardonnay passes out in the back seat. I think she's asleep or comatose or something, really out of it; but she leans against the side of the door, groans and opens her eyes. And after long minutes we are home.

From The Journal
of Crystal September

Wayne said, I see the way you are with that boy you go out with, that Keegan Arnold. That is what Wayne said to me. Don't tell me you don't want it. And he said, it's better the first time with someone you know. It is your duty, he said. A favour to your mother. How can I disturb Benita with my needs when she's still in mourning about her miscarriage? These are the things Wayne said to me.

The first time, Shardonnay was out. Benita was on night duty.

When I started to argue, Wayne put his hand over my mouth. I couldn't scream. No one was there to hear me anyway that first time. He did what he wanted.

Tonight though, I was not expecting him. I could hear the sound of the TV on downstairs. Some cop movie Benita had fallen asleep in front of. Benita was off tonight, but I'd stayed out of her way. Shardonnay still out at her dance, all dressed to the nines, and laughing before she left, going on about what a wonderful time she was going to have. Every minute of her time is spent out of the house. I've tried to go out and have a nice time. But that doesn't change what goes on in this room.

Ricardo was snoring gently next to me. Curled next to me, rooting for his bottle, snuggling into my warmth. I love him when he is quiet like this and has forgotten what I have done.

I heard the kitchen door. He was home. I listened to the way Wayne climbed the stairs, slowly, stopping after each creak in case Benita had heard him come home. Then he was at my door.

He closed it quietly. Turned the key. Locked us in. The way he does these days when he comes to my room, which is most nights after his shift.

I begged him. Wayne, not tonight. Leave me alone tonight. Please. Benita is home.

But I knew he wouldn't leave till he got what he came for.

He said, put the baby in his own bed. This is my right. If your mother can't perform, you girls are next in line. No question about it.

Shardonnay hadn't worked out for Wayne. She'd kicked him in the guts and fractured two ribs. A prisoner out of control at work was how he'd explained his injury to Benita.

Wayne sat on the edge of my bed, ran his fingers down my back. His fingers like snakes, slid over my skin.

Talk is useless. Whatever I say makes no difference. My begging only makes him more insistent.

Crystal, I like you the best, you are special, you are my favourite, he said. And it's not as if I'm your real father, is it? He lifted Ricardo and put him in the cot. Wayne said, I love having a baby in the house. You've given me what I've always wanted.

I closed my eyes. Waited for it to be over. I watched as Wayne pulled the covers right down and climbed on top of me. I watched from above, like I always do. I sat, cross-legged on my cupboard and peered over, as if I was watching an ugly TV show. I watched

Wayne, and I watched the child sleeping in the cot.

He was done, quickly. I heard the sound of Wayne's zip as he closed his flies. And his cough as he opened my door, and the soundtrack of the same cop movie, not over yet, as he stood a while and listened in case Benita had come up the stairs.

He left me. I heard the toilet flush. He took his time in the bathroom. Then he joined his wife, in front of the TV.

Grace asked me today, what do you write about in that notebook? But it's none of her business, is it?

The next morning I owe Martha an explanation, me being responsible and all. I don't know who stuck me with that label first, but I guess I live up to it. I'm ready to talk.

'I had a couple of coolers, that's all. I didn't let my booze out of my sight. I know

I didn't tell you where I was going after the dance, but I knew you'd kick up a fuss.'

Martha leans towards me and hugs me. I don't hug back. I'm not ready for this. But I have so suddenly seen sense that I keep a low profile that week at school.

At the weekend I go to the pet shop. The rats have been sold.

'We should sell those rats with a warning: They breed like rodents!' Melvyn says.

Saturday afternoon I go to the movies with Bianca and Tracey, girls in my class I used to hang out with. Girls with less drama in their lives. Martha drops us at the Blue Route, and picks us up. I stay home on Saturday night. I see Shardonnay leave with Ramon. She hasn't called me. The novelty of having me tag along has worn off. Wayne and Benita argue bitterly, but we can't make out what it's about, me and Martha, straining to hear. Something to do with Shardonnay is it?

'Well, at last they're doing something about her wild ways,' Martha says.

Later I hear Ricardo wailing. I stay out of it. Crystal is doing better with Ricardo, isn't she? She knows she can come over if there's a problem.

I watch a *chick flick* on TV, with Martha. We eat popcorn. Martha's is plain. Mine has salt and butter. She covets mine, but I remind her what's good for her.

The sky is black velvet, with stars sewn on like sequins. The wind streams under my window. I stuff a T-shirt at the crack. Pull the duvet under my chin. I am safe.

Palm Sunday after Lent, Martha renounces the wickedness of the world.

When God created the world, he brought order out of chaos. Ordered prayer life is a small reflection of the order which is God's purpose for the world.

Though I don't tune in much to the words, I hear Father Adam's passion. Whatever he is, he is a good man. Light, like lasers, cuts through brilliant stained glass. Saints of transparent pink, blues, yellows do penance on the floor between the pews as the sun rises.

The Septembers are not at church. Whatever God's purpose, man has other plans.

My project is due on Monday. I write what I know, what I've seen, what I've read. Martha knocks on my door while I'm at it, says she's glad I've taken the project seriously. *You can do whatever you want in the world if you have an education.*

In the afternoon, I hose the yard and give the plants a good soak. I stroke the mutt, watch a nature programme, help with dinner. Maybe I'll go back to being an example. It suits me better.

CHAPTER 12
Like cat and dog

Next Saturday afternoon, I'm back in Sha's room. Shardonnay spreads shaving foam on her legs, drags the razor gently along each calf, leaving pathways of smooth skin, then wipes off the excess foam with a towel.

'Why don't you wax?' I make small talk.

'Way too sore,' she says. Then Shardonnay paints her toenails a jazzy purple, silver stars floating in the varnish, like a night sky. Her toes are spread and separated by tight wads of cotton wool. The purple varnish matches the barely-there silk dress hanging on the back of the chair.

I offer to do her fingernails but she says she knows just how to get the stars in the centre of each nail. I hold the bottle. Sha blows on her right hand so the nails are dry before she does her left. *You can't be in a hurry*, she says, as she floats her hands in front of her, waiting for the varnish to harden. As if this is something really important she's putting her energy into.

She turns up an *Anastacia* hit on the CD player, sings about how nothing is gonna keep her down, keep her from doing what she wants to do.

Shardonnay taps her foot to the beat and rotates her pelvis. Even sitting on the bed she can do it. Practising for her Big Dream. In the meantime looking for love in all the wrong places.

'What about tonight? You coming along, Grace?'

'Is this really what you want to do, Sha? Hang out at Liquid Dreams?'

'Hey, I can do what I like. You had fun clubbing, right? Breaking out of your straightjacket?'

'Sha, didn't you get a wake-up when you were so out of it last time?'

'I can hardly remember yesterday, never mind about last week, or the week before. So what if I overdid it a bit,' she laughs, ha ha. 'And what I like is going out with Ramon. We going over to Tashreeq's first. Nothing wild, we'll talk, have a few laughs. Benita's off tonight. Best I'm not around. Anyway, what's it to you, Grace?'

'I'm scared for you, Shardonnay.'

'Your brain is working overtime, Grace.'

'Listen, Sha. At the club, Freddy was about to screw me in the passage at the men's room if I gave him half a chance. I had to get Martha to come pick us up. You remember that part, right?'

'Hey, don't overreact, Grace – shit

happens. I'm cool, Grace. We cool. Me and Ramon are cool. That's all that matters.'

'I'm worried about you, Sha.'

'Don't stress, Grace. Even if I felt like talking, there's nothing to say. Nothing that would matter.'

She stands in front of the dressing table mirror, stickers of Tinkerbell and the Ninja Turtles peeling off the glass, stuck in the corners from when she was a little girl. Pale blue underwear, with lace on the edges of her bra and at her hipbones along the top of the G-string, shows off the flawless honey of her skin. Her hair is damp from the shower.

Then I notice the marks.

'Hell, Shardonnay, I hope Ramon didn't do that to you.' I'm looking at a set of bruises, purple and yellow, in shades of healing on the outside of her thighs.

'Oh, that.' She makes up what sounds like an excuse. 'Ricardo kicked me. He was having a tantrum. You won't believe the power in that tiny body.'

Shardonnay, usually not shy about parading in her panties, pulls a towel from the bed and wraps it around her waist. 'Hey, Grace,' she says, 'just wait in the kitchen why don't you? Till I'm done dressing.'

I'm about to leave the room when Crystal barges in, goes straight to the CD and switches it off.

'Hey, what did you do that for?' Shardonnay is annoyed.

'I said to iron Wayne's prison shirts, Shardonnay.'

'Get out of my room, Crystal.'

'Who d'you think you are?' Crystal yells. 'Think you can live here and not do your share? I work my butt off packing bags at the *Friendly* and you can't even do a little ironing when I ask you? For your stepdaddy?'

Crystal sounds just like Benita, almost the same words coming from her mouth, the tone escalating to a cutting whine. 'You never do a thing around here. I'm the one who has to carry the load.'

I'm suddenly worried about Ricardo. 'Crystal, where's the baby?'

'Sleeping.' She flashes the barbed wire look that warns Stay Out. 'Don't fuss about my kid, Grace.' Then turns to Shardonnay. 'You'd think I'd have a minute to myself when the little guy is asleep, but no, the shirts aren't done. If I leave them like that Wayne will shit all over me. Jesus, Shardonnay, can't you ever help me out?'

'You supposed to do the housework. Wayne said,' retorts Shardonnay.

'Are you taking Wayne's side against me?'

'I'm saying I've got schoolwork, Crystal. Besides, I never see any of your money. You about to tell me you put food on the table with your little job? Mommy puts food on the table, not you. They pay you peanuts down there. Why d'you humiliate yourself? Did I ever tell you how sexy you look in that grass-green overall, effing *Friendly* logo splashed across your boobs? A real turn on to the guys. I've got to babysit and I'm not the one who got herself pregnant!'

'I'll kill you,' screams Crystal, going for Shardonnay with the same craziness flashing in her eyes as her mother. Crystal yanks Shardonnay's hair. Sha, in some bizarre moment of self-preservation, tries to keep her nails from getting ruined. Her hands flap uselessly at her sides as she twists her head and kicks out at Crystal. I pick up the full glass on the bedside table and toss the water at the fighting cats.

Crystal gasps. She wipes water from her face. 'What did you do that for?' At the door, she turns, dazed and shaken and says softly: 'You Sha, you putting on your make-up ready to go out, but me, I'm stuck here with Ricardo. And Grace, Mrs Williams thinks she can get you understand what it's like being pregnant, but what about afterwards? Do you understand what it's like looking after a real live baby? Do you understand there's no future for yourself?'

'It doesn't have to be like that, does it?'

'For me, it is.'

Blood beads along the scratches on Shardonnay's arm.

Crystal is sobbing now in the bathroom. The door is open. She's slouched on the toilet seat, head in her hands. From the doorway I see Ricardo fast asleep in his cot, his mouth pulling on the dummy. He's used to this kind of ruckus. Sleeps through any riot.

Crystal comes down to the kitchen before Shardonnay, with her brown hair combed and clipped off her face, her face washed and shining, her eyes swollen.

'Think you gonna do better with your life?' Crystal looks at me. 'Better than me and Shardonnay?'

Stained

I don't know why, but I think to myself, what if we look closer? What is it brooding in the background? There's something for sure.

I think, *Yes, I want to do better with my life.*

From The Journal
of Crystal September

He cast a dark shadow across the wall, like the monsters that used to scare me in my dreams when I was a small girl. I knew that finding me asleep wouldn't put him off. Nothing ever puts him off. I wanted to stretch my mouth wide and scream Benita out of her bed, scream Shardonnay into the room with me. I wanted to scream the house down. But it was too late. Benita was passed out. Shardonnay had gone with Ramon.

His smell got to me first, always the smell of sweat mingling with the cheap cologne he splashes on before he comes to my room. As if he is trying to please me.

I relaxed my eyes, kept them still behind the lids. Slowed my breathing right down. Surely, surely he would leave me alone tonight I prayed. He knew I was not well. He sat on the bed. He stroked my cheek. I smelled the stale smoke concentrated in the brown stains on his fingers. He coughed into his hand. A sickening rattle. He couldn't stop coughing.

Wouldn't do to wake Ricardo, he said, and got up, went into the passage and finished his coughing fit there.

I heard Benita call, are you home Wayne?

Who does Benita think it is? Mommy, half knocked out by those sleeping tablets she steals from the pharmacy at the old people's home. Mommy, not knowing what is going on under the roof of her own house.

Wayne called to Benita, yes, it's me. Go back to sleep.

He waited a moment. Then he said, I've missed you. It's been a few days. You must be better by now.

He used to come only when Benita was away on shift. But he comes more and more now. He doesn't care if Benita is in the house. He tried again with Shardonnay a few nights ago. I heard it. She struggled. He thinks I don't know, but I do.

Tonight he opened his zip. Pulled himself out. Brought himself closer. I tasted the salt of him.

I watched what I was doing, from above, where I sat, my legs hanging loose. I was surprised he couldn't hear the banging of my heels against the top of the cupboard door. Then I brought my knees up to my face. I turned away, shivering. Waiting to climb back into my skin.

When I was back in my bed, I couldn't sleep.

So I write. I am not sure of anything. This is why I write, to make my life real.

Later, much later, Shardonnay has let herself in. It is close to three in the morning. Partying till all hours, her liquid flesh poured into that clingy dress, showing every curve. Shardonnay is the golden girl. The one who can say No.

And who am I? Who is Crystal September? Nobody.

CHAPTER 13
The lost soul

'Have a nice time,' Martha calls after the minibus. Not like her to miss a church picnic, but it's the weight that gets in the way. No sofas at Silvermine Nature Reserve to .spread herself on. 'Wish I could go with you, but I'm baking for the confirmation celebration next weekend.' Cupcakes sprinkled with hundreds and thousands, coconut doughnuts, blueberry muffins.

Today, the choirgirls in North Stars and jeans and T-shirts chill out. I connect with Bianca and Tracey. We talk about our project, about how Mrs Williams really cares, how she goes the extra mile. Bianca goes on, *what will you do when you finish school?* I shrug. There are still two years. I don't tell about Martha's endless enquiries, to UCT and Pen Tech and Rhodes. *Education is the key.* To WITS, to UWC, Stellenbosch. She's got every brochure, every form, for every university, every college.

Shardonnay and Ramon are there too, lying on a plaid blanket, all lovey-dovey as if nothing has ever come between them. Crystal is nearby, cradling Ricardo in her arms. Even Wayne and Benita settle down together on a blanket in the laziness of the day, in the dappled light, under the canopy of pine branches.

We pig out on sausage grilled on the *braai*, and chops and ribs, and roasted corn on the cob. Baked beans, coleslaw, beetroot. Fruit salad, trifle, cake and pastries.

At the end of the day, I lie on my back, eyes closed, lulled by the peace of the forest. I feel the breath of the slightest breeze on my face. I turn my head and look at the stretch of dam alongside the picnic area. Water the colour of Coca Cola, afternoon sun glinting gold where I'd rinsed my feet earlier and watched Crystal skipping stones, watched the ripples spread and the water settle again. Way above, tree trunks slope in, converging to a common point, the light sparkling through the top branches.

From The Journal of Crystal September

I stood at the edge of the water, the wind lifting small waves over my feet and back again. The water lapped gently, like an animal licking at my toes. I picked up a shiny stone that had caught my eye. The late sun glancing off it, I noticed how flat it was. Sticks, pine needles, stones and the dark mud swirled as I circled my foot in the water. I watched the silt settle. I lifted my head towards the long rays of the sun. Warm on my face. I rubbed my thumb across the slate surface of the stone.

Then I turned again to the water. Blacker and blacker the further the dam stretched, till it seemed to me as dense as coal. No one would find anything lost in the water. Anything lost would be there forever.

I pulled my arm back as far as I could, twisting sideways, aimed and skimmed the stone across the water. One, two, three, four, five, six skips, then the stone was gone. I watched as the circles touched the shore, and a moment later the water was smooth again.

Wayne was standing on a boulder high up on the slope like he was on top of the world. He waved to me. I turned back to the water.

I unhooked the bracelet. The one Wayne gave me for my eighteenth birthday. The one with a gold charm of a baby dangling from it. A gold bracelet, nineteen-carat and worth a few hundred I'm sure. But I didn't think twice. I threw it. I watched as it flew through the air, the charm suspended for a split second, before it fell, and disappeared, with a quiet splash in the black water.

Look Ricardo, look, it's like a giant sandpit here, I said to my child. Play with the dirt Ricardo. And I watched as his tiny fingers clutched at the earth, and small stones and pine needles. Watched him laugh as he played.

The debris of the picnic was all around. Scraps of cheese curls and crusts, and smears of mayonnaise on paper plates. Empty bowls. Crushed cool drink cans and used serviettes. Somebody had to do it. Somebody had to clean up the mess. The day had to end. So I got on with packing the cooler box, not that the crowd had left much. I put the leftovers of grapes and cheese in the giant cooler box. I wrapped them first in tin foil. They took up a small space.

You had a busy day, Ricardo. He was done with his playing. You tired, aren't you? His eyes were heavy. Have a rest, baby, I said. I picked him up. Wrapped him in his blanket. He curled up and sucked the last bit of milk from the bottle. He was so tired he went straight to sleep.

So beautiful when he is sleeping.

I looked around after I was done. The picnic site was tidy. I put the lid on the cooler box. Airtight. I rinsed my hands in the cool water. Dirt was caked under my fingernails. Fingers still greasy from cleaning up. I went to the toilet, where I could wash my hands with soap.

I hear the sounds of packing up. Scraping, scrunching, the rustling of bags.

A little later Crystal stands near me, asks: 'Where is he?'

'Who, Crystal?'

'Ricardo. He was there a minute ago. I left him right there. I went to wash my hands.' She points to the toilet block. 'He was fast asleep. He couldn't have rolled down to the water, could he?' Her voice suddenly anxious.

'No way Crystal. There's not much of a slope. There, he's with Benita over there.' I point to the group of women, Benita and her nursing friends I recognise from the congregation, chatting, their backs against large boulders. Benita holds the bundle in her arms, holds Ricardo close against her chest.

'My baby,' Crystal sighs. 'You know Grace, in one split second I can imagine all the dreadful things that can happen to my son in this world.'

'Stop it, Crystal. Nothing is going to happen to Ricardo. He probably started crying and Benita picked him up.'

'He always wants something.'

'Soon he can go to a Day Mom, can't he? At least for a few hours a morning? There's that playgroup run from a house just down our road. Then you can finish school. It's only a couple of subjects you need, right?'

'Two more exams to do. When he was born he was so puny I had to almost live at the hospital for a month before I could bring him home. No way I could finish. Most days,' she sighs, 'I feel stuck. I think I'll never get further than I am.'

'Don't be negative Crystal, you can do it. *Obstacles are those frightful things you see when you take your eyes off your goal.*' I laugh. 'That's one of Martha's favourite sayings. By Henry Ford. Stuck on our fridge. She laps up these words of wisdom. And you, Crystal, can do anything you set your mind to.'

'You really think so, Grace?'

'I do.'

Benita walks over to us, saying what a pleasant day it's been and that it's getting late and we'd better go before the sun sets.

'Whose child is that in your arms, Mommy?' Crystal asks.

'Michelle Heyns over there, this is her grandchild.'

Sleeping against Benita's breast is another girl's child. Not Crystal's.

'But where is Ricardo, Mommy?'

I sit up. My stomach lurching.

'What are you talking about, Crystal?'

'Ricardo, Mommy. I thought that baby you holding was Ricardo.'

'Crystal, you not asking me where your son is, are you?'

'I am asking you. I thought he was with you.'

'You had him ten minutes ago, Crystal.'

'I was packing up. I went to the toilet. Last I saw he was sleeping on the blanket near the picnic area.' Panic rises in her voice as she starts to call frantically for him. 'Ricardo?'

'Crystal, don't worry,' Benita says. 'Probably Wayne has him.'

Crystal runs now, to the group of men and boys returning from the nature walk. She trips on a tree root but quickly gets up again. She's torn her denims. Her knee is bleeding.

Ricardo is not with the men either.

'He can't walk. He can't crawl. No way he could roll into the water,' Wayne says.

'Then where is he?' Crystal screams. 'Where is my baby? I left him on that blanket for one minute. Who has my baby?' She runs from this one to that one. *Do you have my baby?*

Shardonnay says, 'It's OK, we'll find him, it's OK.' She holds Crystal, keeps her from collapsing to the ground. I have a bad feeling in the pit of my stomach. I'm standing there hearing everything around me and watching people go frantic. Like I'm part of some second-rate reality TV show. This can't be real.

Shardonnay says, 'Crystal, he's probably with one of the younger girls. They love playing with babies. They should tell you in future if they pick him up. He's so cute they probably couldn't resist. See, everybody's coming back now.'

I climb onto a boulder the size of a car. I look around. I see rocks, hollow logs, piles of leaves. I see people running around looking for Ricardo.

Fear clutches, squeezes hearts. We stare at the expanse of water, so dense nothing can be seen in it. The lengthening light of the late afternoon, like knife blades, cuts the surface. Crystal runs in circles screaming for Ricardo, *Where are you, where are you?*

Wayne is on his cell, talking to the police. Emergency services are on the way.

Wayne says, 'We'll find him.' He rounds up the children. 'Has anyone been playing with the baby? Did you pick him up and put him down somewhere? Tell Uncle Wayne now.' But the children shake their heads and look scared. The children know that the nightmare they have been warned about is happening right here.

'Who could have taken him? This was a church do, wasn't it?' someone says.

'We weren't the only people here. We've been playing ball, walking,' Wayne says. 'You left him alone, Crystal.'

'You saying it's my fault, Wayne?' Crystal says, dead eyes looking at him. 'I shouldn't have left him, not for a second.'

We cannot find Ricardo.

Ricardo is gone.

Police divers go down with torches, the lights a dim haze in the water.

The divers pull a rusted bicycle frame from the far end of the dam. And a carcass of a large dog. Someone's pet wearing a collar. A stretch of two-toned hair still attached to his hide. Maybe a German Shepherd. The water has done its work and there are leeches on his hind legs.

Found something. A diver holds up a baby's bottle. But Crystal does not recognise the ABC pattern.

Benita wraps her arms around Crystal. Crystal pushes her away.

Crystal won't let anybody touch her. She sits on a tree stump with her legs folded and drawn against her chest, her chin resting on her knees. She rocks back and forth, back and forth.

Police comb Silvermine. They search the dense brush. And still the divers search, but there is no baby.

It could have been a baboon that took the baby, someone says.

'Take the mom to the station to fill in the forms,' a police detective says to Benita. 'Then take her home. This is traumatic.

We'll let you know. There is nothing you can do here.'

I call Martha on my cell. Martha says, 'Grace, we can pray. Later we can bring the September's some dinner. I'll make shepherd's pie. They have to eat.'

Ricardo is officially missing.

CHAPTER 14
All these questions

Crystal sits on a bench in the charge office. Me and Sha on either side of her. Benita is at the counter. A policeman hands Benita a clipboard and a pen, and asks her to help her daughter fill in forms. *The pen is yours to keep,* he says, as if he's trying to make up for the family's loss.

A man staggers into the charge office, a knife handle sticking out at right angles from the side of his skull. *My friend stabbed me. We got in a fight.*

A junior policeman, new to the job I'd say, panics, says *Must we pull it out or what?*

Another, older and calmer, says *No man, leave the knife there. Call the paramedics. You pull out the knife he'll bleed more.* They lead him away.

Crystal is dazed. Confused. She is no help with the forms. She sits on her hands. Slumped forward. Stares at the injured man's trail of blood spilled on the tiled floor. No one comes to clean up. He could be HIV positive. He could have AIDS.

A blond man, next in line, reports his cell phone stolen. *Don't leave the temptation on your dashboard next time*, a new cop on duty says.

There's yelling and swearing from the holding cells below, echoing and bouncing off the passage walls right into the charge office. The walls of the office a sickening pink, like diluted blood.

A pin-board takes up nearly half of one wall, covered in black and white composite drawings of suspects wanted for questioning in cases of robbery, rape, and murder. On another board are the photographs and printouts of faces of the missing – babies, teenagers, old people – with promises of rewards for information.

A policewoman brings Crystal some tea in a pretty mug, with butterflies on it. The mug and Crystal, too pretty for this police station. *Lots of sugar in there,* the policewoman says. *For the shock, you know.* But Crystal doesn't drink the tea. Her hands wrap around the mug, draw warmth from it, till the tea turns cold. Till the policewoman takes it from her.

Crystal says, 'What am I doing here? Why can't I go home?' She wipes dirty hands on her T-shirt. Her denims are torn and blood-streaked, her nails broken, her fingers raw from digging to uncover her baby at the picnic site. Crazy with grief she was, screaming that if Ricardo wasn't in the water she'd find him buried there somewhere in the forest.

A detective sits next to her, with forms of his own, asks, 'What was the little man wearing?'

'Red track pants, right, Crystal?' Shardonnay says. 'And the red jersey with a yellow taxi on the front. Bright clothing. From Pep Stores. Good value. I swear we keep that shop going. We get shoes there, and pyjamas and things like that. Not only Ricardo's clothes…'

The cop buts in, 'What about distinguishing features?'

'Like a birthmark or something?' Sha asks.

'That's right. Anything to help us identify him.'

'He has a big gap between his front teeth,' Sha says. 'But most babies do. He has soft, dark hair, just starting to grow nicely. He was a baldy but he's not any more. Here's the photo they asked me to bring.'

'See, he has dimples like mine. Like my Daddy had,' Crystal says. 'And he has blue eyes. Eyes like ice. Cold eyes. Like his father's eyes.'

Benita gets up, pulls a smoke from her bag, lights up as she leaves the charge office.

Shardonnay hands over the photo of Ricardo taken when he was just three months old. Five minutes later, the cop pins up an A3 photostat enlargement and Ricardo's face laughs out from the missing person's board. He is bigger now. But still the same.

Benita September is called to the counter, to the phone. An urgent message. She tells us nothing when she puts down the phone.

Benita and the policewoman whisper together, the policewoman's hand on Benita's arm. Benita comes back to us. To Crystal sitting stiffly on the bench between Sha and me.

'Come,' she says. 'It's over, Crystal. Let's go home.'

CHAPTER 15
The door is open

A Monday evening six weeks later, Martha calls me to watch *Behind Closed Doors*, one of those TV programmes where reporters find the truth of what's happening out there, and they tell the world the real story. Like what happened to Crystal September.

Martha bangs on the door. 'You may as well glue those earphones to your head,' Martha teases. What does she expect with the latest Robbie Williams out? She should be pleased I'm lightening up a bit.

I sit at her feet, a pillow behind my back against the *Lazee Boy*. Though it's warm in the lounge, I put one of Martha's throws over my shoulders and pull it tight for comfort. Even the mutt knows something is up. He tucks his snout in my lap. This is the programme we've been waiting for.

The camera pans across a group of girls squashed in a tiny room. These are Crystal's friends, wiping their tears, linking their arms, looking around the room as if they can't believe what's happened. The room is empty now, but I remember how it had looked: Crystal's bed, with the pink duvet with the big red roses printed on it, and matching pillows and a ruffle around the bed. On a shelf were stuffed animals. Jammed between the window and the bed was Ricardo's cot.

Letisha Abrahams, Crystal's best friend, pulls out a heart-shaped cushion from a cardboard box in the corner of the room. One of those cushions boys give girls on Valentine's Day – *I heart u* embroidered in white on the red satin. There are hangers in the box, and a baby's blanket, a pair of scuffed school shoes – leftovers from Crystal's life.

'Keegan Arnold, her boyfriend, gave her this. Before she got pregnant,' Letisha says, squeezing the cushion against her chest. 'We thought Ricardo was his baby. Keegan loved her, you know that? If only she talked to us, we could have helped.'

'It's not as if this doesn't happen,' Zelda Africa says. 'Around here girls get pregnant a lot.'

Letisha says, 'We could have told someone. A teacher. Or maybe phoned Childline or Helpline. Heavens, there are lots of numbers. Like Loveline. The number is staring you right in the face right there on a billboard outside Capricorn High. The number the size of a man.'

The reporter asks: 'You think that would have helped? To call one of those numbers?'

Letisha says, 'They say they can help you. Then they must help you.'

'None of us knew how bad she was feeling,' Zelda says. 'We said, *Come out with us Crystal, have a night out, everybody needs a night on the town. Come, girl, eat ice cream at the market.* But she just said she had to look after the baby. Crystal didn't want to see her old friends any more. We didn't bother much after that. Her whole life was the baby and cleaning up after the others in that house.'

Letisha says, 'But whatever was going on, Crystal didn't have to kill herself!'

The next shots are at the cemetery. Letisha and Zelda stand at the foot of Crystal's grave. *Beloved Crystal September. Daughter. Sister. Mother.* On the grave a vase of plastic roses. Jars of daisies, *vygies*, lavender; flowers people left on the grave after they heard the story.

'I can't believe she did that,' Zelda says. 'How can life be so bad you have to go and *hang* yourself in your own back yard? Leave yourself there for your family to find you?'

'Why didn't she tell someone what was going on?' Letisha asks the reporter, as if maybe the reporter has the answers to it all.

Crystal September hanged herself from the steel post at one end of the washing line, on the night of the church picnic. She stood on a plastic chair in the back yard. Kicked it out from under her. The rope around her neck did the rest.

Martha and I heard Shardonnay's cry early the next morning, heard the cry become a wail.

We heard Benita scream, 'Call Wayne, oh my God, get Wayne.'

When I looked over the wall into their stark yard, not a flower planted there, I saw Benita holding her hands on either side of her face, staring at her child, at Crystal's face, purple and swollen and silent.

In the documentary, Letisha's voice is hardly a whisper: 'And as far as the story with Crystal's baby goes, I still can't believe Crystal put little Ricardo in the *cooler box*.'

From The Journal
of Crystal September

Ricardo, sleeping so peacefully and so deeply, didn't even stir as I placed him down in the box. The small breathing body of my baby boy, wrapped warm and snug in his blanket. My boy, asleep. So beautiful.

When he looks at me, I see you, Wayne.

Then he is not my baby.

Then he is your son.

Never my baby, when he looks at me.

But when Ricardo's eyes are closed, the eyes I can no longer bear, and he cannot remind me of you, then he is mine.

Only when he is sleeping is he my baby.

The day Crystal is found, the police talk to everyone on the street. They come to me and Martha. They are interested in the things I know about Crystal.

The police say, 'We hear you've been taking notes. Asking Crystal September questions for some kind of school project?'

I tell them, 'You know she had a notebook too. Some kind of journal.'

What's in there, Crystal, I asked her a few times. *What are you writing about?*

Hiding that tatty notebook in the pocket of her big sweatshirt or her *Friendly* overall, pulling it out and scribbling in there, holding it close, writing her secret life when she thought no one was looking.

'Try to find the journal,' I say to the police.

But I'm the one who finds it. I get there before the police. They're still doing paperwork or whatever they're doing.

Crystal's body is being taken away. Shardonnay is in her room. She is curled up on the bed. I go into Crystal's room, and it doesn't take me long to find the journal under her mattress. I find Crystal's journal, with an elastic band wrapped around it, as if she thought this would stop anyone from looking in there and reading about her life.

I read every word, take in every hurt, in her life and Ricardo's; every date of Wayne's visits to her room recorded there, in black and white.

From The Journal
of Crystal September

Wayne, you swore that for the rest of my life you would be watching me.

I am trapped, like that bird in the cage.

I am sorry. I thought I was somebody, once.

I give the journal to Martha. Martha gives it to the police. I hardly speak for days.

Of course it all comes out. The police come again to question Benita and Wayne and Sha about Crystal's suicide. *You can't take suicide at face value,* they say. *It's our job to investigate whether or not there's foul play involved.*

Crystal killed herself alright. But they discover, when they look in her journal and read every word, exactly why she did it.

And then the TV people get hold of Crystal's story.

The reporter in *Behind Closed Doors* asks Letisha, 'Crystal's stepfather, Wayne, found Ricardo that evening didn't he?'

'Ricardo slept through for hours in that cooler. He must have been so tired from the picnic. They say there was no proper seal on that box. And the lid was loosened from the ride in the minibus,' Letisha says. 'They say Crystal said she didn't know how the baby got in there. They say she killed herself because the baby was back, because it had been found. Her stepfather's baby. That is what they say.'

After the credits, Martha says, 'Ricardo's better off you know, Grace, with the foster family.'

Martha holds out her arms and I sink into her warm flesh.

'You can always come to me. You know that, Grace. If you have a problem you can come to me.'

This time I hug her back. For the first time in a long time.

Death seems everywhere. It wasn't even two weeks after Crystal's death when

Freddy died in a crash on Prince George's Drive. Ramon wasn't drunk or drugged-up when he crashed his car – it was just another accident like the ones that happen every day. I went with Shardonnay to see Ramon in hospital. They broke up for real this time when he got out.

And a couple of weeks after that, Benita and Wayne split up, with the investigation and all the publicity and finally Wayne's arrest. Wayne is out on bail now. The prisons are so full, they only keep the murderers locked up. The rapists and abusers are walking around out here. He's gone. I don't know where. And overnight Benita and Shardonnay moved out without even a goodbye.

People said, *Didn't Benita know? Didn't Crystal's mother have any idea what was going on? What about Shardonnay? Didn't she know?*

I don't know about Benita, but Shardonnay knew what was going on. It's written right there in Crystal's journal.

Wayne had tried it with Sha. Those bruises I saw on her, were from Wayne, I bet, though I never came right out and asked her.

Sometimes, when I can't sleep at night, when the wind keeps me awake, I wonder if it all could have been different. Why didn't Sha say something? What about me? I didn't see what was staring right at me. Those pale blue eyes of Ricardo's, just like Wayne's, staring me right in the face. Or maybe none of us could face the truth.

I'm glad people know the whole story. That Crystal tried to love her baby. That it was Wayne who made her crazy. That's the way I see it.

Next door, there'll be a new family moving in one of these days.

I haven't heard from Shardonnay. I wonder if I'll ever see her on *Idols*?

I see Ricardo, in my mind's eye with his sweet smile like sunshine brightening my day. And I see myself – in Martha's arms, when I was a baby – just like Ricardo is now in the arms of another mother.

Later, in my room, after the TV doccie, and after supper and I've washed the dishes, I take from my bag the photographs I've been carrying around. The young woman on the swing in front of the bougainvillea, with the soft light around her, is a stranger. As is the girl in the fuchsia dress.

My mother is starting to look more like Martha Hunt.

I am Grace Hunt, Martha's daughter.

I tear the pictures into tiny pieces. Store them in an envelope. Tomorrow, over at the *vlei,* I will toss these pieces into the wind. I'll watch them lift like confetti, as they blow across the park, over the highway, across the dunes and to the sea.

I am Martha's daughter. I am Grace.

THE NIGHT
BEFORE
CHRISTMAS
OF THE
LIVING DEAD

A novel by

M.V. MOORHEAD

DOCKYARD PRESS

ISBN 978-1-913452-50-6

PART ONE

CHRISTMAS EVE EVE

1.

For Brian, the nightmare began at straight-up midnight on Christmas Eve.

He was parked on the couch, trying to get himself into something resembling the holiday spirit. He'd been watching *Miracle on 34th Street*, but after he'd found himself imagining Maureen O'Hara naked—the 1940s Maureen O'Hara, of course—he'd decided that popping a boner over an actress who was born before his grandmother wasn't likely to help him feel any more wholesome and festive. He'd switched the channels, and found *Christmas in Connecticut*, but stayed focused on wrapping presents, not letting himself stare at Barbara Stanwyck too long at a stretch.

Of course, "wrapping" wasn't really the word for what he was doing to the presents, he realized. He was stuffing the items he'd bought for a handful of family members and friends into gift bags. The gift bag, he reflected: The single man's best friend. Or, maybe, the single man's second best friend. After Jergens lotion.

Just as he had placed the bracelet he was already glumly certain Trina would hate—or at best be indifferent to—into a small green pouch with a retro-looking Christmas tree on the side, he heard the key in the door. Ah, it's the mostly-absent roommate, thought Brian. The single man's third-best friend.

In came Teddy Mrozowski, bringing a blast of wretchedly cold wind and a swirl of white powder with him.

"Snowing out there?"

"Just started. It's been colder than the middle of a TV dinner all night, though. That fucking wind off the lake, Jesus."

"How was work?"

"Sucked less than usual, I guess. Lots of drunks, good tips. Bagging presents, I see. You may give me mine unbagged, help the environment."

"Glad to hear it. My unbagged gift to you is one of the two pieces of cold pizza over there on the counter."

"Just what I wanted, how did you know? You want the other one?"

"In a few minutes. I don't want to get greasy fingerprints all over this shit."

Mrozowski, divested now of coat, hat and gloves, retrieved his slice of supreme from the Barbato's box on the counter, zapped it in the microwave for eighteen seconds—the perfect timing for room-temperature pizza, he insisted—then sat at the far end of the couch.

"Barbara Stanwyck," he said dreamily. "I'd like to bend her over."

"As she was circa 1945, I assume you mean."

"No, Bri, I meant I'd like to violate Barbara Stanwyck's freshly exhumed corpse, as it is this very moment. That's my hot sexual fantasy."

"I should have realized that's what you meant."

"Mind if I see what else is on?" asked Mrozowski, picking up the remote.

"Nah, go ahead. I've just got Logan's present to do anyway, and then I'm going to bed."

Instead of changing the channel, Mrozowski watched as Brian opened a large red gift bag emblazoned with Santa, set it on the floor in front of the couch, stuffed it with green tissue, then picked up a large box from beside the couch and began to slide it into the bag.

"Doesn't Logan already have *Return to Dino-Dragon Island?*"

Brian looked sharply at him.

"What?"

"He does, I know he does, actually. I played it with him last time we were over there."

"What the fuck are you talking about? He's got *Dino-Dragon Island*. The first one. He doesn't have *Return to Dino-Dragon Island.*"

"Dude. *Return to DDI* is the first one."

"The fuck it is."

"Dude. *Return to DDI* is the first one. It came out last year. *Treasure of DDI* is the new one. That's the one nobody can find this year."

Brian stared at Mrozowski for several seconds, and then he said, "Are you fucking with me? Please tell me that you're fucking with me."

"Bri, I am so not fucking with you. I'm sorry, dude, but you've totally got your son a Christmas present he already has."

Just then, the digital clock on the DVD player switched from 11:59 to 12.00. It was now officially Christmas Eve, and for Brian Morgan, the nightmare had begun.

2.

Mitchell walked through the door into the dark serviceway, and the stink hit him hard. He swore out loud.

As a security guard at Micromegas, wandering the bowels of the plant for hours on end, he had encountered plenty of bad smells—slurries seeping out of pipes, hot electric odors exuding from rows of terminals, and, for that matter, the farts of Missy, his boss. But this one was, he thought, the worst of the lot. It was like...what was it like? It was like piss mixed with kerosene mixed with Gatorade.

A red alarm light blinked over the gauge on the twin panels above the overflow tanks, but when he looked down over the rail into the first concrete pit, he saw only a few inches of yellow-green fluid collected at the bottom. There was nothing unusual about that. There was always a little spillage there.

He walked out onto the metal catwalk and looked down into the second tank, then stepped back, turning his face away. This tank was quarter-full—at least four feet deep—of purplish fluid from which, even under the dull glow of the bare light bulbs down here, rising fumes were visible The stink, terrible before, struck Mitchell like a punch in the nose. He felt dizzy, thought for a moment he might pass out then realized that he was going to vomit instead.

He just barely had time to lean over the rail, and out came the two Chik-fil-a sandwiches he had eaten in the truck on the way to work, and the hissing plop that the puke made as it dropped into the fluid sounded so revolting that it brought on round two: Mitchell piked forward again, and there went the Dr. Pepper, mixed with the eggnog and the cookies that he'd found in the breakroom just before his shift, left over from the sad little Christmas party that the office staff had thrown that afternoon. His upchuck formed a little pink island in the steaming purple lake below.

"Fuck," he spluttered, as he straightened up and reeled toward the door at the far end of the serviceway.

He banged through it into the stairwell and sat down on the bottom step. The fresh air felt blessedly cool on his lungs, but it took him several minutes to stop coughing.

Jesus, he thought. That was really bad. That didn't just stink, I think it was poison.

He pulled his radio off of his belt and called Brooksbank.

"Zero Nine to Zero Four."

"Zero Four."

"What's your 20?"

"I'm in the out building. Wassup?"

"I'm under Section F South, by the overflow tanks. There's a situation. Can you come down here?"

"Sure. Gimme a coupla minutes."

"Bobby? Come down the east stairwell, OK? Don't come in through the serviceway."

"Uhm...OK. You OK?"

"Yeah. Come on over, all right?"

"On my way."

Mitchell put the radio back on his belt. He didn't get up. He still felt a little dizzy, and he couldn't get the smell, even the taste, of the purplish fluid out of his mouth. He spat, and there was a purplish cast to the gob that landed on the step.

"Fuck," he said again.

3.

Bobby Brooksbank spewed the same word as he slipped his radio back onto his belt-clip. What now? he thought.

When Mitchell's call came through, he had been down on one knee, next to one of the stand-alone gauge units that were arranged in rows in the outbuilding, like the speaker-stands in an old drive-in. Once again, a yellowish liquid was seeping from the base of one of the units, but this time, the puddle that had gathered in a sloping corner of the room was big enough to have some depth. The floor was painted blue, and the latex-enamel paint was coming up in strips from the concrete and drifting, slightly, in the fluid, like the tentacles of an anemone.

Bobby hated the outbuilding anyway. It was always deserted, at least during his shift, and the fact that it was a quarter-mile walk from the main plant was somehow unnerving. Why was the distance necessary?

Before he rose from his knee, he patted the little ankle-holster that held the Browning HP he wore at work. He felt ridiculous carrying a gun on this job—felt, indeed, like a typical cop-wannabe security guard even though he had never wanted to be a cop. The people who hated this place, for the most part, were environmentalists. Probably, thought Bobby, their hatred was well justified. But you didn't generally need a gun to defend yourself from environmentalists.

But he couldn't help it, the place gave him the creeps, and the weight of the gun on his ankle was somehow a comfort to him.

One side of the building held a row of four enormous cylindrical furnaces, which periodically roared to life with a noise so deafening and startling it made your scrotum shrink three sizes if you happened to be wandering through the otherwise quiet place when it started. If you looked through the small window at the end of these furnaces when they were quiet, you saw only a flicker of fire, as if from a pilot light, but if you looked through during this roaring, the empty inside of the cylinder looked like a scene from Dante's *Inferno*. What in the name of God, or whoever, Bobby had often wondered, was all that heat for?

Bobby walked past these furnaces, silent at the moment, past the rack of headphones he was supposed to wear while patrolling in the building to protect his ears from the machinery's din—but which he, like the other six officers of which he was assistant shift supervisor, almost never did—and out the door. The fierce wind off Lake Erie hit him hard in the face. He headed back across the wide yard toward the main building, walking carefully as the layer of snow now thickening on the asphalt was slippery beneath the street shoes he was idiotically required to wear.

He dutifully marked the leakage on his clipboard as he walked, certain that the notation would be ignored. Anytime that he or any of the other Triple S officers pointed out leaks or puddles or alarm lights to Missy in their daily reports—

nd there were many such occasions—Missy, ever hungry or glory, would feverishly call her liaison with Micromegas management, Howard Fuller. She would then be politely hanked and told that the problem would be fixed. He would ell her to tell her officers that if they noticed the problem igain, record it on their log.

But every shift, Bobby would see the same leaks, the same puddles, the same alarm lights. He never had the slightest sense that any of them had even been worked on. In the five months he had worked for Sentinel Security Solutions, now subcontracted to Micromegas, he had gained the distinct sense that he and his fellow officers weren't really there to observe lapses in plant safety or security. They were there, he suspected, to gradually begin to ignore such lapses, and to fail to record them, so that if anything serious happened, Micromegas could scapegoat them.

This was paranoid thinking, and he knew it—the sort of scenario you build in your mind over an eight-hour shift in which you have too much time to think. But he couldn't help it; he believed it was true. Despite the squawking of a few local environmental groups, the City of Erie had begged and pleaded and bowed and scraped and promised the moon to get Micromegas to build this plant here on the otherwise boarded-up west end of 12th Street, all in hopes of revitalizing the town's decrepit industrial sector. He believed that the company's interests would be protected at all costs, and he was determined not to be a sacrificial lamb to that end—he kept obsessively recording every leak and red light.

He arrived at the serviceway and was pulling out his ring of keys when he remembered that Mitchell had said not to come in that way, so he hurried around the side of the building.

4.

Brian stared at the box in his hands, then back at Mrozowski.

"I've got to ask you one more time. You're fucking with me, right? I won't be pissed if you just admit it to me now."

"I'm totally not fucking with you. Look it up online if you don't believe me. *Return to Dino-Dragon Island* is last year. *Treasure of Dino-Dragon Island* is this year. That's the one people are offering thousands of dollars to get."

"I don't believe this. Why would the original be called 'Return?' It doesn't make sense. 'Return' is always what they call the sequel, right?"

"Not this time. You see, it's the backstory of the game. Treasure hunter Luke Rankin had been to Dino-Dragon Island before, with his old partner Lizzie Brock, and he'd seen her fall off a cliff into the path of a styracosaurus stampede, so he'd presumed she was dead, right? So he was trying to drink his sorrows away in this barroom in Singapore when he heard these two sailors talking about a weird distress call they'd heard on their ship's radio that Luke realized could only be from Lizzie, because it was…

"Jesus, you're not making this up, are you? This really is the wrong fucking game."

"I'm sorry, Bri, but yeah, it is."

"*Return to Dino-Dragon Island.* Fucking *Return to Dino*-fucking-*Dragon* fucking *Island*. Son of a bitch. I should've known, when I just walked into the store and found it, no problem. There were, like, twenty of them on the shelf. I remember thinking, what's the big fat fucking deal? I should've realized it was too good to be true."

"Sorry, Dude."

"Actually, when I think about it, it's that bitch Trina's fault."

"What do you mean?"

"Give me a break. She knows damn well that I don't know about this crap. She had to know that any normal person who didn't follow this shit would assume that '*Return*' meant that was the new one, right? I think she wanted me to fuck this up, so I'd look like an asshole to Logan on Christmas morning. That fucking bitch."

"Look, Bri, Trina's kind of a bitch, I'll be the first to admit it. Except for how her ass looked in blue jeans, I never really got what you saw in her. But do you really think she'd deliberately fuck up her kid's Christmas morning just to make her ex look like an asshole?"

"No, I guess not," said Brian after a moment. "She knows her ex doesn't need any help to look like an asshole."

"Do you have a back-up of some kind?"

"I have some coloring books and shit. They were just supposed to be, you know, little extras. I figured if I had this…" Brian gestured at *Return to Dino-Dragon Island*, and shrugged. He realized he was amazingly close to crying.

"Well, look, this is a long shot," said Mrozowski. "But I have a friend. A guy named Don Engelsdorf. He used to be a dishwasher at Nelson's, but now he's in the stockroom at JayDee's Toys up at the Mall. If anybody could hook us up, it's this dude."

"Really?"

"Yeah. Like I said, there's probably nothing he can do, but you never know. But we'll have to head up to the Mall early. First thing."

"I think they're opening at, like, dawn or something."

"Before dawn. We should get there right when the doors open. How much money do you have?"

"That pizza was pretty much the last of it."

"Well, you'll return the game you got, that'll give you a little."

"Believe me, I'll return '*Return*' with the greatest of fucking pleasure."

"OK. And I got pretty good tips tonight. If we're lucky enough to find one, and you have to pay extra, I should be able to cover you."

Brian felt even closer to crying now. "Thanks Dude," he said, getting up. "I'm going to bed. I'll set my alarm for five. Have the last piece of pizza."

5.

"You look like shit," said Bobby, as he walked into the stairwell, where Mitchell was still sitting on the bottom step. He wasn't being playful. Mitchell's eyes were purplish-red, he looked pale, and he was sweating.

"I'm OK," said Mitchell.

"What the hell happened?"

"I got a whiff of some shit in one of the overflow tanks in there," said Mitchell, pointing to the serviceway entrance. "Some nasty purple shit, a couple feet deep, giving off fumes. It's the worst thing I ever smelled."

"A couple feet deep? How fast was it filling?"

"I'm not sure. Not too fast, I don't think."

"Well, why didn't Steve notice it and call it in?"

"Fuck if I know. I haven't seen him. That's where I was going when I walked in there, to relieve him for lunch," said Mitchell, and then he let out another wheezing cough, and spat another purplish lunger.

"You need to go to the Emergency Room," said Brooksbank.

"No, I think I just need to get home and lie down, maybe drink some hot tea."

"Bullshit. You're going to the hospital. Hamot or St. Vincent's, take your pick. I'd call 9-1-1, if it didn't mean Missy would have me writing the *War and Peace* of incident reports. So get going before she sees you."

"All right, I'll go to St. Vincent's and let the nuns take a look. No shit, though, Bobby, I'm feeling a little better."

"I'm glad to hear it, but go to the hospital anyway."

"Sorry to leave you shorthanded."

"We're security guards, Mitch, not air traffic controllers. Besides, I've got Amos and Burl, and Steve, if we ever find the son of a bitch."

"He's probably out back, asleep in his car again."

"No doubt. I wouldn't mind that so much, 'cause he's about as much use asleep as awake, except one of these days he'll freeze to death out there, and his family'll sue us. But don't worry about it, we'll be fine. Should be a quiet night. Just get to the hospital. You look like fucking death."

"OK," said Mitchell, heaving himself to his feet. "Merry Christmas."

"You're very funny," said Brooksbank.

Once Mitchell had walked out the door into the swirling snow, Brooksbank spoke into his radio.

"Zero Four to Base."

"Base, go ahead," croaked Missy.

"Missy, be advised, we have a situation in Section F South."

6.

Christmas in Connecticut was just ending on TV when Corinne came out of the bathroom in the red teddy and looked at herself in the mirror. She grinned. God didn't give you much of a face, her mother had said—more than once—after she had hit puberty. He gave your sister Kelly the face. But it looks like He decided to make it up to you in the body department. You'll never go hungry with that stuff you got from the neck down, honey. Just keep a bag handy, in case they want to put it over your head.

When she was drunk—which was quite a bit of the time— Mom might add "Or put a flag over your face. That way they can say they're fuckin' for old Glory." Mom had even dragged out that old favorite in front of Mitchell a few times.

Yeah, you were a real sweetheart in the building-self-esteem department, Mom. But you know what? You were right. Buck teeth—heavily nicotine-stained, now that she was in her late twenties—a big nose, even a couple of die-hard zits just didn't matter when you looked like a girl from a comic book from the shoulder blades south. Add a couple of strategic tattoos, and boys would be able to refuse you just about nothing.

Mitchell would love this. One quick fuck—with Mitchell it was always a quick fuck—and the surliness she'd noticed in his mood would be banished for weeks.

His quiet, grumpy attitude had led her to wonder lately if he suspected about the visits Eddie had been paying her in the afternoons.

That was over now. She'd told him, the last time he'd been over—two days ago—that the visits had to stop. She'd turned her face up toward the headboard and pictured Dierks Bentley as Eddie's remarkably gifted tongue did its work down below, and her orgasm was almost over before she realized that she was yelling so loud that even out here in the Millcreek sticks, the neighbors might hear her.

It had been fantastic, until Eddie had gotten off his knees and slithered onto the bed next to her, with his big gut—even bigger than Mitchell's—and his missing front tooth and his tufts of werewolf hair across his back, not to mention the swastika tattooed over his heart. Corinne didn't know any Jews, and though she had to admit she wouldn't kick Kayne what's-his-name out of bed, even after what he'd done to Taylor Swift that time, she wasn't too partial to blacks. But somehow the swastika creeped her out anyway, as it did when Eddie started up his shit about how someday there was going to be a homeland for the superior white race. More than once she'd thought to herself that when she looked at Eddie naked, "superior" wasn't the word that occurred to her.

Except for his tongue. He really was superior when it came to his tongue.

She'd taken a long look at Eddie's flabby body and his homely face and his small dick and she'd told him, in a tone of earnest regret, that the visits had to stop, that their time together had been very special but that she had a good thing with Mitchell and she didn't want to ruin it.

Besides, she reminded him, you were Mitchell's best friend.

Eddie had shrugged. "If Mitchell was banging Sandra, I wouldn't care," he said. "But whatever. How about a going-away blow job?"

Corinne had obliged. It was like eating a Vienna sausage, she thought. But it hadn't taken very long, and then he'd left and she hadn't seen him since. No, she figured, if she threw Mitchell one or two quick fucks over the holidays, then his suspicions would be banished, he'd cheer up, and she'd be able to stand living here with him, and she wouldn't have to move back to her mother's house, nor would she have to get a job.

All she'd have to was close her eyes and picture Dierks Bentley again, and be sure to say "Oh, Mitchell" instead of "Oh, Dierks."

If only Mitchell had a tongue like Eddie's. The memory made her smile.

It made her a little wet, too.

Funny thing about memory, she thought. It could take inches off a guy's waist and belly, and add inches to his dick. It could even erase the swastika on his chest.

Corinne looked at her herself again in the mirror. I must be way hot, she thought, if I can get turned on looking at myself. She laid back on the bed. She slipped her fingers under the crotch of the teddy, and began to stroke herself. She closed her eyes and pictured Dierks Bentley, but she gave him Eddie's tongue. Within a few minutes, she tightened up and shuddered and groaned. But after she relaxed, and lay there staring at the ceiling, she had to admit that her ring finger just wasn't as talented as Eddie's tongue.

She looked over at the clock next to the phone. Just after midnight. It was Christmas Eve now. It would be hours before Mitchell came home.

And Sandra would be working graveyard at Country Fair.

And Eddie had to work until midnight, so their kids were at his parents' place.

He'd just be getting home, right about now. Half a mile down the road.

Fuck it, thought Corinne, lighting a cigarette. If she was going to settle in with Mitchell, she deserved to give herself a Christmas present first.

She picked up the phone and dialed Eddie's number.

"Hello?"

"Hey. You home yet?"

"No, I'm still over to Slingshot's. What do you care, anyway? I thought we was all done with each other."

"You eat yet?"

"No, I'm having a couple Buds."

"Well, don't order anything."

"Why not? I'm hungry."

"Cause I got something for you to snack on. One last time. I just warmed it up for you."

7.

As Mitchell passed St. Vincent's hospital heading up Sassa-
fras, he briefly considered stopping at the emergency room
there, and it occurred to him how really bad he felt. Almost,
he thought, like he was...

No. He didn't feel so bad. The fumes had just turned
his stomach, and throwing up had left him achy and shitty,
that was all. Really shitty, but it wasn't like he was in pain
or anything. It was just like having bad flu. He needed to get
home, that was all. Corinne had her faults as a wife, but she
was always really nice to him when he was sick.

This would pass. He just needed a little rest. By morning
he'd be up and around.

8.

Steve Beeson was indeed in his car, but he wasn't sleeping. He was pretty sure he was dying, actually.

He admitted it—he slacked off a lot on this job. Even setting aside the fact that his wife had left him, that his kids hated his guts, that he was broke, and that the country was going to hell, even setting all that aside, he still didn't see why he shouldn't slack off.

Because, after all, he was working for Japs. Japs. He was working for the same bastards that had turned his old man into a vicious drunk. Working for the same race, or close enough, that Steve himself had fought against in Vietnam.

There was a whole team of them that worked in the labs upstairs—nervous, uppity little fuckers who glanced contemptuously at Steve when he passed through on patrol, doing his job. Some of them worked in "clean rooms," and you had to put little booties over your shoes and hats on your head—ridiculous in Steve's case, since he didn't even have hair up there—before you walked through. He resented the implication, especially from these foreign pricks, that he was dirty.

None of this, however, was why Steve was sitting in his Ford Crown Vic in the parking lot at Micromegas, swigging Old Crow and coughing. No, that was because he had walked into the south serviceway, heard the sound of running liquid, leaned over the rail for a look, seen some kind of purple crap pouring into the overflow tank, and gotten a faceful, and a lungful, of the nastiest fumes he'd ever smelled.

He'd run out the door opposite, coughing and hacking, through the stairwell and outside to get a few breaths of fresh air. The first few gulps had felt wonderful—not as wonderful as Old Crow, but close—and then the dizziness hit. He decided it was time to take a little unscheduled break in the Crown Vic, complete with some private Christmas cheer.

While he was sitting there with the window rolled down, coughing and spitting purple lungers out onto the snow, he'd heard Mitchell call Brooksbank over to the serviceway, and he knew that they'd found what he'd found, and no doubt Missy, that sad excuse for a woman who was in charge, would blame him for not having called it in sooner. He'd have to claim that he started his rounds from the other end of the building, for variety, but he doubted she'd believe him.

He didn't care. He felt so awful from breathing that stuff that he was thinking about going home. And if this Jap crud had fucked him up for real, you could bet there'd be Workman's Comp, and a lawsuit too.

Mitchell and Brooksbank would get credit for finding the spill, of course. Steve despised Brooksbank, a snotty college boy, and Mitchell wasn't much better; a dopey, pussy-whipped redneck. But neither of them was quite as bad as Missy the Ballbuster.

"Zero One to Zero Eight."

28

Speak of the Devil. Speak of the She-Devil. There was Missy's voice, melodious as a buzzsaw, coming through his radio. He decided to ignore it, until he could honestly answer her inevitable demand of "What's your twenty?" with something other than "In my car, having a drink." He took another swig of Crow, screwed the cap on the bottle, then slipped it back under the seat.

"Zero One to Zero Eight."

"Yeah, yeah, I'm coming bitch," said Steve, and pulled the door handle with his left hand, and that was when the pain slammed into his chest like a cannonball, and his left arm locked up and he slumped against the door and it came open and he tumbled out onto the pavement.

"Oh God," he gasped. All of a sudden Missy seemed less like a bitch and more like somebody who could call 9-1-1. He tried to pull himself up to the level of the front seat, so that he could grab his radio, and a second wave of pain pushed him back down and he groaned and then he stopped groaning and lay still. Snowflakes began to collect on him.

"Zero One to Zero Eight, do you read?"

9.

Missy, standing in the stairwell next to Bobby Brooksbank, tried it one more time: "Zero One to Zero Eight, do you read? Steve, do you read? What's your twenty? Please respond."

Nothing. She re-holstered her radio.

"Want me to go look for him?" asked Bobby.

"Shit no," said Missy. "We got more to worry about than that old drunk. Where are the other two idiots?"

As if on cue, the inner door banged open, and there were the other two idiots, walking together as always. Rosencrantz and Guildenstern, as Bobby called them, though only to himself; he didn't want to seem like a snotty college boy. Amos and Burl, he called them to their faces—Amos pudgy and graying, Burl slender, with copper-red hair and a thin, dapper red mustache.

"What's up?" asked Amos.

"Have you guys seen Steve?" asked Bobby.

"Look in the gutter," said Burl.

"No, you look there," said Missy. "I have to go call HAZMAT."

"HAZMAT?" asked Burl. "What for?"

"Explain it to them," said Missy to Bobby. "I'm going to go call HAZMAT, and then Mr. Fuller."

"You don't think maybe you should call Fuller first?"

"That's not what it says in the post orders. And I'm tired of Fuller always telling us to just log everything and leave it at that. What the hell are we here for, after all?"

"You got me there," said Bobby.

"Get these two up to speed, then get back to the office and get the caution tape, and tape off the serviceway. We don't need anybody else going in there."

"So what's going on?" Burl asked Bobby as soon as Missy was gone.

"Ah, there's been a spill. Some thoroughly nasty shit, right in there. It's contained in the overflow tank, I guess, but the fumes made Mitchell so sick I sent him to the hospital."

"No shit?"

"No shit. So now Missy gets her dream come true. She gets to call the HAZMAT team in. I have a feeling Fuller's going to be pissed as hell."

"Having to deal with this on Christmas Eve?" said Amos. "He'll be pissed alright. So Mitch is really sick?"

"Seemed like he was. I almost called 9-1-1, to tell you the truth."

"Just from the fumes, huh?" asked Burl. "You think maybe Steve got a dose of the same shit, and he's lying dead somewhere?"

"I doubt we're that lucky," said Bobby. "Probably just out in his car, taking his medicine as usual. You guys go look for him, then get back to the office. And whatever you do, don't go in that serviceway."

Then Bobby went off after Missy, while Amos and Burl zipped up their jackets and pushed open the outer door and felt the winter air assault their faces.

"Jesus, it's cold," muttered Amos.

They hustled, hands in pockets, to the east end of the building, crunching through the snow toward the gravel lot where the security guards parked. There was Steve's Crown Vic, and as they got closer they could see that the driver's side door was wide open, and Steve's radio was on the front seat.

Steve himself, however, was nowhere to be seen.

10.

Eddie Stuckert fishtailed a little as he came down the steep sloping driveway toward Mitchell and Corinne's house, tucked in a little hollow in the woods on the outskirts of Millcreek, just north of the Mall. Not for the first time, he had a moment of terror as he turned the wheel at the sharp right bend in the drive, and found that the truck seemed to want to continue straight ahead, down the bank and into the screen of maples.

But as before, at the last moment the truck obeyed, lurched grudgingly to the right, then fishtailed some more before coming to rest in front of the house.

Eddie found the front door unlocked, as he knew it would be. The downstairs was dark, but he was able to navigate it easily, by long experience. He felt a pang of anxiety at what he was about to do. Eddie was no wimp, but he knew in his heart, much as it pissed him off to admit it, that Mitchell could beat the living shit out of him with no trouble.

He felt a pang of guilt, too. Fucking his best friend's wife once was perhaps forgivable, the sort of thing that might happen to anyone. But fucking her dozens of times, as he had done over the last few months, didn't seem like the sort of thing one ought to do to a guy you'd grown up with.

But he squelched the guilt. A superior man didn't feel guilt about betraying a betrayer. And Mitchell, though a nice guy, was a betrayer—a race traitor. Ever since his own awakening to racial pride, Eddie had repeatedly tried to share his new interest with Mitchell, who could have been a powerful warrior against the mongrels, to no avail—the literature he gave him went unread, and there was always some excuse why he couldn't go to the meetings. Finally, Mitchell had told him point-blank that if white people were the superior race, a lot of the ones he knew did a great job of keeping it a secret.

So, fuck him.

And fuck his wife.

Which Eddie was about to do. He came to the top of the stairs, unbuttoning his shirt, and there Corinne was, dimly illuminated by the flicker of the TV screen, reclined on the bed.

"Hey," he said. He pulled his shirt off, revealing his chest. He knew his swastika tattoo turned her on.

"Hey back," she replied. "Merry Christmas."

Her big-nosed, buck-toothed face wore a grin. Her creamy-skinned, blow-up doll body wore a red teddy.

But not for long.

11.

"You've got to be kidding me," Brooksbank was saying into his radio, as he walked into the security office. "Well, search the parking lot, make sure he's not a drunksicle out there somewhere, and if he isn't then start looking inside. Keep me posted."

"Watch the unprofessional comments on the radio," said Missy distractedly, hanging up the phone. Her heart wasn't in reproving him. "So I take it they couldn't find the souse?"

"Worse than that. Rosenc...uh, Amos said that his car door was open, and his radio was lying on the front seat, but he was gone."

"Great. Just what we need."

"Did you call HAZMAT?"

"Yes I did."

"And did you talk to Fuller?"

"Yes I did."

"In that order?"

"Yes."

"How did he react?"

"Not so well. He's on his way down here."

12.

Howard Fuller had hung up the phone, sat on the edge of his bed hissing obscenities for a minute or two, then rose and began hastily dressing. His wife had stirred and asked him what was going on, and he had explained that the miserable self-important battle axe rent-a-cop supervisor down at the plant had called in a HAZMAT crew without asking him first, and he had to get down there before things got any more out of hand.

He told her he'd be back as soon as possible and shut off the phone and she and the kids would have his full attention and they'd have a nice Christmas Eve together. Then he kissed her on the forehead to avoid her breath and went into his home office. He removed a large envelope from the bottom drawer of his desk. He threw on his coat, slipped into the garage, got in his car and opened the envelope.

It contained a cell phone and a slip of paper with a phone number and a name on it.

He entered the number, then backed out of his garage into the swirling flurries and cruised passed the handsome homes of his Glenwood neighborhood. He flipped on his wipers. His heart was pounding. Much as Missy's action infuriated him, much as it was rooted in the need that so many people at the lower-paid end of the security field seemed to feel to generate drama and feel important, he still couldn't be sure that it hadn't been the right thing to do.

The sad truth was that at the end of the day, he really had no idea what product or service the staff at Micromegas, including the grim-faced, unfriendly "Kyoto Team" that had started there in July, was trying to create or produce or discover.

The place, especially its upper floor, was a warren of cleanrooms and cages full of shrieking lab animals and huge interconnected vats of evil-looking solutions in primary colors. He had a hard time believing that there was no danger in all that stuff, or that the purposes for it being made or studied or whatever had only benign ends. He was simply an operations manager, supervising the day-to-day maintenance and clerical and security support for a plant the actual purpose of which was shadowy and secretive. He was paid very well, but dealing directly with his employers scared him silly.

He had turned off Glenwood Park Avenue onto the 38th Street and passed the Erie Zoo before he finally steeled himself to hit the call button on the cell phone. On the second ring, a pleasant voice answered.

"Good evening, Mr. Fuller."

"Hello, may I speak to Marvin please?"

"This is Marvin, go ahead."

"Marvin, this is Howard Fuller with Micromegas in Erie, Pennsylvania."

"Yes sir, how can I help you tonight, Mr. Fuller?"

"Uh, well, a while back I was given this phone and this number and told to use it if, well, if any of a couple of different situations arose at the plant. I've just been informed that one has."

"We appreciate the call, Mr. Fuller. Tell me all about it."

13.

Dr. Tanaka gritted his teeth at the thump on the cleanroom door. He didn't look up from his microscope.

He tried to temper his irritation—it had been hours, after all, blessed hours since he had been interrupted. The Americans had left after their holiday party, most of them, and in the resulting blessed quiet, with no one around to bother him, he had accomplished an astounding amount, so he had just kept working through the evening and on past midnight. He'd had to waste a half-hour writing up an incident report about a mistake one of the techs had made, opening the wrong disposal valve for the solution he was flushing, but so long as the outer safety valve was closed, it wasn't a serious matter, and since then the time had been splendidly productive.

Another thump.

He glanced at his watch, and sighed. He ought to be getting back to his efficiency apartment anyway, he supposed. But the more he got done, the sooner this wretched project would be complete, and he could leave this miserable, frozen city and return to his wife and children in Kyoto.

43

Tanaka finished entering the figure he was working on, then turned to the door. Immediately his irritation flared into anger. One of the imbecilic security guards was standing in the airlock, staring in at him. He was wearing no booties, no face mask, nothing, and he had the palm of his hand against the glass door.

The man slapped the glass again with his open palm. Tanaka recognized him—the tall, bald one who stared at him and the rest of the Kyoto team with what looked like undisguised hatred. He had thought once or twice of reporting him, but decided it was better not to make waves.

But that wasn't the look on the man's face now. He didn't look well at all. His face was bluish-gray, his eyes wide and glazed, yet imploring, his mouth slack. He looked like he needed help. Oddly, he was wearing his keycard on a lanyard around his neck. He could have swiped himself in.

Tanaka got up and crossed the room. He felt some apprehension. Perhaps the man was just drunk, and if so he could be dangerous. And it made Tanaka furious that the cleanroom would have to scrubbed because of this. But he put his anger aside. He wondered if he could remember his CPR training. The man might need it. He looked just terrible, half-dead.

Tanaka opened the door.

14.

"Hello?"

"Mr. Snyderwine? This is Marvin at White Lake. Sorry to bother you at this hour, on Christmas Eve."

"No problem. Go ahead, Marvin."

"We've just been contacted by Mr. Fuller, in Operations at the Micromegas plant in Erie. His security staff apparently came upon a chemical spill of some sort. They called him at home, of course, and he's on his way to the plant now, so he didn't have many details. But apparently the shift supervisor has called in an outside HAZMAT team."

"Why in the name of Christ did he do that?"

"It was a she, sir, and Mr. Fuller says she's somewhat officious. Apparently the spill is emitting fumes, and one of the guards felt ill after inhaling some of them, and the post orders there say that you can call in HAZMAT if it's a life-threatening situation."

"One of the guards inhaled the fumes?"

"That's what Mr. Fuller was told, yes."

"Jesus. Alright, Marvin, where's what you do. Call this guy back. Tell him to hold the HAZMAT guys there at the plant, but don't let them do anything."

"You're aware, of course, that they'd have to report the incident to the EPA whether they do anything or not."

"Yes, Marvin, I know. I'm going to send somebody down there to talk to them about that. In the meantime, I need you to make some calls for me. I forget the name of the Governor, but he's a friendly, right?"

"Yes sir."

"Call him, and tell him we may need the Pennsylvania National Guard tonight, and that we may need to put some of your advisors in there with them, in their uniforms."

"Yes sir."

"Then call our friends at the FCC. Tell them we need a serious clamp on the media. Anybody starts telling them stories, any cell phone calls from inside the plant, they can't put the stories on the air. Not one. On pain of getting their licenses revoked. Got it?"

"Yes sir."

"If the print assholes get a hold of it, we'll deal with that later. Hopefully it won't come to that anyway, but we'll need to be ready if it does."

"Yes sir."

"That's all for now, but call as soon as you hear anything else."

"Yes sir."

"Thanks for calling, Marvin. Stay on top of this. I have to go call my son-in-law."

15.

OK, so he was right, thought Mitchell. I should have gone to the hospital.

Nausea and dizziness consumed him as he turned off Peach onto the dark, wooded side street that led to his house. Another stomach cramp hit him hard, and doubled him over behind the wheel. He had to puke again. He pulled over, opened the door, undid his seat belt, leaned out and retched, but everything he'd eaten that day was long gone. Nothing came up but purple fluid, spattering onto the snow-dusted pavement.

"Holy shit," he spluttered. "I think I'm going to die."

The fear that came with this realization focused him. He sat up, closed the door of his Jeep, and drove on.

OK, he thought, the hospital it is. I'll call 9-1-1 as soon as I reach the house. Then at least I'll be warm while I'm waiting.

I just hope I'm still warm when they get here, he thought grimly, as he reached the turn into his own driveway. The Jeep rolled down the slope, the headlights shining down into the woods, and just before the bend to the right another cramp doubled Mitchell over, and the truck went straight instead of to the right, straight off the drive, straight toward the biggest of the maples, and that stopped the Jeep but it didn't stop Mitchell, who wasn't wearing his seat belt. He continued headfirst, like a torpedo, right on through the windshield.

His shoulder caught the edge of the maple's trunk, and that spun him around four times in midair and dropped him in the snow with a thud, bits of windshield glass tinkling down after him like snowflakes.

16.

He couldn't be sure over the racket of Corinne's approaching orgasm, but Eddie thought he heard something. He raised his head from her crotch.

"Oh God, don't stop."

"You hear that?"

"Hear what?"

"I thought I heard something, outside. Like a crash."

"Could've been up on the road."

Eddie listened for another few seconds, then shrugged, and went back to devouring Corinne.

17.

"Hello, Missy," said Howard Fuller, as he walked into the security office.

"Hi, Mr. Fuller."

"Well, you got your wish. It's going to be a big night. They're going to send some bigshot down here from the company, and it may very well cost me my job, and in the meantime none of us are allowed to leave. So get comfortable."

"I'm sorry, Mr. Fuller, but the post orders…"

"Yeah, yeah, I know. Is the HAZMAT team here yet?"

"No sir," said Bobby Brooksbank.

"OK, well, how about you go wait for them at the gate, and call me when they get here."

"Will do," said Bobby, and slipped quickly out the door.

"Sir, one of the Japanese gentlemen left an envelope in your box earlier this evening," said Missy.

Fuller found it and tore it open. It contained an incident report from Dr. Tanaka, the alpha male, as far as he could tell, of the unfriendly Japanese upstairs. The command of English was shaky—though he had to admit that it was probably better than that of his oldest son, a sophomore at Penn State—but Fuller got the gist of the report, and of what had happened. Somebody left a valve open assuming that a drain pipe wouldn't be used, somebody else accidentally used the pipe but hadn't made a big deal out of the mistake, assuming the valve was closed.

"Human fucking beings," muttered Fuller.

18.

The theme to *Airwolf* played in her dark bedroom. After a few seconds, Ellie Cotteri drifted awake, said "Shit, George, take a hint," rolled over and fumbled for the cell phone on her bedside table.

She squinted at the readout. It said "HUBIE." She hit answer.

"Hubie?"

"How'd you like to fly the A Star?"

"What? What time is it?"

"It's late. It's early, actually. You want to fly the A Star, or not?"

She was looking at her clock. It was 3:08 a.m.

"Right now?"

"No, I'm calling you at 3 a.m. to set it up for next week. Yes, right now. Like I needed somebody here half an hour ago, that kind of right now."

"Fly the A Star? Fly it where? For who?"

"For some big wheel from the company who owns it. He's flying in right now on a Lear, and he needs somebody to give him a lift to a plant down on 12th Street where they're having some kind of problem that only a corporate genius of his caliber can solve."

"No shit? And Arthur doesn't want to this?"

"Arthur took his family to Florida for the holidays. That's the point. You're the only person I know around here who's even qualified on the simulator for the A Star. So if you don't get down here, I'm screwed. Plus, care to guess what he'll pay you?"

"No, I can't guess at this hour. Just tell me."

He told her.

"Wow," she said, and kept *Not bad, considering I'd pay him to fly the A Star* from slipping out after.

Hubie said, "Santa came this year after all, right? Now hurry up."

"I'm on the way," she said.

19.

They had searched the parking lot and the sides of the building as quickly as they could, then gratefully retreated inside. There, at a much more leisurely pace, they had searched the break-rooms, the rest-rooms, the office conference room, and all the other comparatively cushy spots in the plant where Steve Beeson had been known to nip and nap away his shift. But Amos and Burl hadn't found him anywhere.

"Hey Amos, you don't think he went up into the clean rooms?"

"Doubt it. He hates those Japs."

"But the Japs ain't there now."

"Yeah, but he hates it up there anyway. He bitches all the time about having to put the booties on, and besides, all those monkeys and rats give him the willies. Can't say I blame him on that one."

"We should probably go check it out anyway."

"I guess."

They climbed the stairs, and emerged into the hallway that led down the first row of cleanrooms. The atmosphere changed—they were no longer in a dim, dingy Great Lakes factory. This area, brightly lighted by fluorescents, was clean and sleek and sterile, like a spaceship in a science-fiction movie. It was no less creepy for its cleanliness, as far as Burl was concerned.

On their left was a long gallery of windows looking in on the rows of animal cages—the area was darkened now—and on their right were the first three cleanrooms. The hallway then turned to the right and the left, each direction leading to three more labs on their right, and a long narrow gallery of large white vats full of brightly-colored liquids on the left. The security guards were forbidden to enter this gallery.

The first two cleanrooms on their right were dark, but they could see a light was on in the one at the end of the hall.

"Somebody's working late."

"Looks that way."

They walked to the end of the hallway and looked through the window. There was a computer still on and glowing at the work station, next to a microscope, and right in front of the inner airlock door was…

"Oh, fuck," said Amos.

…a small lake of blood on the floor.

"That old drunk finally lost his shit for real," said Burl. He slipped his radio off his belt.

But just then Steve came around the corner, followed by Dr. Tanaka.

20.

Even with the snow, it took Ellie Cotteri less than twenty minutes to drive to Grandhill Aviation from her apartment house near Behrend, the pretty Penn State campus where she was belatedly starting the B.A. that everybody seemed to think you needed to get ahead in this world.

She was thirty and had gotten her helicopter-pilot's license nearly a decade earlier, and she made a modest living teaching other aspirants to the whirlybird at Hubie Grandhill's little airport and flight school south of I-90. But it appeared that getting a Bachelor's Degree, a less difficult if more tedious and expensive task than learning to fly a helicopter, would be needed if she expected to do better than just make a living.

So she taught flight school and took 101 courses at Behrend and tried to keep the presence in her life of her ex-boyfriend-now-verging-on-stalker George to a minimum and still get enough sleep to be an alert helicopter pilot. It wasn't always easy, but she had to admit that she felt very alert at the moment.

Hubie's call had woken her up fast.

Speak of the devil. As she turned into the driveway of Grandhill Aviation she saw Hubie through the light flurries, short and cylindrical in his parka, facing away from her, staring off over the treeline beyond the glowing greenish lights of the runway. He had already dollied the sleek Eurocopter AS350, or "A Star," over which Ellie had been drooling for more than a year, out of the big hangar onto the pavement. Ellie parked, pulled on a stocking cap, and climbed out of her Jeep.

"Nice timing," said Hubie. He pointed to the south. "I think I can hear the Lear."

"Who is this again?"

"I don't know his name. If it's the same guy that was here before a couple of times, he's a gigantic fuckhead."

"And I'm taking him to 12th Street? Why doesn't he just fly into Tom Ridge, and take a cab?" Erie International Airport, or "Tom Ridge Field" as it was now officially known, was located on west 12th Street, minutes from the long strip of mostly closed industrial plants to the east.

"Probably for the same reason these people hangar this beautiful chopper out here in bumfuck at my place, instead of downtown where it belongs—because they're a bunch of cloak and dagger dipshits who don't want anyone to know what they're up to, and they think the local media won't notice them coming and going from out here. Which they won't, at that. These people really hate publicity."

"Why? Who are these people?"

"It's Micromegas. That chemical plant that all the environmentalists were screaming about last year."

"No shit?"

"No shit. Lot of good the screaming did. The city would OK a puppy-strangling plant, if they thought it would bring ten jobs into town."

The sound of the Lear's engines grew shrill as it sprang into view out of the snow, and landed with a small screech on the powdered runway. Hubie and Ellie watched as it taxied to a stop in front of them, and a minute or so later the door opened, the stairs dropped, and a tall man in a heavy black winter trench descended, carrying a metal briefcase.

"Gigantic fuckhead?" Ellie asked.

"That's him," said Hubie. "Go get powered up."

She walked over and climbed into the A Star. As she hurried through the checklist, she glanced up periodically at the guy, who talked briefly to Hubie, and handed him an envelope. He was dark-haired and bearded and good-looking. Strikingly good-looking. He was so good-looking that Ellie was prepared to be skeptical of Hubie's judgment.

The man came over and climbed in the front passenger seat, opened a smartphone, and began tapping at it feverishly.

"Let's get going," he said.

"Hi, I'm Ellie."

"I'm Rick. Let's get going."

"Full disclosure, Rick. I don't know if Mr. Grandhill told you, but I've never flown this helicopter before. About two months ago I qualified on a simulator, but I've never had a chance to actually fly one, and I just thought you should know before we…"

"Are you going to crash?" he asked, not looking up from the smartphone.

"No," said Ellie.

"What a shame. You'd spare me this clusterfuck downtown. Let's get in the air, OK? I trust you implicitly. Although you're right, that rascal Hubie somehow managed to omit that you were new at this. Or that you were a girl, for that matter. Smart fellow."

"Yes he is," said Ellie, and kept *He was right on the money about you* from coming out after.

21.

Bobby Brooksbank opened the gate for the HAZMAT van, then closed it behind them. He tried calling Rosencrantz and Guildenstern on the radio, but neither of them responded. Just like Steve. Radio silence reigned at Micromegas tonight.

It was snowing hard, and the wind was persistent, pushing the flurries sidelong. But Bobby lingered out by the gate all the same. It felt like something was really wrong here tonight. He felt no wish to go back inside the plant. For some reason it came into his head to get into his car and leave, just quit.

Instead, he took out his cell phone. He decided to call Mitchell, see how he was doing.

22.

The theme from *SWAT* played in Mitchell's pocket, rousing him to semi-consciousness. He didn't move. Phone's ringing, he thought dimly. Probably work. Probably want me to pull an extra shift, the fuckers. I'd rather stay here and sleep.

He was lying face down in the snow, surrounded by shards of windshield. He was bleeding in more than one place, but the snow slowed it to seepage, and it cooled his feverish flesh. He'd been lying there for well over an hour, more comfortable than he'd been since he walked into the serviceway and breathed the purple fumes.

His cell phone stopped ringing, and the woods around Mitchell's house were quiet again, except for the creek trickling and gurgling a hundred yards or so to his left.

And, somewhere up above, the sound of a helicopter passing over.

23.

Ellie Cotteri set the Eurocopter down gently on the helipad of the plant. The roof door was open, and holding it was a slight, anxious-looking man in a long coat, with sheet of paper in his hand.

"There's the little twerp," said Rick. He looked at Ellie. "Leave the meter running, as they say. Stay here, and be ready to take off at a moment's notice."

"I'll be here," she said.

Rick climbed down with his metal briefcase, and hustled through the flurries toward the door.

"Good evening, Mr…"

"Inside," snapped Rick.

The door closed behind them, and they stood at the top of the stairwell.

"All right Howard, explain to me why I'm here on Christmas Eve Eve."

"Sir, according to Dr. Tanaka's incident report, one of the Kyoto techs accidentally opened a flush valve, and it drained several hundred gallons of Solution B into an overflow tank that was only meant for Solution A."

"Why do I care? Don't we have techs to pump it out ourselves?"

"They're all off until the day after Christmas."

"Are you fucking kidding me? We have their phone numbers, don't we?"

"Yes sir, but a couple of the night security guards came upon the spill, and before I could stop her the shift supervisor called an outside HAZMAT crew. They're downstairs, waiting to pump out the spill now."

"What made her think she should do that?"

"It's in the post orders. She was going by the book."

"Fucking Barney Fife. I pled with my father-in-law to let me hire inside security instead of these contract morons. OK, please tell me nobody's called the EPA."

"Well not yet, I don't think, but the HAZMAT company will have to."

"Nah, this briefcase should take care of the HAZMAT people. Just make sure nobody from here calls it in. It'll be hard enough to talk the Jap out of it. Alright, let's see his report."

Fuller handed it to him, and he skimmed it.

"Take me to his lab, please."

"Right away."

The two men descended the single flight of stairs to the cleanroom level and approached the labs from the west end of the building. They froze when they turned the corner. The floor was covered with red smears and bloody footprints, leading down the hall away from them, to the south stairwell.

"Oh dear God," said Fuller in a high, weak voice.

"Take it easy, Howard," said Rick. He took out his cell phone. "It's going to be alright, but I need you to hang in there for me, OK? You said the HAZMAT guys were here already, right?"

"Yes, sir."

"Do you have guards you can post at the street gates?"

"We only have one street gate, and I think there's already a guard on it."

"Good. Make sure he stays there. Nobody comes in, nobody goes out."

While Fuller repeated these orders in a quavering voice through his radio, Rick keyed a number into his fancy smartphone.

"Marvin? This is Rick with Micromegas. I'm boots on the ground at the Erie plant. We're going to need to mobilize the National Guard, but in the meantime call the local P.D. and have them block off the street and set up a perimeter. Tell them it's a serious HAZMAT situation, they should keep their distance but don't let anybody in, and above all don't let anybody out. Tell them it's no joke, they should shoot to kill if anybody tries to come out, aim for the head, and don't touch the body afterwards, we'll collect it. Got it? OK, I'll call you back."

He slipped his phone back into his coat pocket. Fuller stared at him, wide-eyed and pale.

"Sir, shouldn't we...shouldn't we maybe think about... evacuating?"

Rick gave him a calming smile.

"Sorry, Howard, we can't do that just yet. Let's go have a chat with the HAZMAT guys."

24.

Teddy Mrozowski sat on the couch, smiling.

After Brian had gone to bed, Teddy had done a few bong hits and finished watching *Christmas in Connecticut* while he ate the last of the pizza, and he'd kept watching straight through *Miracle on 34ᵗʰ Street*. And when that was over, he turned off the TV and opened his dear old record player and did a few more bong hits while he listened to music, a fine program of holiday tunes on his beloved vinyl, not on cold, sterile CD.

He listened to the Kingston Trio's *The Last Month of the Year*, and then to a stack of singles: James Brown's "Santa Claus Go Straight to the Ghetto," and Amos Milburn's "Let's Make Christmas Merry, Baby," and "Santa's Messin' With the Kid" by Eddie Campbell.

By the end of all this, Teddy was feeling really festive.

It was time, he decided. After all these years, it was time. For the sake of this cranky, self-pitying old-movie buff that he'd lived with for the last four years, and some reason couldn't help but like. It was time.

He picked up his cell phone, searched for a stored number, and dialed it.

"Hello," rasped out a voice on the fifth ring.

"Donnie Engelsdorf!"

"Who is this?"

"Teddy Mrozowski. Merry Christmas, Donnie."

"Teddy? Why the fuck are you calling me at...Shit, look at the time. I got to get up in an hour or so for work. What are you, baked as usual?"

"Sorry about the time, Donnie. I'm calling because I know, I *know*, that you have a *Treasure of Dino-Dragon Island* stashed away somewhere, and that you're probably going to be selling it today."

"You don't know any such thing."

"Right, so you *don't* have one? I'm wasting my time with this call?"

"No, you're wasting *my* time with this call. If, I'm saying *if*, I had a *Treasure of DDI* for sale, it wouldn't be for an amount of cash Mr. Teddy Mrozowski could afford."

"What would that price be?"

"You couldn't afford the cash price, Teddy. Unless you've started selling more than you're using. You got just one thing that I want, and you don't want to give it up."

Teddy smiled.

"This year I changed my mind," he said. "For a *Treasure of DDI*, new in box, I'll give it up."

"If this isn't just the weed talking, be at the store first thing in the morning."

25.

There are moments in life when you feel destiny is on your side, and Rick had such a moment when he and Fuller came up the hall from the north stairwell and he saw the sofa, just to the right of the security office door. It was just an ordinary dark-brown leather sofa which, like the other furniture in the shabby, unwelcoming lobby, had seen better days. But it gave Rick an idea.

On the other side of the door was a large window looking into the office. Through it, Rick could see a thick-bodied middle-aged woman in uniform—the notorious Missy, no doubt—and two thick-bodied middle-aged men in overalls. The HAZMAT guys.

Yes, if things go right and I keep my head, thought Rick, this little excursion might just work out nicely for everybody.

Well, for me.

He and Fuller entered the office. The door, Rick observed, opened out. Better and better. Just inside, somebody had hung mistletoe. Optimistic of Missy, if it was her.

"Hi, everybody, I'm Rick," he said pleasantly. "You're Missy, I'm guessing. On behalf of everybody at Micromegas Corporate, I just want to say that we appreciate your diligence and professionalism tonight."

"Thank you, Rick," Missy beamed. Rick wondered if it was the first praise she'd ever received in her life. Quite possibly, he decided, all things considered. She shot a told-you-so glance at Fuller, then seemed to register how stricken he looked.

The two guys in overalls didn't look so easily flattered. One had a sober, goateed face, the other wore an angry expression. Rick addressed the latter.

"Are you Mr. Lyman?"

"No, I'm Mr. Deutsch, this is Mr. Lyman," said the angry-faced man irritably.

Rookie mistake, thought Rick. The pissed-off guy is usually the boss.

"Sorry about that," said Rick, and then, to the other, "I'm sorry, but it appears we brought you two gentlemen down here on Christmas Eve for nothing."

"Well, not for nothing," said Mr. Deutsch.

"No, you're right, not for nothing," said Rick. "We'll pay double your usual fee, of course, plus a little something extra for each of you in cash, for your trouble. But we'd prefer to have our own techs pump out the spill."

"That's fine with us," said Mr. Lyman. "We ain't eager to do it. Just so long as you understand, we got to file an EPA report."

"I do understand that," said Rick. "That's why I was hoping to have a word with Mr. Lyman in the hallway."

"You can have the words you want," said Lyman, "As long as none of them are about us not doing an EPA report."

"Thank you, sir," said Rick with a chuckle, and then, to everyone else in the office, he said. "Listen folks, turns out the spill isn't as serious a matter as I thought, but we do have an unstable, even dangerous situation here tonight. There's no need for alarm at this point, but as a precaution I need you all to stay right here in the office. Howard, I need to use the men's room. Could I borrow your keycard, please?"

"Sure," said Fuller, slipping the lanyard off over his head. The frightened man met Rick's eyes as he handed the card to him; gave him a significant look. *He's telling me that we're on the same page, that he won't say anything, won't cause a panic,* thought Rick. *Perfect.*

He and Lyman stepped into the hall, and around the corner to the short corridor where the restrooms were. Rick shot a pensive, impatient glance up the north hallway.

"Mr. Lyman, I don't have time to be coy, so I'm going to cut to the chase. Instead of a bunch of words about the EPA report, how about a bunch of these?" He popped open the metal briefcase and revealed it to be full of bundled hundred dollar bills.

"Well, shit, nobody ever offered us this much before," said Lyman in a gloomy tone.

"Make for a pretty Merry Christmas for you and Mr. Deutsch, wouldn't you say?"

"I ain't taking it. Neither is Deutsch."

Rick glanced up the north hallway again. *Did he hear something?*

"Mr. Lyman, if you give me a couple of minutes, I could probably get my bosses to authorize..."

"The amount ain't the problem," said Lyman. "Shit, in Erie me and Deutsch could probably both retire and live pretty well for the rest of our days on this. But first of all, for all I know you're some undercover Fed looking to set us up, make headlines..."

"I promise you, we…"

"And second of all, even if I knew for sure you weren't, I wouldn't take it. Because it's too much. Whatever you're willing to pay this much to cover up is something I don't want covered up. This is my town. May sound corny, but it's how I feel. This is my town. I live here, so do most of my kids. Same with Deutsch. So you can keep your money, and we'll file that report, and I hope to Christ the EPA inspectors follow up on it. Course you could try making the same offer to them. Bunch of GS-9s, so you might have better luck."

Just then Rick heard the north stairwell doors open. He saw the silhouettes of four men emerging into the hallway. He smiled at Lyman.

"Mr. Lyman," he said, "I had to make this offer. My bosses insisted. But your response is the most inspirational thing I've heard in years. It's made my Christmas season, quite honestly." He closed the briefcase. The four silhouettes were walking very slowly, like drunk men, toward the office.

"Could I get you to go back in the office with the others, please? I need to step into the men's room, and then we'll see about getting you and Mr. Deutsch out of here quickly."

"Sure thing, Santa Claus," said Lyman, still unflattered. He turned and walked back into the office.

Rick, meanwhile, turned and swiped his way into the men's room, then stood there, peering into the hall. At last, the four men stepped into the light. Three inexpensive security guards. Behind them, dammit, a very expensive Japanese biochemist, his head slumped impossibly far forward, because most of his neck was missing.

All of them covered with blood.

"Holy Jesus!" yelled Deutsch. "Who's this?"

"Oh God," wailed Howard Fuller.

The first man, tall and bald, reeled around the corner into the office.

"Oh my God, what happened to you guys?" screeched Missy, and that was the last coherent phrase that issued from the office. As the other three new arrivals trooped through the door, words were replaced by a symphony of shouts and screams and crashing furniture.

Rick stepped out of the washroom, and walked quickly up to the door. As he did, Missy lunged out wide-eyed.

"Merry Christmas, Missy," said Rick, and he shoved her backwards into the arms of the bald man, right under the mistletoe. Rick then hit the lock button on the door handle, and pushed it shut just as the bald man clamped his jaws down on Missy's face.

The office shut, Rick ran to the far end of the sofa and rolled it in front of the door, swearing mildly when he felt a slight twinge in his back from doing so. Why did everything happen to him?

He took out his fancy cell phone, stepped in front of the window, held it up, and began taking video.

26.

Steve was still missing. Rosencrantz and Guildenstern were apparently dead, or at least their radios were. Mitchell hadn't answered his phone. Then a little over an hour ago, Brooksbank had seen a big helicopter land on the roof. About half an hour after that, the Erie Police started showing up.

They blocked off 12th Street from both the east and west ends of the plant, with units across from the gate, but on the opposite sidewalk. A cop with a rifle stood outside his cruiser, gazing in Bobby's direction.

Bobby waved at him, sheepishly. The cop didn't respond.

"Shit," said Brooksbank.

27.

Rick hopscotched over the bloody footprints, used Howard Fuller's keycard to get into Tanaka's cleanroom, then jumped the puddle of blood inside. Tanaka's computer was still on, and when Rick moved the mouse, sure enough, lists of Japanese characters came up.

"Hallelujah."

He opened the briefcase, pulled a flash drive out of the pocket inside the lid, slipped it into the computer, and began to download. Then he keyed his cell phone.

"Marvin? This is Rick at Micromegas. I'm going to transfer some data to you. You may want to wake up a Japanese translator, if you have one you can trust. As soon as you have the files backed up, I'm going to evacuate and this facility can be considered expendable. In the meantime, I'm going to send you a video. Do me a favor, after you watch it, send it to my father-in-law."

28.

Face down in the snow in his own blood, Mitchell was in bliss.

He was making love to Corinne. But there was something a little different about it this time. There was something different about Corinne, for one thing.

Her supple, flawless, creamy body moving below him was as he remembered it. But where her neck used to be, there was instead a tiny flagpole. And at the top of that flagpole a tiny Stars and Stripes fluttered.

Mitchell felt an intensity both of erotic pleasure and of patriotism he had never known before. The true meanings both Christmas and the Fourth of July, the eternal brotherhood of all humanity and the genius of American democracy, filled his soul, and he could see the racist idiocy of his friend Eddie's endless grievances of the white race more clearly than ever.

For another thing, Mitchell noticed that he was really hanging in there. Tonight there would be no complaints from Corinne—if, indeed, it was even possible for complaints to issue from her tiny flag head—about his lousy staying power.

He was close to climax, but it was OK. They had been at it a long time now. Indeed, they had been at it so long he was out of breath.

Very out of breath, actually...

Mitchell's breathing, already almost imperceptible, slowed, hitched, hitched again.

And then stopped.

And then his eyes opened.

29.

Then the army showed up.

Large green vehicles with stars on the side rolled up alongside the police cruisers, and the cops departed their positions hastily and, it seemed to Brooksbank, without reluctance, and headed off to some outer perimeter. Soldiers with M-16s climbed down from the vehicles and took their places.

It was still snowing, and the wind was still cutting, but Brooksbank was sweating. He really, really wished he had left when he had the chance.

But clearly that chance had passed. These guys weren't letting anybody out tonight.

But there was that big helicopter on the roof.

Brooksbank began to wonder if whatever big shot had flown in on that was going to be allowed to fly back out. He also wondered if he could somehow talk his way into a ride along.

He glanced across the snowy street again, at the soldiers staring at him in the same unfriendly manner that the cops had, and decided it was worth a try. He headed for the building, unholstering his radio as he walked.

"Zero Four to Zero One, I'm coming in."

No reply.

That wasn't like Missy at all. She usually pounced like a cat on any radio transmission directed at her.

"Zero Four to Zero One. I have to come in, Missy."

Still no answer. He walked into the lobby, grateful for the warmth, and then...

"What the fuck?"

It took him a few seconds to register what he was seeing.

Missy and Fuller were inside the security office, as were Rosencrantz and Guildenstern, crowded around the window. So were the HAZMAT guys, and one of the Japanese guys from upstairs.

They were all looking at him.

Then he noticed Missy's face. A large chunk of it, around her mouth, had been ripped away. Her nicotine-stained teeth were exposed. She put a hand on the window, as if she was reaching out for Brooksbank. The glass was already smeared with blood.

The others palmed the window as well. Fingers were missing on some of the hands. Brooksbank saw that they were all injured. Horribly injured, blood-covered. One of the HAZMAT guys was missing his right hand, and the right-hand side of his face.

He glanced at the door. A couch was blocking it. Somebody had barricaded them in there.

Missy brought her torn face close to the glass. Her exposed mouth gaped, her tongue waved at him like a lure.

"Oh, Holy Fucking Christ," Brooksbank squeaked. His head spun. He raised a hand to his colleagues in the office, as in conciliation, and began to back away. He almost turned and bolted back outside for the gate, M-16s or no M-16s.

Then he remembered the helicopter on the roof.

There was no part of him that wanted to remain inside this building. But there was a large part of him that did want to live. He turned and ran down the hallway toward the north stairwell.

30.

"Oh, shit," said Corinne and Eddie, in near-perfect unison. Eddie scrambled off the bed, hunting for his underwear.

The door had opened downstairs, and they heard heavy, slow tread crossing the living room.

"Shit, is that Mitch?" said Corinne. "He doesn't get home for…" She glanced at the clock. "Who's there?" she called. "Mitchell? Mitch, is that you?"

The tread was coming up the stairs.

"Mitchell…Mitch…Eddie's here. He, um….he stopped by, and…"

"Hi, Mitch!" called Eddie. He stopped looking for his underwear, and settled for grabbing his pants and holding them in front of his crotch.

Mitch's big shape stepped into the doorway.

"Mitch, honey, I…I didn't plan to…"

"Mitch," stammered Eddie, "I'm sorry, man, she called me over, said she needed help with something around the house, and then she put the moves on me. She's trash, man, she…"

"Oh, fuck you, Eddie," said Corinne, "You weren't saying that when…"

Then she noticed that Mitchell didn't seem interested. He was slowly advancing into the room, staring down at his nude wife with bleak-eyed hunger.

"Mitch?" she asked. "Honey, you want to party, is that it? You want to show Eddie how it's done right? OK, baby, why not, I'm game, let's…"

And while Eddie watched, Mitchell opened his mouth and lunged for his wife's belly.

31.

"Look, I know, I know, it's not how you want to do a human trial, but it amounts to a human trial just the same," said Rick, into his cell phone. He stood on the second-floor landing of the north stairwell, briefcase in hand, like he was waiting for a cab.

"I'm telling you," he went on, "compared to what Tanaka's done here, the rhesus monkeys in Chattanooga seem like a science fair project...I told you these Kyoto guys were the shit...Yes, they're still too slow, and they don't make any distinction between good guys and bad guys, we have to work on that, but the important thing is that Tanaka's absolutely cracked the cortical override of vital functions. Dismemberment, exsanguination, vital organ loss, none of it matters. As long as the frontal lobe's intact, they just..."

Rick paused when heard the first-floor stairwell door bang open down below.

"Hang on," he said, and then another bit of theatre occurred to him. He paused a few more seconds, then whispered, "Oh God, oh my God, they're coming..."

And then he cut off the call. He was beginning to think it might be in his interest to lay low this Christmas. Maybe in the Caribbean, someplace like that might be nice. Step one was getting back to the Lear, however.

He went down to the landing below and peered cautiously down the stairwell. Had they gotten out of the office?

No. It was a young guy in a Triple S security uniform coming up, moving fast, wide-eyed with fear. He wasn't one of them.

The guy from the gate, of course. He'd gotten cold or bored and come inside. What a surprise he got.

The poor guy got another when he turned onto the next flight and saw Rick standing there at the top.

"Fuck!" he yelled.

"It's OK, be cool!" said Rick.

"No it isn't, man" said the kid. "You're the corporate guy, right? Don't go down to the lobby."

"Why not?"

"They've all gone bugshit, and they're tearing each apart down there. This shit you brew here must have gotten to them somehow. They don't even look like they should be alive."

"My God!"

"I'm not kidding you, dude. Besides, there's no way out down there. The fucking Army is blocking the place off, and they don't look like they're going to let anybody out."

"The Army? Well, it looks like we better evacuate. I've got a helicopter waiting on the roof. Maybe you better come along."

"Oh, God, man, thank you."

"You weren't exposed to the...the fumes, or whatever it was, were you?"

"No, no, I kept my distance. I feel fine."

"All right then, let's get the hell out of here," said Rick, unbuttoning his coat. "I'm a little turned around in this place, though. Can you lead me up to the helipad?"

"It's right up these stairs," said Brooksbank, gratefully bounding ahead of him.

"Thanks," said Rick, as he drew a .38 semiautomatic out of his coat, and shot Brooksbank in the small of the back. The guard stiffened, then tumbled backwards, falling past Rick and collapsing on the landing.

32.

Ellie Cotteri had tried to doze for a while with little success. Then, searching under the seats of the Eurocopter, she found an old issue of *Vertical* magazine, and was more than halfway through it when she saw the roof door open. Out came Rick, briefcase in hand, buttoning his coat.

As before, he looked like he was in a hurry. She began to snap switches on the console, readying the resting bird for flight.

Rick climbed into the cabin.

"All done," he said. "Get us out of here now."

"It'll take a couple of minutes," she said.

"Well, then, get us out of here fast."

He was trying to play the same sardonic smoothie that she'd brought down here, but she could see it was a put-on. He was very uptight.

This made her a little uptight, too.

The beautiful helicopter gradually stirred to life, and at last her rotors began to spin, sending the snowflakes into a frenzy around her, and she rose grandly from the roof.

Ellie glanced out the window to her left, toward 12th Street, then did a double-take.

"Hey, is that the Army down there?"

She never got an answer. The next second they heard, just barely over the roar of the rotors, the crack of a gunshot.

"Jesus, are they shooting at us?"

"Fly us the fuck away from here," hissed Rick. "Now."

33.

"Got you, I think, you dirty fucker," said Bobby. He fired again at the rising helicopter, just in case he was wrong, and then again. Knew my Browning would come in handy one of these days, he thought.

He wasn't in pain, but he felt weak and he sat down hard on the roof, the gun he held clunking down beside him. He could feel the warmth of the blood that had run down his legs, over his ankle holster, and soaked his socks. He knew he was about to lose consciousness.

The helicopter turned sharply away above Brooksbank. He raised the Browning and took one last shot into the night air.

34.

Ellie wheeled the Eurocopter to the south and east, back the way they came, and then there was a loud cracking thud below, as something hit the undercarriage. Rick looked out his window, and sure enough, there by the access door was the young guard he had shot, sitting on the roof, with a gun of his own. As Rick watched, the kid dropped over backwards and lay still in the snow.

Fucking Barney Fifes. This was an unarmed post, but they could never resist packing. You couldn't count on anybody to follow the rules.

He cursed himself for not using a head shot. Head shots were so messy, though, and he'd managed not to get any blood on his jacket so far.

"We're hit," said Ellie.

"Well, can you get us back to Hubie's?"

"I'll try."

"Try hard. We don't want to land anywhere nearby."

"There wouldn't be many options if we did want to," she said, staring hard out the window.

The Eurocopter thrummed on through the blackness, but Ellie could hear it—a faint, urgent whine in the engine that wasn't there before. Something was wrong.

Then the craft wobbled a little in mid-air. Ellie's simulator training kicked in, and she corrected without thinking.

"We've lost generator power, and we're losing fuel fast" she said. "I can smell it. I don't think we can get back to Hubie's. There's a shopping mall a few minutes up ahead here, though, the Millcreek Mall. They have a helipad. Hopefully it won't be occupied. It's maybe ten minutes by car from there to the airport. I think we should go to the Mall."

"The woman's answer to every problem," muttered Rick.

35.

The soft snow was beginning to change to freezing rain as the three of them emerged from the open front door and shambled off into the woods together—a big guy in a security guard uniform, and a naked woman with her guts hanging out, and a naked man with a swastika on his chest and a gully torn into his neck.

The cold didn't bother them. Nothing bothered them, except the hunger. Once a love triangle, they now walked quite peaceably alongside each other through the nearly black woods toward a gleam of streetlamps off in the distance.

Somewhere nearby a deer, snoozing in the cover of a tall maple, caught the scent of death from them, stirred, and hurried off. The trio could see its dark shape moving away from them, but paid it no attention. They could see it wasn't the object of their hunger.

They crossed the creek, their feet crunching through the thin ice near the banks and splashing through the current in the middle, and then they blundered up the snowy, muddy slope on the other side, each sliding back down several times in the attempt, but finally reaching and clambering over the steel guardrail at the top.

There before them, across a wide expanse of parking lot, stood the Millcreek Mall.

They were facing the north facade, mostly dark and quiet at this hour, with no public entrance to an anchor store. But distantly, on the other sides, they could see cars and even, faintly, hear voices.

There were people over there.

The trio began to trudge forward, past the free-standing Millcreek 6 Discount Theatre, deserted at this hour, toward the sound of early-rising Christmas Eve shoppers, arriving ahead of the opening.

People. Living people.

Mitchell and Corinne and Eddie—what was left of them—each let out small moans of hunger and anticipation, as they plodded toward the bounty of living human flesh that lay before them.

PART TWO

A MALL AND THE NIGHT VISITORS

1.

Even Santa can't handle this weather, thought Miguel, taking a drag. *Not even for the sake of nicotine.*

Miguel was hunkered against the north wall next to the loading dock, collar pulled up, face turned toward the bricks, finishing his first cig of the morning. Santa Claus had pulled up a few minutes earlier, and scurried across the parking lot, and when Miguel had asked him if he wanted a smoke, the jolly fat man said thanks but no thanks, too cold, in his big jolly voice, and hustled on in, seeming in a rush to get to the locker room. Miguel couldn't blame the guy, who was normally delighted to accept a cigarette in return for a few minutes' chat, for wanting to escape this unpleasant freezing soup.

I really should quit, he thought, as he had thought at least a thousand times since he'd taken up the habit a decade earlier. Now, at 22, with Graciela and Javier and Marta to provide for on a stock assistant's wages, it made even more sense.

And as much sense as it makes, I'm still not likely to quit in this lifetime, he thought sullenly, taking one more drag. *It's probably what will kill me.* He dropped the butt into the slush at his feet and watched it sputter there.

Wouldn't it be great if that was the last one I ever smoked?

As he turned to step back inside, he noticed three people slowly walking toward him through the rain, from the direction of the movie theaters. He couldn't quite make them out, but they were coming straight toward the stockroom door.

Were they employees, or early-bird shoppers who thought they'd be clever and park in an area normally eschewed by the public, somehow making their getaway easier this afternoon? If so, they'd really parked far away. The overnight crew had gone home—or, more probably, gone somewhere to get drunk—and except for his own old beater and Santa's, he couldn't see any other cars over here in the north lot.

Come to think of it, maybe these three were drunks, wandered in from some bar or party over on Peach. They walked like drunks, and like drunks, the cold didn't seem to bother them.

Anyway, if they thought they were coming into the store through the stockroom and beating the rush, they had another think coming. He pushed aside the cinderblock doorstop and let the door swing shut with a bang, locking behind him.

He pulled off his coat, tossed it onto a chair, and picked up a clipboard with the logistics sheet that Lucinda had left for him. Light duty today; there were no deliveries scheduled, and most of the stock left in the store was already on the shelves. He was trying to decide what to do first when the door handle began to rattle behind him.

"Forget it," Miguel muttered.

He kept reading the sheet, trying to ignore the rattling, which only grew louder. Then the pounding started: hard, deliberate thumps on the metal door.

"Shit," said Miguel. "Do I have to kick your drunk asses?"

He thought fleetingly of calling security, but decided that if a former badass like himself couldn't handle three chilly drunks, he didn't deserve the title of former badass. Still, as an afterthought he picked up a box cutter from Lucinda's desk, just in case they were mean chilly drunks instead of friendly chilly drunks.

They were still pounding monotonously away when he grabbed the handle with his right hand, in which he also held the box cutter, keeping it out of sight, and opened the door.

"Sorry, folks," he began politely, raising his left hand. "This is no' really a public entrance, so you have to...Ah!"

The big guy in front grabbed Miguel's left wrist in his cold hand, pulled it to his mouth, and took off Miguel's pinky and ring finger with one crunching, wrenching bite.

Miguel bellowed with pain and fury and pulled back, and the tiny stumps squirted thin streams of blood into the guy's gray face. The guy advanced, his two friends crowding in behind him. He didn't let go of Miguel's wrist, and his grip was surprisingly strong, but Miguel's former badass reflexes hadn't deserted him altogether, and he swung the box cutter up in an arc, hard, jamming the blade under the guy's ribs, into his left lung.

It didn't slow the guy down. He didn't seem to notice, really.

Miguel didn't stop to wonder why. He raised his right foot and kicked the guy in the stomach. That did the trick—the guy tumbled backwards into his two friends, who also stumbled backwards.

Unfortunately, so did Miguel. He landed hard on his back, knocking the wind out of himself.

His attackers slowly got back to their feet, and for the first time Miguel registered that the other two, a man and a woman, were naked, and that all three of them were hurt.

Badly hurt. The woman's—oh *Madre de Dios*, the woman's tripes were hanging out.

He turned and tried to scramble away, but he'd been transfixed too long, and three pairs of hands seized his legs, below the knees. They pulled, and Miguel began to slide backward toward them. He grabbed a pipe running up the wall and held on and tried to kick loose, but the two guys had strong grips, and they kept pulling at him, now in opposite directions like he was a wishbone, breaking both of his knees.

Miguel roared as pain crashed over him like a tsunami. He blacked out for a sweet second or two, and then he was back, still clinging to the pipe, feeling somehow lighter now, and he looked over his shoulder.

The big guy was seated on the floor, tearing pieces away from Miguel's left calf, while the naked, maimed man and woman were listlessly fighting over his sneaker-shod right leg. His jeans were empty below the knees, blood hurrying out of the soaked cuffs into bright red puddles.

Miguel let out a feeble, croaking scream, and scrambled away, pulling himself along on his hands, leaving a wide crimson trail behind him, around the corner and down the hall toward the locker room. By the time it occurred to him that he should take off of his belt and try to tourniquet his stumps, it was too late. He lay on his side, but his fingers only got as far as his buckle before they went slack, and he lay still.

Mitchell, Corinne and Eddie sat contentedly yanking off chunks of flesh from Miguel's legs and chewing on them. After four or five minutes, though, they slowed, and stared at the limbs in their hands with dissatisfaction. The sense of it as fresh meat, as part of a living human, was gone. The hunger rose up in them again, and Miguel's legs could no longer sate it.

Quietly groaning, the three of them climbed to their feet again and plodded off together, following Miguel's blood trail. Around the corner, and not twenty feet down the hall, there was Miguel, now sitting up, no longer bleeding, his half-length legs sticking out in front of him.

They stared down at him, indifferently. He stared back up at them with equal disinterest. After a second or two, they plodded on down the hall, toward the locker room. Miguel crawled after them.

2.

It was still full dark, under thick, gun-metal-gray clouds, when Brian Morgan and Teddy Mrozowski turned off Peach Street and into the parking lot of the Millcreek Mall. The silhouette of the Mall's familiar water tower loomed in the murk at the south end of the parking lot, looking somehow like a mushroom cloud.

"Jesus, look at that," Brian said.

At every entrance, a large crowd of people stood in the freezing drizzle, waiting for the doors to open.

"Look at what?"

"All these dipshits. Freezing their asses off, but they don't even notice 'cause they're drooling like dogs to get at the merchandise inside."

"Well, that would be one way of looking at it," said Teddy. "Or you could possibly see them as filled with the Christmas spirit, and so eager to find the perfect gifts to delight their loved ones that the cold doesn't bother them."

"I'm going to go with my take, I think," said Brian.

Teddy parked, and they slogged their way through the slush to the food court entrance, Brian carrying *Return to*

Dino-Dragon Island in a Jaydee's bag, and joined the milling crowd. Brian scanned the faces, and his initial impression was confirmed—he didn't see much of the cheery holiday spirit that Teddy had just described. True, there was a lot of talking and laughing, but the laughter sounded nervous. These people were anxious, irritated by the weather, the wait, and the competition they saw in each other's eyes for the slim pickings that lay inside.

And who am I, thought Brian, to judge? I'm just another last-minute zombie.

He glanced to his left and Teddy wasn't beside him any more, looked around and spotted him, slipping a dollar into the homeless-looking Salvation Army guy's kettle. God, what a sap. He sighed, dug in his pocket, found eighteen cents, strolled over and dropped it in with a clatter.

"Merry Christmas, God bless you," the homeless-looking guy said, robotically.

And then the security guards unlocked the doors, and the crowd poured through them. As he and Teddy plodded in with the rest, they heard, but paid little attention to, the faint sound of a helicopter, off in the distance, but approaching.

3.

Santa Claus had just finished jerking off. He pulled down some toilet paper and cleaned himself up a little, then hung his head and sobbed, right there in the stall. He pressed his hand over his mouth, determined to stay quiet, even though he had the locker room to himself.

They knew about him. Somebody knew.

The evening before, one of the security guards came to him while he was on break, catching a butt by the JayDee's stockroom entrance, standing behind a wall of stacked pallets so that nobody would see Jolly Old St. Nick cooking one. The guard said that Mr. Roczinski needed to see him right away.

Somehow Santa knew on the spot that the jig was up. The bottom dropped out of his stomach. He went to management office like a sleepwalker, not remembering how he got there, and there by the receptionist's desk was Roczinski, trim and impeccably dressed, smiling with his usual professional geniality.

"Santa! How are you?"

"I'm fine, sir. Busy day today."

"And you're doing a great job. Best Santa ever." To the buxom, frizzy-haired receptionist, he said, "Have you seen this guy in action yet, Sherry?"

"Nope."

"Well, he's as good as it gets. If I hadn't seen him without the beard, I'd be pretty sure he was the real thing."

"Thank you, sir," said Santa.

"Come on in my office, will you? Excuse us, Sherry."

Roczinski's manner was so friendly and easygoing that for a moment Santa thought he might be okay after all. But as soon as the office door was closed, the smile switched off like an electric light.

"We've got a problem," Roczinski said, gesturing at the leather couch as he dropped into the chair behind his big wooden desk. "Have a seat."

"What problem, sir?"

"You know fucking well what problem, man. Don't waste my time."

There was silence. When it became clear that Santa simply wasn't going to say anything, Roczinski said: "Somebody from your neighborhood recognized you. Even with the fucking beard, somebody managed to recognize you."

Silence again. Santa sat, staring at the pile of four naked female mannequins piled against the office wall. But he knew he'd have to say something, so finally he just said, "Somebody recognized me, sir?"

"Yeah, that's what I said, somebody recognized you. One of your neighbors. From when you went to their house. From when you had to go to their house, and tell them about yourself. Tell them all the shit you somehow didn't see fit to tell me."

"I...I see."

"I doubt very much you do see, asshole. I doubt very much you see in the slightest how much I'd like to take one of those big plastic candy canes and beat your pervert ass into the floor with it. How much I'd like to see you trampled by a heard of fucking reindeer."

"I…"

"Wait a minute. Before we go any farther, let me ask you something. Who was it? Was it somebody underage?"

Santa hung his head.

"I'll take that as a yes. Some teenage girl? A Roman Polanski type thing?"

"It was…it was a boy, sir."

"Christ. How old?"

"I was in my thirties at the time."

"Come on, man."

"Well, the, uh, the case where I was convicted…"

"Oh, Christ!"

"…he was. Um. He was twelve, sir."

"Oh, Jesus." Roczinski put his face in his hands. "That's just wonderful."

"That was more than five years ago, sir. There's never been one incident since then. My wife took the kids and left me, and I did my time, and I did the therapy, and I'm clean. Completely."

"That's fucking swell."

"I'm sorry I, you know, deceived you, Mr. Roczinski. I needed work, and I look the way I look, so I was always able to find work as a Santa this time of year."

"Yeah, that's some sense of humor that God has."

"I just needed the money. They let you out of prison, and then they make it impossible for you to get back into society, make a living."

"Yeah, my heart bleeds for the fucking problems of child molesters. OK, listen. Here's the thing. If it was up to me I'd like to give you to the Air Force and let them drop you over the North Pole without a parachute. But there's two problems. First of all, if I fire you, and then you choose to let it slip to the media that I hired you, I'm screwed."

That hadn't occurred to Santa, but now that Roczinski mentioned it, it was true. Of course, his own identity would be revealed, too, but it's not like his own neighbors could think any less of him than they did already, after his door-to-door tour earlier in the year.

"Second of all," continued Roczinski, "I wasn't kidding just now when I said you were the best Santa ever. I've been managing this mall for more than twenty years, and I never saw one that even came close. Not even the ones with real beards."

"Thank you, sir."

"Shut up. We got one more day. So I just need you to answer me one question."

"What's that, sir?"

"Are you going to molest any kids tomorrow?"

"Of course not, sir."

"You said you were clean. Do you ever get the urge, still?"

Silence again, for a few seconds, and then:

"Sometimes...when they're on my lap, yes sir. Sometimes I still feel it. But I've got it under control."

He thought that this answer would send Roczinski into another tirade, but he seemed satisfied by the candor.

"Alright," he said. "I gave the shithead who recognized you a really large gift certificate to keep quiet. His Christmas is pretty much covered this year, so he's in a great mood. Now if you go out there tomorrow and put in one more good day's

114

work, and keep your beard on tight and hope everybody else on your block did their shopping early this year, we can all have a Merry Christmas. There might even be a bonus in it for you."

"I can do that, sir."

"You'd better. If this gets out somehow and comes back on me, I promise you'll be sorry. Rudolph'll be putting flowers on your grave this time next year. OK, go back to work."

"Yes, sir," said Santa, rising.

"Hey," said Roczinski, in a milder tone, before Santa reached the door. He turned back.

"No joke, my life is in your hands. Remember that I didn't just can your ass on the spot."

He probably should have canned me, though, thought Santa now, wiping his eyes. He got up from the crapper, pulled up his red velvet trousers and tied them off, then lowered his red jacket with the fluffy white trim and buckled the wide leather belt around it.

Because, of course, though he had admitted that he still got the urge, he hadn't told Roczinski how intense that urge was. He hadn't told him about how, even though he jerked off two or three times at home in the evening and at least once in the morning before his shift started, he still had to slip into the men's room and jerk off on every break, how every one of those fucking little cockteases gave him a raging hard-on, how he was sure that some of them could feel it and moved their tiny, perfect little asses around on his lap to make it worse for him.

He left the stall and went to his locker to get his Visine. Wouldn't do for Santa to look like he'd been on a crying jag. He sat on the bench and put the drops in his eyes.

"But whoso shall offend one of these little ones who believe in me, it were better for him that a millstone were hanged about his neck,

and that he were drowned in the depth of the sea." I agree with you on that one, Jesus, thought Santa, head rolled back, eyes closed, letting the Visine do its work. *In the depths of the sea, or of Lake Erie. Did You ever think of asking Your Dad why He let people have that urge when they never wanted it?*

He heard the back door of the locker room open with a clang, but he didn't open his eyes.

"Morning," he said to whoever it was.

He heard several sets of feet approaching—heavy, plodding tread, and a mournful little moan.

"Sounds like you guys hit the holiday cheer as hard as I did last night," said Santa, forcing a chuckle. "You can borrow my Visine, if you want."

Then two pairs of hands grabbed him at once, and he felt cold, clammy mouths rip into his face and throat.

4.

Brian and Teddy fought their way into JayDee's Toys, past a pyramid of boxes of last year's *Return to Dino-Dragon Island* at which none of the shoppers around them deigned to so much as glance. Brian glared at the display reproachfully.

"So that was the big deal last year?"

"That was it. You couldn't get one of those this time last year for a night with Angelina Jolie."

"How did Logan end up with one, then?"

"Jesus, you really don't pay much attention, do you? He got it for his birthday. Trina got it for him for his birthday. When is that, again, Bri?"

"Fuck you, his birthday's August 8."

"Thank God to hear you know that, at least. So by August, it was easy to find."

"And the one he wants this year, it's the same deal?"

"No," said Teddy. "From what I hear, it's even tougher to find."

"But somehow this friend of yours, at a shit toy store at a shit mall in Erie, he's somehow going to be able to fix me up with *Treasure of Dino-Dragon Island*? On Christmas Eve?"

"Keep your voice down, will you? You could totally start a riot if people thought there was one of those things in here. Look, I don't know what the guy has. What he said was he thought he could make you happy, for the right price."

"For the right price? Dude, I told you, I couldn't buy a Pez dispenser right now. No way I'll be able to meet this guy's price, even if he does have what I want."

"Look, I just thought it was worth checking out, OK? What's your alternative, at this point? Hey, there he is."

And there indeed Don was, up ahead of them at the end of the aisle—a short, chubby guy with a graying beard, decked out in his purple JayDee's vest, fielding questions from a small mob of shoppers.

"That's him? He looks like the winner of an Oscar Homolka look-alike contest," said Brian.

"He does at that," said Teddy, laughing. "What would the first prize in an Oscar Homolka look-alike contest be? A jar of pickled herring?"

When he saw Teddy, Don Engelsdorf made an elaborate keep-it-cool gesture, inclined his eyes toward the back of the store, and extricated himself, with difficulty, from the frantic questioners.

"If this dude's jerking us around, he's dead," said Brian, as he and Teddy struggled after him through the crowd.

"If he's jerking us around, *you're* dead," said Teddy.

From somewhere behind them, in the main concourse of the Mall, they could hear screaming, but, like the sound of the helicopter, they barely noticed it.

5.

Santa had shrieked when he felt the teeth clamp onto his cheek, shrieked louder when he felt a large piece of his face torn away, and then the shriek was cut off as another set of jaws tore into his neck and a cold tongue shoved into the gushing wound. He'd flailed his arms out and sprang up from the bench, and though he wasn't a strong man his attackers fell back easily, like tipsy drunks, and he got a good look at them.

Demons, he thought. *I blasphemed, and God let the demons come to get me. Just like my mother always told us they would.*

He turned and ran out the other locker room door, trying to hold his hands to his maimed face and throat. But he'd gotten a look.

The two who'd bit him were a heavy-set, tousle-haired guy in a rent-a-cop uniform, and a topless woman with big tits and a big nose. The rent-a-cop had a knife sticking out of his chest, and the woman—well, her belly had been ripped open, and her pinkish-gray guts were dangling to her knees, like an apron.

Behind them was another big, heavy-set guy. He was naked, and he had a swastika tattooed on his chest. His throat was laid open, too, and he was carrying a human leg, in a black sneaker, at his side like an umbrella. And behind him, bringing up the rear, was Miguel or Manuel or whatever his name was, that stockroom kid. He was dragging himself along by his hands, because—well, because his legs were missing.

Sorry you got in the way of the demons sent for me, kid, thought Santa, as he crashed through the door and fled down the long white hallway, blood spilling between his fingers onto the tile floor. The hallway began to spin, and his vision got dim, and he knew that time was nearly up, that he had to get help fast if he was to have any chance at all. He threw his Santa-sized bulk against the door at the end of the hallway, and burst out into the Mall proper, main concourse, blood flying.

The shoppers recoiled, and at first they laughed at him, but with annoyed faces, thinking it was a joke in particularly bad taste. But then they got a good look, saw his eyes, saw it was real. Santa was hurt. Santa was badly hurt. Santa's face and throat were torn open. Santa was about to bleed out. Santa looked imploringly around, then toppled over onto his back, staring up at the skylight above. Just before his vision grayed out, he saw the lights of a helicopter, skimming in low.

6.

Ellie set the A-Star down between the skylights—rather gently, considering the power loss, if she did say so herself—and cut the engine. "Okay, we're down," she said, and kept *Thank God* from slipping out after. "I'm going to hop out and see if I can assess what's up, and then I'll call Hubie."

"Do me a favor," said Rick. "Don't call Hubie until you've looked at the damage, and figured out what it's going to take to get us airborne again."

"What it's going to take? It's going to take a helicopter mechanic, which I'm not. I'm just going to see if it's something obvious I can tell him over the phone. No way I'm taking off until Hubie's come out and fixed it."

"All the same, don't call until you've looked, and talked to me, OK?"

"You're the boss tonight. Listen, on the chance it's a fuel leak you might want to hop out too, and put some distance between yourself and the aircraft."

"I'll risk it," said Rick, now furiously tapping at his Blackberry, or whatever the hell swanky smartphone he had.

"Suit yourself," she sighed, and kept *you hardheaded douchebag* from slipping out after, as she climbed out into the wet cold.

7.

"My God, I think he's dead," said a middle-aged woman. "What was it, one of those pit bulls?"

"Call 911," said a guy in a plaid jacket, as he crouched next to Santa. People were already pulling out their cell phones. "And we need a security guard."

As if in answer to this request, the same door Santa had come through opened, and in lumbered a security guard, a big guy with a box cutter in his chest and blood smeared all over his face like a kid who'd just finished a whole cherry pie.

Somebody screamed.

The bloody-faced guard looked around dully at the crowd, then lunged at the middle-aged woman.

More people screamed.

"Get him off her!" yelled the guy in the plaid shirt, springing up. He didn't notice that Santa had sat up behind him—until Santa sank his teeth into the guy's thigh, right through his jeans, sending out a fountain from his femoral artery. The guy bellowed, but by now everybody's eyes were on the bare-breasted, big-nosed woman who had just come reeling through the same door.

And when they got a good look at her, *everybody* screamed.

8.

"What have you got today?" asked Tristan.

"Anthrax," said Andrea.

"Perfect," said Dipstick.

"Weather really sucks out there," said Andrea, also known as the Morning Goddess, as she closed the door of the plexiglass booth behind her and tossed a box of Mighty Fine Donuts on the counter beside the console. Dipstick's face lit up.

"Mighty Fines! Breakfast of champions. You got me a maple frosted, right?"

"Yes, Dip, in response to your eighteen reminders yesterday I got you a maple frosted," she said. Then, from her purse, she produced a copy of the Anthrax CD *Spreading the Disease*.

"Today's counterprogramming," she said, and popped open the top of the boombox under the counter.

"Hang on, OK, ten seconds," said Tristan, putting on his headphones. "Dip, hold off on the maple frosted until after, OK?"

Dipstick reluctantly dropped the donut back into the box, and he and Andrea also crowned themselves with headphones. Tristan opened the mike, the ON AIR light went on, and he spoke:

"Good morning to the City by Misery Bay, and just to make you a little more miserable here with Tristan, Dipstick and the Morning Goddess on WSER at 5:01 on a Christmas Eve A.M., that was John Lennon with 'So This Is Christmas,' reminding you that you just wasted the whole year, and we're going to follow that up with Band Aid's 'Do They Know It's Christmas,' just to make sure that you feel lousy about having enough to eat..."

"I don't think that's what they intended with that song," said Andrea.

"That ethereal ebon beauty the Morning Goddess just walked in, you guys, and she brought a big box of Mighty Fine Donuts with her..."

"She even brought me my maple frosted..."

"Yeah, Dipstick got his maple frosted, so he may not be much good to us here until he knocks that back, but anyway we've got plenty to eat in here, but like the song says, in Africa...Well, Dipstick doesn't look like he feels guilty, he just looks like he's going to pass out if he doesn't get to inhale that maple frosted in the next five seconds, so go for it Dip, we won't expect to hear from you for a while..."

"You're not supposed to feel guilty," persisted Andrea, "It's just supposed to remind you to help..."

"Right, right, now listen Goddess, Dipstick, this is a big deal..."

"What's a big deal?"

"We're coming up this half-hour on the season's ONE TRILLIONITH playing of Amy Grant singing 'My Grown-

Up Christmas List,' so you're going to want to stick around for that, unless of course you haven't done your Christmas shopping yet..."

"Uh-oh..."

"In which case you should be on your way..."

"Driving carefully of course," put in Andrea, "Freezing rain out there right now..."

"Driving carefully of course, and listening to WSER in your car," Tristan went on, "you should be on your way down here to the Millcreek Mall, where Dipstick and the Goddess and I are hanging out all morning, bringing you, for the fourth year in a row, non-stop, wall-too-wall, back-to-back, all your favorite Holiday music, along with wealthy British musicians of the '70s and '80s scolding us for enjoying our good fortune..."

"That's not what they're doing..."

"Yeah, yeah, whatever Goddess, anyway, if you make it down here to the Mall alive, stop by our glass house here on the Main Concourse and don't throw stones, just wave hello while we bring you all this great Holiday music, and this hour we'll also have the Goddess's Nutty News Flash—it'll be a Holiday Nutty News Flash today, right Goddess?"

"You bet it will, Tristan."

"So we've got that to look forward to, and a little later on Dipstick will bring us the Stick's Pick; today it's Mariah Carey's 'All I Want For Christmas Is You,' right, Dip?"

"No it isn't, Tristan," said Dipstick, wiping maple frosting away from his lips. "No more than it was yesterday."

"Then what have you got for us?"

"As always, it's a surprise."

"Eat another donut, Dip, you look a little undernourished," said Tristan. "And on that note, here's Band Aid with 'Do They Know It's Christmas.'"

He tapped two keys, the ON AIR light went out, and they all pulled off their headphones. Tristan quickly turned down the console volume, and the opening bars of "Do They Know It's Christmas" faded away.

"Blissful silence," he said. Outside the plexiglass booth, however, crowds had begun to flow into the Main Concourse from each of its tributaries.

"Keep up that snotty attitude on the air," said Andrea. "They're going to get pissed again."

"You think O'Leary's listening at this hour?" asked Tristan, picking up a Boston cream. "On Christmas Eve?"

"I think he can hear about anything that's said, any hour, any day. Somebody's always listening. This is just like that crap on the Fourth of July."

"Had to be said."

"You piss them off again, it won't just be Mr. Daring Iconoclast who gets shit-canned, it'll be me and Dipstick, too."

"I don't think he's gone over the line yet this season," said Dipstick. "The only thing he did just know that might piss them off is use the word erth...erther...You know, about Andrea?"

"Ethereal."

"Yeah. What does that mean?"

"It means hot," said Tristan, taking another bite of Boston cream.

"That's not what it means," said Andrea.

"That's what it meant in this case," said Tristan. "As far as Dipstick's concerned."

"Ok," said Dipstick. "I'm with you there." Dipstick's crush on Andrea was painfully obvious.

"You know, they say the economy sucks in this town, but you'd never know to look out there," said Tristan. The crowd outside the booth was indeed dense, teeming. Hardly anyone smiled or waved at the trio under plexiglass, however. Everyone looked too preoccupied.

"They're all spending money they don't have," said Dipstick.

"These stores are really late getting the gates up," said Andrea. "JayDee's is open, but it looks like that's about it. They'd better hurry up; the natives are going to get restless."

"Let's have the Anthrax, OK Goddess?" said Tristan.

"Intro first, please," said Andrea.

"Oh, right," said Tristan. "OK, gang, for your listening pleasure here on the WSER Private Audience-Of-Three So We Don't Lose Our Fucking Minds From Repetitive Insipid Christmas Music Counterprogramming Station…"

"Holiday music," Andrea reminded him.

"…Sorry, *Holiday* music, here's a selection from the heartwarming 1985 holiday album *Spreading the Disease*, by Anthrax. It's 'Madhouse.'"

Andrea selected a track on the boombox, hit a button, and thrash metal filled the booth.

"Jesus, I remember this," said Dipstick. "I remember seeing the video of this on MTV when I was a kid. I must've been 12 or 13, and I remember thinking, Jesus, rock and roll really *is* bad for the youth of America."

"You were a middle-aged man already, Dip, even at 13," said Tristan.

"Hey, did you guys hear that?" said Andrea.

"Hear what?"

"I thought I could hear screaming out there."

"Probably just on the record," said Dipstick.

9.

Rick snapped his smartphone shut—he'd gotten all the information there was to get, at this point—and sat impatiently, listening to the freezing rain patter on the helicopter's windshield. He'd heard the girl open a panel on the aircraft's underbelly and tinker for a minute or so, and now he heard her slam it shut. A few seconds later she was climbing back into the cabin.

"So?"

"You were right, it was a lucky shot," she said. "The bullet nicked a fuel line. Lucky for us, it was return line, with little pressure. Then it took out a wire to the generator; probably a field wire. We can start again, but we won't have much fly time on the remaining juice. But it looks fixable. Hubie can probably get us out of here in an hour, tops."

"An hour? No, that won't work. What about you? A nick to the line, that sounds like something that could be temporarily patched, right? How long would it take you to fix it, just enough to get us back to the airport in one piece?"

"I told you, I'm a pilot, not a mechanic. I can't fix it. If we were on the edge of a volcano that was about to erupt, something like that, I could maybe give it a try. But we're not, so I'm not going to risk it. Even if we made it back to the airport no problem, I could get in a lot of trouble for..."

"I'll give you five thousand dollars if you do it."

"What?"

"You heard me. Five thousand. And I'll give Hubie a thousand to look the other way once we're back, too."

"Why would you pay so much for a short cab ride?"

"What do you care?"

"I'm just curious, OK?"

"You saw what happened back at Micromegas."

"Yeah, I did. I'd still like to know what it was all about."

"No. You don't. I promise you, you don't want to know. And I don't want the cops, or anybody, to know I was anywhere near it. And they won't, if I can get back to the airport and get the fuck out of this shit town. I promise you, this would be the best move for you even without the five grand. Put it this way: You're not that far off about the volcano."

She looked at him hard. For the first time this messed-up Christmas Eve, he didn't seem to be bullshitting her.

And five thousand bucks would buy a lot of Behrend College textbooks. Two, maybe even three.

"I'll need some duct tape," she said. She slipped into the back of the cabin, turned on a light, and rummaged in various compartments for several minutes.

"Fuck, no duct tape," she said finally.

"No duct tape?" said Rick. "All you need is fucking duct tape, and you don't have any?"

"I don't carry it with me, no, and this isn't my helicopter. If it was, I can tell you there'd be duct tape aboard."

"Somebody's going to eat their job for Christmas dinner for this," said Rick.

"Come on," she said. "The mall's open. Let's go find some duct tape."

"I'm staying here."

"No you're not. We can split up, and you can help me find it. If the security guards come up here, wondering why the hell a helicopter just landed on the roof, they'll ask you your name. Do you want that?"

"Shit. OK, you know what, you win. How far is it from here to the airport? By car, I mean."

"Like I said, ten minutes tops, at this hour. Maybe another ten or twenty waiting for the cab to get here."

"Oh, bullshit. I'll find some redneck who needs a few bucks for Christmas, and pay him some of what I was going to give you to give me a lift. As far as I'm concerned, the mall can keep this fancy helicopter that can't take one bullet. Come on, let's go."

He picked up the metal briefcase and they climbed down, and hurried, chins tucked forward, trying not to slip in the loose slush, toward a service hatch at the far end of the roof. Horrible though the weather was, they could detect the first light of dawn, faintly, off to the east.

Ellie pulled on the hatch, sure it would be locked, but it wasn't. She climbed down the rungs set into the wall, Rick following her, clutching his case. They found themselves at the top of a cinderblock stairwell.

Down they went. As they reached the ground floor service hallway, Ellie, brow furrowed, said "What's with all the screaming, I wonder?"

133

10.

"Just give me a minute," said Don Engelsdorf.

Brian and Teddy waited in the outer stockroom while Engelsdorf slipped through a divider of hanging plastic strips. They heard a door open and close on the other side.

"It's like he's bringing out the Hope Diamond," said Teddy.

"This is a waste of time," said Brian. "I'm not going to be able to pay him anything resembling what he's going to want for this thing."

"That's all arranged, Bri. You're going to blow him."

"Believe me, I would, if I thought he'd go for it. But it sounds like he could get Brad Pitt to blow him for one of these things."

"Oh, he told me Brad's been calling regularly, but I emailed him your picture, and you're more his type."

"Yeah, if I was anybody's type, it'd be my luck it was this guy's, but dude, I'm serious, I don't want to waste the whole day with this when…"

"Shut up, OK, Bri? Here he comes."

They heard the door reopen, then close and lock, and Engelsdorf emerged from the hanging plastic strips with *Treasure of Dino-Dragon Island* in his arms.

"Here it is," he said, setting it on a long table. "Unopened, New In Box, as they say on eBay."

The three of them stared down at it in silence. From behind them, they could still hear screams and shouts, getting closer. Engelsdorf knitted his brow, glancing toward the door that led out to the store: "Christ, what's all that about? People are really nuts this year."

"What's the story here?" asked Teddy, pointing to the upper right-hand corner of the box, which was dented blunt.

"Slight damage to the outer container and to the Styrofoam underneath," said Engelsdorf. "Very slight, no damage to the contents themselves. Just enough that I didn't think it should go on our shelves, so I set it aside, in a hidey-hole I have back there, to protect my fellow employees from the temptation that might arise to sell it privately, or take it home to their own kids. Any implication that the damage was caused by an entrepreneurial-minded assistant manager with a rubber mallet is unsupported by evidence."

"That dent bother you, Bri?"

"I wouldn't care if it had dried camel shit on it, as long as the thing inside works," said Brian.

"Not exactly an expert haggler, is he?" said Engelsdorf, and Teddy barked laughter.

Then they were all silent another moment or two.

It's for Logan, Brian thought at last, and then he said, "OK, look, I can give you, say, four hundred bucks for it, if you can just wait while I go borrow it from my aunt..."

"My friend," chuckled Englesdorf, "I have a guy driving in from Buffalo, he'll be here at eight-thirty, and he's bringing me a thousand dollars, cash."

"Well then, thanks so much for wasting our..."

Engelsdorf held up a hand. "Teddy?"

"Yeah, I have it right here," said Teddy Mrozowski, unzipping his coat and reaching into an inside pocket.

That was when they heard the gunshots.

11.

The screaming got a little louder as Ellie pushed open the stairwell door, and she and Rick entered the Mall proper. They found themselves in a short concourse which offered a video-game arcade and a beauty salon on one side and a branch library on the other, and which dead-ended in a Barbecue joint. None of these businesses would be open for hours, so the concourse was devoid of people. The screaming was coming from around the corner, off to the left, the main concourse.

"That sounds really awful," said Ellie. "Sounds like a riot."

"It's the most wonderful time of the year," said Rick.

Ellie said, "OK, if I were duct tape, where would I be? There's a hardware store down there somewhere, what's it called? Redemption Hardware? Resurrection Hardware?"

"Reconstruction Hardware?" asked Rick.

"That's it, Reconstruction Hardware."

Rick laughed. "They have one in this shithole? My wife loves that fucking place. Yes, I'm sure they have some Designer Free-Range Alligator Skin Duct Tape with Hand-

Woven Alpaca Backing and All-Natural Barnacle Secretion adhesive for just sixty-five dollars a roll. But screw the duct tape, you talked me into it, I'm catching a cab. Later." He strode off, in the general direction of the screaming. From somewhere off in the distance, she heard what sounded like gunshots.

"Watch yourself," she said, and managed to keep *Somebody somewhere must care if you live or die* from coming out after.

Before Rick had gotten ten steps, however, he froze, as a bespectacled man came reeling around the corner. He was clutching his throat with his right hand, vainly trying to slow the blood that spurted between his fingers from a wound in his neck. His left hand was missing. He stared at them, wide-eyed, holding up his stump as if to show them that he wasn't kidding around, this was serious, and then he collapsed at their feet.

"Jesus God," said Ellie, as a chunky woman in blood-soaked blue jeans and down vest followed him around the corner, backwards. In both of her blood-smeared mittens she clutched a severed left hand—this man's, thought Ellie, a reasonable assumption, right?—and she was trying to keep it away from perhaps a half-dozen other people who were grabbing and pawing for it, groaning frantically.

She seemed to be trying to get the appendage to her mouth.

Behind this scrum came dozens more people, all ages, all sizes, all races, blood-stained and wide-eyed, plodding and staggering.

"You've got to be fucking kidding me," said Rick, backing away from this throng. "Already?"

Already? thought Ellie. Interesting choice of words. But there was no time to speculate about it.

"Let's get back to the roof," she said.

"Yeah" said Rick, and they ran for the door they'd just come out of. But then Ellie noticed the sign on it that said NOT AN EXIT.

It had locked behind them, of course.

12.

Tristan, Dipstick and Andrea the Morning Goddess watched from their Plexiglass booth, as all around them the Dead became an Army in a matter of minutes.

Driven by all-consuming hunger, and free of the squeamishness that would have inhibited even the most barbaric attacker among the Living, they plunged into the soft places of their victims, the throats and faces and bellies and groins and thighs and calves, they bit and tore and yanked at knees and elbows and shoulders, and limbs were ripped loose as from Christmas turkeys, and blood spurted and gushed, and death swept over the victims in seconds, and seconds later their eyes reopened, blank and unoffended, and just as hungry as their killers, and they heaved up on whatever remained of their frames and joined in the feast, their high shrieks quieted into ravenous groans. They turned and waded backward into the onrush of shoppers, and the panicked dying tried to flee and were trampled, and then rose up to bite and grab from below, and by the time the shoppers realized they were rushing into mayhem, screaming bloody mayhem was all around them.

Nobody managed to leave the Mall. On Christmas Eve, not even the Dead could turn back the last-minute rush.

Tristan called 911, only to be told to stay put, the police were on their way. Andrea called the station to report what was happening. Natalie, the newsroom intern downtown at the station, thought it was a joke at first, of course, thought she was on the air and tried to play along, but then from Andrea's tone and language she realized that something real was happening, and asked if she should come to cover the story.

"Don't come near the place, for Christ sakes," said Andrea. "If I were you, I'd go home and hide under the bed."

On the air, Amy Grant simpered out her grown-up Christmas list. About the time she was finished, the screaming and struggling in the concourses had died down, and the bloody Dead noticed Tristan, Dipstick and the Morning Goddess, and began to crowd around the booth.

13.

"Jesus, that sounds like it's inside the store," said Engelsdorf. He grabbed the box, and darted back through the plastic strips.

"What the hell?" said Teddy. He and Brian crept to the swinging metal doors that led from the stockroom to the store proper, and peered through the window.

It took them a few seconds to decide if they were really seeing it.

Four people, two men, two women, tearing a fifth man to pieces.

"Christ!" said Brian.

"Quiet," said Teddy.

A cop, gun drawn, approached the group, yelling "Let him go! Let him go now!" but even as he said it, the attackers towed the man's left arm out of its socket, amidst a gush of cherry colored-blood. The man's screams went shrill, and the cop fired twice, into the back of one of the attackers, which broke up the scrum.

The shot man, who wore a plaid jacket, stumbled forward—but didn't fall. The victim, who wore the same purple JayDee's vest as Engelsdorf, did fall, gushing blood from the shoulder and from chunks torn out of his other arm. His screams trailed off. The party of attackers turned toward the cop, who suddenly seemed to realize that he was too close to them. He fired again, this time into the forehead of one of the women, and she dropped like a sack of groceries.

The other man and woman kept coming, however, and a second later they were upon the cop, dragging him down, out of sight behind a tall display of baseball equipment. A second later he began screaming, and two seconds after that, his screams also became shrill.

What Teddy and Brian noticed, however, was the man whose arm had been pulled off.

He was getting up.

He struggled to his feet, his bearded face emotionless, and walked toward the group that had attacked him, like a man who had reconsidered an invitation, and now thought that yes, a little snack would hit the spot. He, too, disappeared behind the baseball display.

"Hey Bri," said Teddy. "I think we should get the fuck out of here."

"Yeah," rasped out Brian.

They turned, and there was Engelsdorf returning, now carrying a shotgun.

"Looters?" he asked, rather eagerly. "I thought we might have some today."

"Not exactly looters," said Teddy.

"Where's the back door?" said Brian.

"Fuck the back door," said Engelsdorf, advancing. "If they're tearing up my store, I'm going to..."

Then he looked out the window.

"Jesus Christ!"

"Keep your voice down," said Teddy. "Now where's the back door?"

"This way," said the wide-eyed Englesdorf. He led them back through the plastic strips, down a short hallway, past the entrance to a large stockroom and to the right. Brian caught a glimpse of *Treasure of Dino-Dragon Island* on a lower shelf, and thought, *Am I really here because of that little box?*

Then they were in a long narrow hallway, lit by bare lightbulbs, leading to an exit door. As they neared it, they could see that the handle was chained and padlocked.

"Oh yeah, that's right. Shit." said Engelsdorf, slowing. He glanced at Brian and Teddy. "Problem."

"It's chained?" said Brian. "Why the fuck is it chained?"

"Is that even legal?" asked Teddy.

"I was afraid somebody might jimmy the door, looking for the *DDI*."

"Man, you were really committed to defending that game," said Teddy.

"Where's the key?" said Brian.

"That's the problem," said Engelsdorf. "I don't have my keys on me. I gave them to Myron to open the register, right before you guys got here."

"Fuck. Can we shoot the lock off?" asked Brian.

"I bet that only works in the movies," said Teddy.

Then they heard a moan behind them. They all turned.

The man in the plaid jacket was standing at the end of the hall, looking at them.

14.

Sherry was slipping back into the green and red bra and panties, trimmed with gold, that she'd had on under her clothes.

"You didn't say how you liked my Christmas lingerie," she said. "I got it for you."

"I have to admit, I like it better off than on," said Roczinski. "But they look beautiful. Like you."

He tried to make his remark sound suave and charming, but he knew his voice was harried, distracted. He was dressing, too, hastily. The Mall was open by now; the two of them had to get back into character. He had a vision of his wife suddenly being visited by the Christmas spirit, feeling sorry for him because he'd had to pull an all-nighter in preparation for the last day of Christmas shopping, coming down here with a plate of cookies or some such shit, and rapping on the door of the darkened office while he was pulling his all-nighter with young Sherry on the leather couch next to his desk. God, this girl had stamina.

He finished buttoning his shirt, tucked it into his pants, then opened the door of his office and turned on the lights in the outer office. When he came back, Sherry was still on the couch in the yuletide scanties, reclined now, smiling slyly.

"Five more minutes? One more round?"

"There's nothing I'd like better," Roczinski lied. "But the doors are open by now. You need to get out at the desk. Christ, hear that screaming? The nuts are already on the warpath out there. Raincheck, OK?"

"Three minutes, then," said Sherry, dropping to her knees in front of him and fumbling with his belt and zipper.

"Three minutes," he said. "I guess we could spare that much."

He sank backward onto the couch as he felt her warm wet mouth close around him. He managed to get hard, too—by thinking about his wife, oddly enough. He'd stumbled upon this oddly effective technique just recently in the course of their furtive grapplings, which had been going on since just before Halloween. Now that the initial thrill of tussling with his ridiculously well-built and talented young receptionist had worn off slightly, he'd found himself running out of erection at times before she'd run out of appetite. Then one time as he was feeling a bit panicky about his inability to stand at attention, he randomly thought of himself orally gratifying his wife, and that did the trick.

Maybe the sheer perversity of fantasizing about your dumpy nagging wife while getting blown by a luscious twenty-five-year old appealed to him, or maybe Sherry was just really on her game this morning, but in any case he was suddenly glad she'd talked him into the extra three minutes. Indeed, he was beginning to ruefully feel that three minutes might longer than he'd need.

Still, he knew he had to find a way to end this thing. He had no illusions that she actually found him an irresistible stud; to her he was a grateful older guy, by her standards a rich guy, and she thought if she could convince him that she was an insatiable slut, he'd leave his wife for her.

And he could do it, too, he supposed. The kids were grown and gone; he'd get hosed in the divorce, and rightly so, but if he got regular service like this, it would be worth it.

But that was the point. He wouldn't get it. This was the free trip to Vegas; after he'd bought the timeshare, so to speak, he knew perfectly well that this girl's legs would slam shut, and her knees would lock into upright position, within a few months at most.

Nah, he thought, as he neared climax. Use your head. Stick with the devil you know. Sometime after New Years I'll find a good opening to have a talk with...

They both froze.

"What's that?" said Sherry.

"Ah, Jesus," he said, jumping up and buckling his pants. "It sounded like gunshots. What the fuck's going on out there?"

Just then, he heard a loud thudding and pounding. Much closer. Somebody pounding on the door of the outer office.

"Oh, shit," said Roczinski. "Somebody's at the door."

"I'll get dressed," said Sherry.

"No, no, just stay in here and don't move. The lights are off in here, it would be too obvious what's going on. I'll get rid of whoever the fuck it is."

As Sherry drew back toward the pile of mannequins against the wall of the darkened office, Roczinski stepped into the outer office and saw, through the locked glass door, who the fuck it was.

Santa.

Santa was at the door, and Santa had clearly had a rough morning. One side of his face was laid wide open, and the fluffy white trim around his neck was soaked with blood.

"Jesus H. Christ," said Roczinski. "So somebody recognized you, did they?"

Shit, he thought, as he headed for the door. There goes my career, if anybody finds out I knew.

As he turned the bolt, he noticed for the first time that there were other people crowding behind Santa, in the shadowy hallway.

A lot of other people.

Santa pushed open the door...

15.

"Back the fuck off, dude," said Engelsdorf, as the man in the plaid jacket advanced down the hallway at them, limping from a deep divot out of his left thigh. Two exit wounds on his chest gaped, from the cop's bullets, but no blood came from them.

When he was halfway down the hall, Engelsdorf leveled the shotgun.

"If you shoot, the others'll know we're back here," said Teddy.

"And if he doesn't shoot?" asked Brian, but Engelsdorf wasn't interested in the debate. The shotgun boomed, deafening in the tight space. The blast hit the man just under the chin, mangling his neck and flinging him to his back.

"Come on," said Engelsdorf, removing the spent shell and pulling another from his pocket. "Let's go find Myron."

"Is Myron a tall guy with dark hair and a beard, by any chance?" asked Teddy.

"Yeah, that's him."

"Then we're going to have a hard time getting your keys back, I think."

The three of them hurried up the hallway. As they stepped around the man in the plaid jacket, his arm came up and grabbed Brian by the calf.

"Shit," said Brian, shaking and kicking loose. Engelsdorf took aim again, but didn't fire. The three of them watched as the man lurched up into a sitting position. His head, barely tethered to his body by his spine and a few straps of neck muscle, hung down backwards between his shoulder blades like a hood, yet his eyes were wide open, and staring at them. He continued to rise to his feet.

"Holy Christ," said Engelsdorf.

"That really does look like it should be a fatal wound," said Teddy.

The plaid-jacketed man stepped forward, away from them, then paused, seemingly perplexed when they receded. He turned, the front of his body now facing them, his backward-hanging head now facing away, stepped forward, then turned again so he could see them, stepped away, paused, turned away, and repeated the process. It was a graceful, dancer-like effect, a series of pirouettes that kept him in place.

"Let's go," said Brian.

They reached the door leading into the store and peered through the window. The store appeared to be empty. Beyond the entrance, however, out in the concourses, the mall itself seethed with people, Living and Dead, grappling with each other in scenes like the one they'd just witnessed.

"It doesn't look too great out there," said Teddy.

"No, it doesn't," said Engelsdorf. "Maybe we should just wait here, for more cops to get here or something?"

"I think that would be a really bad idea," said Teddy.

"Me too," said Brian. "Let's get the fuck out of here."

"I'd love to get out of here, but how do we do that?" asked Engelsdorf. "Look how many of them there are out there."

"Yeah, but whatever's wrong with these people, they seem to move really slow," said Teddy. "If we run for it, and keep our eyes open, we should be able to get through them."

"So what do we do? Just make a break for it?"

Teddy pointed to the baseball display. "I want one of those, first. How about you, Bri?"

"Why not?"

"OK, let's go," said Teddy. "We stop to grab a weapon, then run like hell, straight out the way we came in. A highly sophisticated plan." Then he added, "We'll just have to hope things are better outside than they are in here."

"Better than being trapped like rats, anyway," said Brian. "I don't want to die in a mall toy store. No offense."

"None taken," said Engelsdorf.

"OK, on three. And Don? How many shells do you have left?"

"Just two."

"Don't use them unless you have absolutely no choice, OK? I think the noise'll only make it worse."

"Got it."

"One, two, three!"

They pushed into the store.

16.

"Jesus H. Christ. So somebody recognized you, did they?"

Sherry, standing still behind the door in the shadows of the inner office, heard her boss say this, then heard him turning the bolt on the door.

"All right, come on in, we'll get you fixed up," she heard him continue, and then "Hey folks, you'll need to stay out there, this isn't a public…This man needs medical attention… Hey! Hey, let go of me, what are you doing? Hey, listen, I didn't know he was a child molester…I didn't know…I…Let go of me! Are you fucking crazy? Hey! *Hey!*"

And then his voice rose into a startled scream, and she heard a ripping sound, and his scream turned into a high, panicked gargling, and then another ripping sound and it stopped, and there was a sharp thud, like a bowling ball hitting the floor.

And then Roczinski's head came rolling through the door, into the middle of the office, trailing blood from where it had been raggedly torn away from his neck.

A scream came hurtling up through Sherry toward her mouth, but somehow she stopped it. She clenched her teeth, and nothing got out but a tiny squeak. The outer office was full of more ripping and snapping and splintering sounds, and wet splashings and ploppings, and soft moaning and chewing and slurping, and the shuffling of many pairs of feet. She took a few steps backward, and almost screamed again when her heel made contact with something. She glanced back and saw the pile of mannequins against the wall. Her foot had bumped the foot of one of the soulless naked girls that had witnessed her coupling on the couch with the boss.

Shadows filled the doorway. Whoever was out there, they were coming in. She wasn't at her desk to tell them to please sit down and wait; Mr. Roczinski would be with them in a few minutes.

Sherry sat down hard, alongside the mannequins, and leaned back against the wall. Without thinking, she narrowed her eyes to slits, as Santa Claus walked into the office.

Santa was in his red suit, the fur trim drenched in blood. His white beard was missing, and so was half of his face. A piece of his left cheek the size of a silver-dollar pancake was torn away, exposing the teeth and gums below, and a crater was ripped from his throat as well.

Behind him came a large man in a blood soaked security guard's uniform, and another big man, naked and covered with Nazi tattoos—he was holding Roczinski's arm, pulled out at the shoulder, peeling back the shirtsleeve like a chicken skin and chewing at the meat below. Behind him came a naked woman with an open abdomen and dangling guts, and behind her six or seven other people. They all milled around, staring blankly like they were in a trance. And they were all hurt. It occurred to Sherry that they were all hurt so badly they should be dead.

And then it occurred to her that maybe they were. Maybe they were.

Santa bent down and picked up Roczisnki's head, and stared down into his face.

Sherry held still, clenching her teeth, clenching her bladder, holding her eyes half shut. The intruders drifted close to her, gazed down at the mannequin pile, but then looked away in disinterest. After an endless minute or two, Santa seemed to lose interest in Roczinski's head. He let it fall from his hands, and it hit the carpet with another thump. Santa turned his head from side to side as best he could, scanning the room. Then he let out a groan, turned and plodded back out. The others followed him, and soon Sherry was alone in Roczinski's office again.

Well…not altogether alone. As she let out a shuddering sigh, her eyes fell upon Roczinski's head, lying on its side in the light from the outer office.

His head was alive. He was staring at her, eyes blank like those of the others, his mouth and tongue working, his teeth snapping.

The scream wanted out of Sherry even worse this time, but she held it in. She sat there holding it in, as the sounds of groaning and shuffling feet receded back down the hallway toward the concourses.

17.

On the other side of the swinging doors that led from the stockroom into JayDee's Toys, the groans of the Dead were louder. So were the screams of the Living, though they were becoming less frequent.

"Come on," whispered Teddy. He and Brian and Engelsdorf moved quickly, keeping the tall baseball equipment display between them and the milling Dead beyond the entrance. They passed Myron's severed arm, they passed the body of the woman that the cop had shot in the head, they reached the display, took cover behind it, and peered around the front at a small ocean of blood on the floor. The cop had either joined the ranks of his attackers, or they'd dragged his body off somewhere to eat it.

Teddy reached around and pulled out a baseball bat from the basket in the display.

"Bri?"

"Thanks." Teddy handed him the bat, then took one for himself.

"Don?"

"No, I'll stick with my shotgun."

"Suit yourself. OK, we break for it on three…"

"Hey, look, a gun," said Engelsdorf, pointing. A .38 lay on the floor, next to the pool of blood.

"It must be that cop's," said Brian. "He fired his clip, though, didn't he?"

Engelsdorf crouched, stretched his arm out, picked up the gun, and popped open the cylinder.

"Nope, he's got one bullet left." He offered the gun to Teddy.

"Never liked guns," said Teddy.

"Neither did I, but I'll take it anyway," said Brian. "One bullet's better than no bullets." He stuffed the revolver into his coat pocket.

"Hey, one more idea," said Teddy. "When we get out there, how about we try walking fast at first, instead of running. If they don't see us running, maybe they won't notice us for a while."

"Worth a try, I guess," said Brian.

"All right, no use putting it off any longer," said Teddy. "On three. One, two…"

"For Christ's sake, let's just run," said Brian.

And so they did. The three of them jogged to the front of the store, past a large blond man sprawled on his back with a bullet hole in his forehead—the cop's first target, apparently. He had somebody's ear, torn away with a scrap of skin and bushy gray hair, clenched in his teeth.

Brian slowed to a brisk walking pace as he stepped out into the concourse, and Teddy and Engelsdorf followed suit. Within a few seconds, however, it was clear that Teddy's idea about blending in wasn't going to work. A stout black woman, her left leg missing above the knee, spotted the trio at once, groaned with hunger, and blundered toward them, and then, from all around, they heard groans turn loud and eager, as they were noticed.

"Fuck it," said Brian. "I'm running."

He broke into a sprint, and Teddy and Engelsdorf followed. The chorus of groaning swelled, as the Dead, one after another, wheeled around, gazed blankly at the running trio, and then began their slow, stumbling pursuit.

Brian wasn't in the peak of physical condition, and he was further weighted down by his parka—with a gun in the pocket—and a baseball bat, but he wasn't doing too badly so far. Even when they weren't hobbled by missing or maimed legs, which a majority seemed to be, the reaction time of the Dead was really, really slow.

They seemed to have no tactical sense—they just came straight at you, arms wide, like a relative greeting you at the airport. When you dodged left or right and ran around them, they'd stand there for a second or two, astounded at your brilliant evasive skills, then turn and start plodding after you again.

Even so, there were so many that a few inevitably got close. A severe, schoolteacher-ish-looking old lady actually grabbed the arm of his parka, and he slammed his elbow backwards, knocking her down. A big, moonfaced, football-player-type kid with a torn-open chest and ribs pried forward lunged at him and got a hold on his arm that wasn't so easy to dislodge, and he had to place a hard kick into the kid's open midsection to knock him backwards. As he ran on, he heard a dull smack behind him, and glanced over his shoulder. The football-player kid was on the floor and twitching, with a cylindrical recess in his skull, as Teddy ran past him. His baseball bat had worked.

They rounded the corner into the short concourse leading to the exit they'd come in, and then, just as they came even with the corn-dog place, they slowed to a stop.

They weren't going anywhere.

18.

Ellie tugged at the handle, but the door didn't budge.

"So we're locked in, for real?" said Rick.

"Looks that way."

She turned, and saw the bloody, slack-jawed mob, eyes fixed upon them, getting closer. She noted with interest that the bespectacled man with the missing hand had gotten up and joined the crowd, tracking his own blood behind him. He was following the little group that had been trying to steal his hand from the woman in jeans, which had broken up when they saw Ellie and Rick.

Rick was moving away from her, toward the other side of the concourse. This whole nasty, bloody turn of events sure didn't seem to surprise him as much as it did her.

"OK, Bond Girl, here's the thing," he said. "I'm going to make a run for it, and to the extent I care, I strongly suggest that you do the same. Don't let these monkeys back you into a corner, or up against a wall. Just like at the office Christmas party, right? You're better off running straight through the middle of them."

With that, he whirled his steel briefcase at the woman who was reaching for him and it whacked her in the side of the head. Ellie heard a crack, the woman dropped, and Rick bolted through the crowd like a running back, weaving in and around bodies, using the briefcase to smack away any hands or mouths that got too close.

He disappeared around the corner.

Some of the crowd followed him, but dozens more turned back to gaze again at Ellie, all by herself now against the dead-end of the barbeque joint.

They started plodding toward her.

She really wished she had a steel briefcase to swing at them, like the gallant Rick. But she didn't. She had, however, run a half-marathon in the last six months. So here went nothing. She ran toward the crowd, ran into it, past the heap of woman Rick had brained, past the other would-be hand robbers, past the bespectacled man, past the woman in jeans, who was sitting on the floor in front of the beauty parlor gnawing at the bespectacled man's hand.

She ran, dodging and weaving through the Dead, around the corner and down the main concourse, toward the heart of the mall.

19.

"Jesus," murmured Brian.

The doors leading outside were completely blocked. They were blocked by a drift, piled more than six feet high, of human debris—limbs, organs, heads, torsos, whole bodies—jammed against the glass and piled above the doorframes, many of them still moving and groaning, wriggling and writhing and flapping, but too intertwined with each other, and too hopelessly damaged and uncoordinated, to get up. Scores of other Dead who could walk free were staring at the drift, perhaps hoping to spot somebody still Alive in the mass.

Brian was pretty sure it was the worst thing he had ever seen. He felt absurdly sorry that he hadn't eaten anything that morning, because he wanted to vomit.

Teddy and Engelsdorf came up abreast of him.

"Jesus H. Christ," said Engelsdorf, too loud, and the footloose Dead wandering at the base of the drift all turned, fixed on the trio, and began to advance.

"I'm thinking maybe we should head back," said Teddy.

"Sounds good," said Brian. They turned, and there, a few feet behind them, was a stocky bald man with two good legs but both arms missing, approaching relatively quickly, reaching forward with his head, mouth agape. Brian let fly with his baseball bat and caught the man in the temple, hard, and the man flopped over sideways and lay still.

Just beyond the armless man, however, were hundreds of the stumbling, shambling Dead that had followed them from the toy store, coming right at them. Dozens more were coming at them from behind.

So there was no choice. Brian and Teddy and Engelsdorf charged forward, and began weaving their way through the throng, toward where they'd come from.

The rush back to the heart of the Mall didn't go nearly as smoothly as the rush away from it, however. They were still able to dart left and right, but more and more of the Dead got close to them and had to be knocked aside by Brian and Teddy's bats or the butt of Englesdorf's shotgun. And as they fought their way into the Mall's main concourse, they couldn't see any sign that the hungry crowd was getting thinner.

I'm going to die here, thought Brian. Five minutes from now I'll be dead. Maybe still walking around, but dead. In a fucking shopping mall, on Christmas fucking Eve.

Then, all of a sudden, it looked like it would be a lot less than five minutes. More like five seconds. They were all around him. Gray or blood-stained or chewed-up hands grabbed his arms or his legs on all sides, and open mouths surged for his throat and face, snapping, missing him by inches as he flailed and kicked. He lost his bat, heard it clatter to the floor. One woman's teeth ripped into the sleeve of his coat. He managed to push her away with nothing but a mouthful of fake leather and lining, but in so doing he fell.

Suddenly he was eye-level with the feet and stumps of the Dead, like a forest. He rolled over in time to see the woman who had bit his coat, leering down at him. She opened her mouth, letting the scrap of sleeve fall away, raised her arms, and started toward him.

Not bad looking, Brian thought. Bet she wouldn't have given me the time of day yesterday, but now she can't wait to get her hands on me.

And as he was reflecting that if he was capable of stopping for self-pity at a moment like this, he deserved to die, the baseball bat whirled into his line of vision, and slammed into the hungry woman's forehead, knocking her backwards.

"Thanks, Teddy," said Brian.

But when he looked up, it wasn't Teddy.

It was a lean, athletic-looking young woman, holding his bat in her left hand. She extended her right hand down to Brian.

"Come on," she said. He grabbed her hand, and she pulled him to his feet. She ran, and he saw no good reason not to follow her. So he did.

20.

The Dead crowded around the booth, patting and pawing ineffectually, leaving bright-red palm prints on the Plexiglass. They tugged listlessly at the door, but it held. After a few minutes they gave up, and just stood there, staring in at the Morning Threesome, who stood back-to-back in the middle of the booth.

"Now we know what a goldfish feels like when it's home alone with the cat," said Dipstick.

"Shut up, Dip," said Tristan. "They've calmed down; don't stir them up."

So they stood silently. Somewhere in the middle of "I Want a Hippopotamus For Christmas," the sound cut off.

"Shit, where's our signal?" whispered Dipstick.

"Right there," said Andrea, pointing. A young man with his right flank torn open and his colon hanging out like a holster was holding a cable he'd pulled loose from the corner of the booth. He stared at it for a few seconds, then dropped it, having apparently decided it was inedible.

"The ISDN line," said Dipstick. "Shit, there goes the phone."

"We've still got our cells," said Tristan.

Some of the Dead seemed to lose interest and wander off. Then several gunshots rang out somewhere nearby, and still more left, to investigate.

Then, a minute or two after that, the Dead outside turned, all at once, and plodded off in the same direction, groaning, and the Threesome was alone again in the blood-smeared booth.

"They're after somebody else, looks like," said Andrea.

"Thank Christ," said Dipstick. "Should we make a break for it, you think?"

"To where?" said Andrea. "The only direction that isn't full of them is that way, toward the Burlington's, and the gates are still down."

"The cops told me we should stay put," said Tristan.

"Oh yeah," said Dipstick, "We should always listen to the cops, right?"

"OK, fair enough," said Tristan, "But those fuckers don't seem like they have the energy to break in here. If we leave, and we can't get out of the Mall anywhere, we might not be able to get back to the booth. And the cops know we're here. If they come in guns blazing and we're out there, they might not stop to ask what side we're on. I'm staying here."

"Sold," said Andrea. "Let's sit down on the floor, while they're not looking."

She and Tristan did. Dipstick still wasn't sure they shouldn't slip out the door and take their chances, but he gave The Morning Goddess a long look, and then he sat down, too. They were the Threesome, after all. Might as well keep it intact, one way or another.

The three of them stared at the stragglers among the Dead, still drifting past the booth.

Dipstick said "What's going on, do you think?"

"Fuck if I know," said Tristan. "Obviously."

"Think it's going on everywhere?"

"Fuck if I know," Tristan said again.

"Natalie didn't know anything about it," said Andrea.

"The 9-1-1 lady said they'd had reports from here," said Tristan. "She didn't say anything about anywhere else. Not that she would, I guess, but..."

THUMP! Somebody slammed against the Plexiglass. The Threesome jumped, and Dipstick let out a little scream he wished he hadn't, in front of the Goddess. They looked up.

A good-looking guy in a really snazzy trench coat had struck the door with a large metal briefcase. He pointed at the knob.

"He's OK, I think," said Andrea. "He's not one of them. We better let him in."

"There isn't enough room," said Dipstick.

Andrea stood up. Two other men were running up as well, a long-haired guy in a leather jacket, carrying a baseball bat, and a chubby, bearded guy in a purple vest; Andrea remembered seeing him at Jay Dee's. He was carrying a shotgun.

Behind them, lurching and stumbling and crawling back toward the booth as fast as their bodies could move, were the Dead. Hundreds of them.

"Shit," said Andrea. "We've got to let them in. Now."

She moved toward the door, but Dipstick grabbed her.

"There's no room," he said again. But just then the other two guys arrived at the door, and the Jay Dee's Guy pointed the shotgun at the doorknob. Andrea held up her hand, stepped forward and opened it.

"Christ, this is perfect," said Trench Coat Guy as he barged in. "Stuck in a fucking hamster cage with the Morning Zoo."

"You're welcome," said Andrea.

"That's the Morning Threesome to you, asshole," said Tristan. "Hey, close the fucking door."

"Yeah, OK," said Leather Jacket Guy, but he was holding the door ajar and looking back anxiously. "I'm just hoping my friend..."

"Close the fucking door," said Trench Coat Guy.

"Wait a minute, here comes somebody," said Andrea.

Outside, two more people, clearly Not Dead rather than Undead, had broken out of the throng and were approaching the booth—a fit-looking young woman with short hair, also carrying a baseball bat, and, well behind her, a paunchy guy in a bulky down parka with a ripped-open sleeve.

"I said close the door," said Trench Coat Guy, reaching around Leather Jacket Guy and pushing at the door.

"Back off, dude," said Leather Jacket Guy, turning. "They have time."

"Yeah, it's my booth, and I changed my mind," said Tristan. "I say they have time."

Fit Woman slipped through the door, then turned and yelled "Come on, hustle, you can make it" to Parka Guy.

And he did, but just barely. Fit Woman shut the door behind Parka Guy, and seconds later the Dead were all around the booth again.

"Everybody sit down and be quiet," said Dipstick. "They'll go away in a minute."

Everybody sat down, and stared at the floor. Sure enough, within minutes the Dead began to wander off.

When they were all gone, Leather Jacket Guy said, "Thanks for letting us in."

"No problem," said Andrea, without looking up. "What's your name?"

"Teddy."

"I'm Don," said Engelsdorf. "You're The Morning Goddess, right? I listen to you all the time."

"I'm Andrea."

"Ellie," said Fit Woman.

"Brian," said Parka Guy, and then, to Ellie, "Thanks."

"No problem."

"Jesus," muttered Trench Coat Guy, flipping open his cell phone.

"Anybody know this dickhead?" asked Dipstick.

"That's Rick," said Ellie. "He's with me, sort of, and your characterization seems to be basically on the money."

"OK, I apologize if the situation doesn't exactly bring out my most sociable side," said Rick the Trench Coat Guy. "I realize that it's important that we bond. But since I thought I might also like to live to see Christmas morning, how about we discuss something useful, like, say, where's the nearest exit?"

"Right around the corner, and past the corn-dog joint," said Brian. "But it's fucking blocked."

"Blocked? Blocked by what?"

"People," said Teddy. "A pile of people, like the ones out there. And pieces of people. It's pretty bad."

"Jesus," said Andrea.

"It was pretty fucked up," nodded Engelsdorf.

"The cops told us to stay put," said Tristan.

"Yeah, but are they really coming in here?" asked Dipstick. "Could they get in here if they wanted to?"

Rick chuckled to himself, and continued to surf on his phone.

"It doesn't really matter if the cops are coming or not," said Teddy. "We were just out there, and I'm telling you, we have no choice but to stay here. Go out there if you want, but if you do, you're dead meat."

"Literally," said Ellie.

"Can I have one of those donuts?" asked Brian, and hands went to mouths to suppress snickers.

"Sure, man," said Tristan, discreetly reaching up to take down the box, and passing it to him. "Have 'em all. I seem to have lost my appetite."

Just then there was a knock on the door.

21.

"Mr. Snyderwine? This is Marvin, at White Lake."

"Go ahead, Marvin."

"Sir, the data transfer seems to be complete, and your son-in-law has advised us that we should now regard the Erie facility as dispensable. We agree."

"So do I. After that fucking video he sent, I think it's a fucking liability."

"Yes, the video suggests a serious outbreak, and we recommend prompt sterilization of the site."

"Agreed. What's the quickest option?"

"An airstrike on a target like this can be arranged very quickly, but there's a wrinkle."

"What now?"

"Sir, we've lost contact with your son-in-law. He's not answering his phone."

"Yes, I was having a conversation with my son-in-law that ended abruptly. He said that someone was coming, and then the phone went dead."

"I see. We've also had reports from the guard units on the street outside that a helicopter took off from the roof of the plant, and that three or four gunshots were heard, possibly directed at it."

"Ha! Yes, that would be my son-in-law. He likes to play with guns. I suspect that the pilot did the smart thing and left without him, and that my son-in-law was showing his displeasure."

"Then you believe your son-in-law is still in the building?"

"That would be my guess."

"Should we initiate an extraction operation?"

"Let me get back to you on that, Marvin. I want to discuss my son-in-law's handling of this project with a few of my associates. In the meantime, get the airstrike option locked and loaded, but don't give the green light without my say so."

"Of course not, sir."

"Call me back when we're ready to go, Marvin. By then, maybe we'll have figured out my son-in-law's future with the company."

22.

Everyone in the booth turned to see who had knocked. It was a tall, very old-looking man in a vinyl jacket, wearing an Erie Seawolves cap. He gave a slight wave, and a gesture indicating that he'd like to come in. He was calm—not smiling, but not panicked either. Nor did there seem to be any reason why he should panic. The Dead weren't chasing him. A few of them wandered nearby, without even glancing at him.

"Who the hell is this?" said Dipstick.

"I don't know, but he doesn't seem to be one of them," said Teddy.

"Let's let him in," said Andrea.

"No way, he may be trying to trick us," said Dipstick.

"Trickery doesn't seem to be their style," said Teddy.

"Anyway, there's no more room," said Dipstick. "We're sardines as it is."

"Nobody's letting anybody else in here," said Rick, without looking up from the cellphone he was still surfing. There was a note of assured, almost parental authority in his voice, the tone of a man used to unquestioned obedience.

"Dipstick, open the door," said Tristan.

Rick looked up from his cellphone.

"But..." Dipstick began.

"Just open it, OK?" said Tristan. "He doesn't look like he's got the ...I don't know, the disease or whatever that the others have. We don't take orders from this butthole, and we aren't at the point of leaving old people to die yet."

"Are you sure we aren't?" asked Dipstick.

"Just open the door, OK?"

Dipstick shrugged, and reached for the door handle.

"Hey," said Rick. "I told you, we aren't..."

"This is my booth, man," said Tristan calmly. "You're a guest here. I decided we're inviting one more person."

"Oh. Your booth. I see," said Rick. "Sorry. I didn't know I was treading on sovereign jurisdiction."

Dipstick opened the door, then closed it after the old man stepped in.

"Thanks," said the newcomer.

"Welcome," said Tristan. "Excuse the delay."

"No problem," said the old man, in a growling voice. "I'd'a thought it over first myself."

Rick smiled, shook his head and returned to his cellphone.

"What's your name?" asked Teddy.

"I'm Bartlett McClain," said the old man. "You can call me Bart."

"Hi, Bart," said everybody, softly.

"It's like a twelve-step meeting," muttered Brian.

"Why weren't they chasing you?" asked Engelsdorf.

"Yeah, how do you rate?" asked Dipstick.

"Hell if I know," said Bart McClain. "Because I'm old, maybe. Craziest damn thing I ever seen, but it looks like all them people out there is dead, right?"

"That's what it looks like to us," said Andrea. She was dialing her cell phone.

"I'm 90 years old. Maybe I'm close enough to dead to where they don't think of me as no different from them. Anyway, I was out there, and they was tearing apart everybody they could find that was still alive, but they didn't pay no attention to me."

"Interesting," said Rick, almost to himself. "No hunger response to extreme old age."

"Yeah, interesting" said Ellie.

"So what in the name of Christ is going on out there?" asked McClain.

"None of us know," said Ellie, and managed to keep *except maybe Rick here* from coming out after.

"I tried to get out, but the exit was...blocked." McClain grimaced, and shook his head. "Never saw anything like it, not even in the War. Christ, I wish I'd'a listened to my wife. She couldn't believe I was dumb enough to come down here today. But they had a good price on these digital cameras, and I wanted to get one for my granddaughter."

"Oh yeah, down at Baylor's," said Engelsdorf. "Those are a good buy."

"Does anybody know if this is happening everywhere?" asked McClain, pulling off the Seawolves cap to reveal tousled white hair. "Or just here?"

"We don't know yet," said Tristan. "There was nothing about it on our radio station a while ago, but they pulled out our remote line and now we're cut off."

Andrea had been murmuring quietly into her cell phone. She said "I love you," hung up, and wiped her eyes.

"I just talked to my Mom," she said. "She says it's on the news, that something's going on here, and somewhere down on 12th street. Nothing about anyplace else, not yet anyway."

"Sweetheart, could I borrow that cell phone?" McClain asked. "I'd like to call my wife."

She held it out, but before he could take it Teddy said "Holy shit, look at this!"

They all looked where he was pointing. The Dead outside the booth were turning and stumbling off toward the West Concourse, where another mob of Dead were chasing after somebody alive.

It was a young woman with curly brown hair and a lush physique, wearing only green-and-red holiday bra and panties.

"Oh, man, she looks like one of those underwear models," said Dipstick.

"What's that she's armed with?" asked Brian.

"A leg," said Ellie.

The woman was, indeed, wielding a narrow, shapely leg like a club. The business end was smeared with blood.

"It's not a real leg, though," said Engelsdorf. "I think it's a mannequin leg."

"Yeah," said Ellie. "She's going to need it, too, I think, in just a second."

Underwear Model was well ahead of the hundred or so Dead in pursuit of her, but now she was heading straight into the crowd from around the booth.

"Hey, there's Myron!" said Engelsdorf.

Tall, bearded Myron, who had lost an arm back in the toy store but still had a pair of good strong legs, came up swiftly on Underwear Model, reaching out with his remaining arm. Underwear Model set her teeth and swung the mannequin leg like a baseball bat, and it connected hard with the side of Myron's head. He went sprawling. But his fellow Dead were bearing down on her fast.

"She's not going to make it," said Brian.

"Yes she is," said Teddy, getting up and grabbing his baseball bat. "I'll get her."

Ellie was on her feet as well. She had Brian's bat.

"I'll go too," she said.

"Not a chance, stay where you are," said Rick, but Teddy and Ellie were already out the door, yelling and banging their bats on the floor. The Dead paused en masse, turned, and headed for back for the booth.

"Come on!" yelled Teddy to Underwear Model. "Run to us, we'll keep them distracted."

She didn't need a second invitation. Underwear Model began weaving her way through the crowd, swinging the mannequin leg to clear a path to Teddy and Ellie, who were cracking heads with their bats. She reached them just ahead of a multitude of greedy, grabbing hands, darted between them and straight into the booth. As Ellie and Teddy turned and ran after her, one of the Dead, a stout, scraggly-haired woman in a bulky black coat, got her fingers into Teddy's long hair and yanked his head backwards toward her snapping teeth.

He elbowed her hard in the chest, and she fell backwards, knocking over several of her fellow pursuers.

Ellie charged through the door, with Teddy a few seconds behind. Dipstick closed it after them. And then the Dead, their numbers swelled by those that had been following Underwear Model, closed around the booth again, darkening it, pawed and patted at the glass, moaned with longing hunger at the nine alive within.

"Everybody sit still," said Andrea. "They seem to lose interest pretty fast."

"Not this time," said Dipstick, "Too many."

"Yeah," said Engelsdorf, "They can tear this place open in ten seconds."

But they couldn't. They patted and tugged halfheartedly, but the Dead couldn't or wouldn't organize themselves even to the minimal degree it would have taken to break through the plexiglass, or push the booth over. They had no strength in numbers; though they moved together none of them really seemed aware of the presence of the others. It was as though they were all there separately.

Within a few minutes, sure enough, they began to move off.

Bart McClain took off his jacket and draped it over Underwear Models's shoulders.

"What's your name, sweetheart?"

"Sherry," she said. She put her face in her hands and began to cry.

"You know what?" said Dipstick. "It's really cramped in here. No room at the Inn. How about if anyone else comes along, we let them find their own shelter?"

"Yes, Dip," said Tristan. "The Girl In Her Underwear has arrived. That's everybody."

23.

"Mr. Snyderwine? This is Marvin, at White Lake."

"Go ahead, Marvin."

"We're getting close on the airstrike, sir, we're just having a little trouble locating one of our friends. He's on Christmas leave, in the Bahamas."

"The Bahamas? When you reach him, remind him gently that we need to know about things like that in the future."

"I certainly will, sir. But I'm calling to tell you about another wrinkle."

"What now?"

"We're starting to hear reports in the local Erie media from a shopping mall in the area, the Millcreek Mall it's called. Maybe ten minutes or so from the 12th Street plant. Rioting, serious violence, bad injuries, fatalities…"

"Well…it's a shopping mall on Christmas Eve. That happens, doesn't it?"

"Sir, there have already been unconfirmed reports of dismemberment and cannibalism."

"Son of a bitch. How in Christ's name could it have reached the Mall that fast?"

"We're trying to figure that out, sir, but in the meantime…"

"In the meantime, the media clamp goes double for the fucking Mall. No more eyewitness accounts, no more cell phone calls, plus they should say the earlier reports were exaggerations, teenagers or whatever, it's a serious situation but not that bad. Then we need another guard perimeter around the place. Pull your people off the plant if you have to, until you can get reinforcements, and anybody who tries to leave that Mall gets a bullet in the brain, be they alive or be they dead. Especially be they alive. Got it?"

"Yes sir."

"And Marvin?"

"Yes sir?"

"When you do reach General Beach-bum, tell him that we may need to avail ourselves of his services more than once today."

24.

Then they all played with their cell phones for a while, those that had them. Those that didn't, like McClain and Engelsdorf, borrowed Andrea's. None of them found their calls very satisfactory except for Bart McClain, who told his wife that he was trapped in an emergency at the mall but offered no details, and just exchanged short, heartfelt avowals of love with her.

Next best was Engelsdorf. He reached his ex, who didn't believe what he told her, but allowed him to chat for a few minutes with his daughter, holding back tears. Dipstick's Mom didn't believe him either, swore at him for waking her, and hung up on him. Ellie thought about calling her mother, decided against it, thought about calling Hubie to explain about the helicopter, but decided against that too. Brian tried Trina but got her voice mail, and left a message telling her to tell Logan he loved him. Teddy, oddly enough, declined to call his adoring Mom or sisters.

Tristan had the most frustrating time of it. He tried his girlfriend, his Mom, and his brother, got voice mail each time, then called Natalie in the newsroom at the station so that she could put him on the air.

"I'd love to, Tris," she replied in a confidential whisper, "But they won't let me."

"What?"

"They won't let me. O'Leary's here at the station, and he says we can't put on any eyewitness stuff from inside the Mall. Or from the plant on 12ᵗʰ Street, either. He says we'll get fired if we try, says the FCC's leaning on him and...oh shit, here he comes, Tris, I've got to go, good luck sweetie we're all praying for you guys down here..." And the line went dead.

"Are you fucking kidding me?" said Tristan. He then called friends who worked at several radio and TV stations and got the same result each time—the News Director or the GM were there, or both, and they were saying that nothing from inside the Mall could be used on-air. Direct orders from the FCC, they said, a matter of national security, and besides they didn't want to start a panic.

If they didn't want to start a panic now, thought Tristan, when would the time be right?

After calling the last media friend he could think of, he said out loud "Something really fucked-up is going on out there."

"You think, Tris?" asked Andrea.

PART THREE

WORST. CHRISTMAS. EVER.

1.

"Mr. Snyderwine? This is Marvin, at White Lake."

"Go ahead, Marvin."

"We're just calling to inform you that we have the Millcreek Mall closed off. Local police and regular Guard forces have blocked off the streets going in and out for about a mile all around, and our operatives have an inner line set around the parking lot."

"What about the media?"

"We're getting them to back off the initial stories, but there hasn't been much of a problem since the first few minutes of the outbreak. We had some reports of panicked calls from people hiding in dressing rooms, lavatories, that sort of thing, but these were calls to police or to loved ones, not to the media. And as far as we can tell, they all ended abruptly. The only cell phone calls to the media from inside were from a morning radio show that was doing a remote broadcast from a booth in the middle of the mall. The station didn't put them on the air. They tried calling some other stations and got the same reception. We haven't head anything from them in almost two hours, so we're guessing that either they gave up or they're dead by now. Probably the latter."

"All right. Not bad. Rumors will fly, of course, but we can deal with that. Now, what about the Mall? What can your guys see?"

"Sir, our operatives report that every unlocked public entrance is blocked."

"Blocked? Blocked by what?

"By what appear to be...human bodies. Pile-ups of human bodies."

"Jesus. What about the ones that got out?"

"Nobody appears to have gotten out, sir. The force of the crowd going in and the crowd trying to get back out appears to have been roughly equal. The people who never got inside at all are being detained at a nearby church gymnasium and a few other facilities in the area, but so far our operatives are reporting that none of them seem to have been compromised."

"No employee entrances? Loading docks?"

"We have them all covered, but none of them have been used as far as we've seen. Reportedly only a few of the stores participated in the early opening, so most of them are probably inaccessible from inside."

"Good work, Marvin."

2.

Most of the Dead that had followed Sherry to the booth had dispersed by now, but Santa Claus lingered, throat and face laid open, gazing down at them.

"Oh, God," said Sherry, "Why won't he go away?"

"Somebody really did a number on his jolly apple cheek," said Tristan.

"Poor Santa."

"Poor Santa my ass. Santa Claus is an asshole," said Brian.

"What, this one in particular?" asked Andrea.

"No, Santa Claus in general. He pisses me off. Like in Rudolph. Ever notice what a bigoted dick Santa is in that show? He totally supports Rudolph being an outcast. But in the end, when he eats shit because he needs Rudolph to lead his sleigh, Rudolph says 'It will be an honor, sir!' Even as a kid, I used to wonder how it was an honor. But I'll tell you what pisses me off the most about Santa."

"Must you?" asked Rick, taking off his trench coat and draping it carefully on his briefcase. "Christ, it's hot in here."

"Yes, he must," said Tristan. "Go ahead."

"It's 'Here Comes Santa Claus,'" said Brian. "That Elvis Presley song, you know? Where he says 'He doesn't care if you're rich or poor, he loves you just the same.' Well, maybe, but somehow the rich kids end up with all the really good presents."

"Gene Autry."

"What."

"Gene Autry," said Teddy distractedly. "Elvis Presley didn't write 'Here Comes Santa Claus.' Gene Autry did. Columbia Records, '47 or '48, I forget which."

"Oh," said Brian. "Sorry."

"Don't say nothing bad about Gene Autry," said Bart McClain.

At this point the half-faceless Santa finally wandered off.

"I could tell you things about that Santa," said Sherry.

"Really?" asked Engelsdorf. "Like what?"

"I probably shouldn't say," said Sherry. "I promised I wouldn't. I better not break a confidence. Forget I said anything."

3.

"Mr. Snyderwine? This is Marvin, at White Lake."

"Where's my airstrike, Marvin?"

"We've located our friend at his resort, and he's working on authorization for the 12th Street facility. He thinks he'll have authorization within about two hours."

"Way too long. We'll have to re-think our relationship with him when all this is over. Anyway, green-light him as soon as he gets it. Did you mention the other target to him?"

"I did, sir. He was very unhappy about it. He said it would take considerably longer to get authorization for that."

"Well, I couldn't give less of a shit that he's unhappy about it, but I admit it's a tough position we've put him in. A factory with a few security guards is one thing, but getting that candy-ass on Pennsylvania Avenue to sign off on bombing a shopping mall on Christmas Eve is another matter."

"Yes, sir."

"Call me back when you're done downtown."

4.

By early afternoon, the silence was oppressive. Engelsdorf broke it:

"Anybody seen any of the big holiday movies?"

"I ain't seen a movie in a theater since I took my boys to see *Big Jake* with the Duke," said Bart McClain.

"Who?" asked Sherry.

"The Duke," said McClain, gazing at her incredulously. "Forget it."

"I saw that one with Adam Sandler, where he's the general of the army of teddy bears," said Sherry. "Took my nephews to it. It was cute."

"Christ. Sounds great," Brian muttered.

"Yeah, my daughter wants to see that," said Engelsdorf.

"I want to see that one where the Vikings battle the sea monster in Lake Superior," said Dipstick. "With that guy from that TV show."

"Oh, yeah, I like that guy, he's good-looking," said Sherry.

"He is good-looking," said Ellie. "But that one's in 3-D, isn't it? I hate 3-D."

"Somebody told me that that's based on a true story," said Engelsdorf. "Except that it really happened in Lake Erie, right here, off Presque Isle."

"Somebody told you that it's a true story?" asked Brian. "The one with the Vikings and the sea monster?"

"Yeah," said Engelsdorf. "What about it?"

"Well, first of all, if it happened on Lake Erie, or Lake Superior for that matter, it wouldn't be a sea monster," said Teddy. "It'd be a lake monster."

"I've just been so busy with the holiday, I haven't had a chance to get to anything," said Andrea.

"Oh, but you should," said Rick. "You really should make the effort. I see every big holiday blockbuster the first day it comes out. First show. If I'm not first in line, I consider it a personal failure. I have a sleeping bag just for camping out at the multiplex. If the movie opens on Friday, I go and set up camp no later than noon Wednesday. The theater management used to get mad at me for coming so early, until I got smart and started bribing the managers to look the other way about it. So now I don't have to budge for two days."

He looked around. Everyone was looking at the floor or staring into space. Only the paunchy guy, Brian, was glaring at him.

"OK, I know what you're going to say," he continued. "You think I'm exaggerating when I say I don't budge. Well, a couple of years ago, you would have been right. I used to have to get up and use the men's room every few hours. But somehow that didn't sit right with me. What if while I was gone, somebody took my place in line? Oh, I'd straighten it out when I got back from doing my business, make no mistake, but I didn't like the idea that I was even briefly not first in line. Know what my solution was?"

"You let the shit build up in your head, would be my guess," said Brian.

"Very witty, young man, but no. What I did was go to my doctor, and have him install a catheter bag and a colostomy, so that I can excrete and urinate right there in my sleeping bag without moving. I used to take sandwiches and big bags of chips and long novels to help me pass the time while I waited, but gradually I realized that these indulgences were just clouding my mind and weakening my response to the blockbuster. So now all I take is drinking water and plain soda crackers, and if I have to have reading material I take magazines with articles about the blockbuster I'm going to see, or maybe promotional materials, press releases and the like, that I've downloaded from the internet. That way I cleanse and mortify my body, and it sharpens my mind to really take in the profound meanings that the filmmakers wish to impart to me through their epic tales of wizards and robots."

"Enough, OK, dude?" said Teddy.

"I know all this may sound a bit extreme," said Rick. "But when you think about it, is it really a big price to pay? I mean, you know that these have to be the best movies there are, since the studios have gone to the trouble of spending all those millions on them, and since all those media outlets have chosen to promote them. I have a friend who says he prefers to go the Wednesday or Thursday evening after a blockbuster opens, because the crowds have thinned and he can get a good seat and enjoy the blockbuster in a less hectic setting. But he doesn't seem to understand that Jesus puts a check mark next to his name for every day he delays going to a blockbuster, and that's another day he's going to have to spend in Purgatory. Now, if two blockbusters are opening the same day, well, my goodness, the problems that causes for me. To begin with…"

"Shut the fuck up, Dude," said Teddy. "Seriously, shut up." He put his face in his hands.

"Yeah," said McClain.

So he did. They were all silent for a while. A woman in her twenties in a blood-smeared winter coat stumbled up to the glass and stared down at them. When they didn't move for two or three minutes, she stumbled off.

Sherry began to cry. Ellie pulled a pack of tissues out her jacket pocket and handed it to her.

"I take it back, I did go to a movie at a theater," said McClain suddenly. "My wife and I seen that one about the sled dogs a couple of years back. That was a hell of a movie."

"The talking sled dogs, or the regular sled dogs?" asked Engelsdorf.

"Just the regular sled dogs," said McClain. He looked sidelong at Engelsdorf. "They made a movie about talking sled dogs?"

"Oh yeah," said Engelsdorf. "We have the DVD. My daughter loves it."

"Talking sled dogs," said McClain. "Jesus Christ."

"You tell 'em, Greatest Generation," said Rick. "What's the world coming to, right?"

A long, sullen silence settled over the booth. Occasionally one of the Dead paid them a visit, but it would last only a few seconds.

"Worst. Christmas. Ever." said Andrea.

"That gives me an idea," said Dipstick. "Tris, Goddess, you remember the call-in contest we did last year? Worst Christmas ever? People called in and told their stories. Why don't we play it now?"

"Jesus," muttered Rick, to himself.

"That's a pretty good idea, Dip," said Tristan, eyeing Rick. "It'd give us something to do, anyway. Let's do it. What was everybody's worst Christmas ever?"

"Aside from this one, you mean?" asked Brian.

"Well, yeah, obviously," said Tristan. "But remember, it's not Christmas yet, if we get out of here alive then tomorrow will probably be the best Christmas any of us will ever have."

"Fair point," said Ellie.

"So come on," said Dipstick. "Somebody start."

Nobody seemed to want to.

"OK," said Andrea. "I'll start. You guys remember Lundahl's Department store?"

Dipstick and Tristan groaned in unison.

"That was going to be mine," said Dipstick.

"Mine too," said Tristan.

"Fine, sorry, you guys can have it," she said.

"No, you do it," said Tristan.

"Yeah, you're the best storyteller out of the three of us," said Dipstick.

Andrea smiled at the compliment.

"OK, this one can be for all three of us" she said. "The first year Tristan and Dipstick and I did a Christmas remote it was at Lundahl's Department Store, which used to be down on Peach Street but isn't any more."

"Old school department store, one of the last of them," said Engelsdorf.

"Right. Well, they were doing an event with a bunch of kids, and Santa was going to be there. And they had some sweet old guy who'd worked there forever, and the big highlight of his year was getting to play Santa. He looked the part, and he had a sweet disposition, and he loved it, and he was great at it. But unfortunately this year he was really sick."

"Like, terminally," put in Dipstick.

"Right. He was very ill, not long for this world," Andrea went on. "So we're there doing our stupid little bits, keeping it fairly wholesome by our standards, and the time comes for the kids to meet Santa. So Tristan gives him a big build-up, and the kids all cheer..." She shook her head at the memory.

"And they brought Santa out in a wheelchair," said Tristan. Dipstick giggled.

"It was really well-intentioned, you know?" said Andrea. "They wanted to reward the poor guy for all his years of dedicated service and all that. But they hadn't thought through the implications. A sort of a hush fell over the kids in the room. And then they started putting them up on his lap, and of course a lot of them were scared, but some of them weren't and he's up there asking them what they want and they keep plunking them in his lap and he's getting more and more tired, and he's starting to cough and wheeze, and finally about halfway through they have to call it off. And as they're wheeling this poor man out, you can hear the kids saying stuff like 'Is Santa sick?' 'Is Santa going to die?' And a bunch of them start crying."

"Oh, man," said Engelsdorf.

"That's really sad," said Ellie.

"Yeah, it is," said Dipstick. Then he convulsed with giggles again. "But it's kind of funny, too."

"You'll have to excuse Dipstick," said Tristan. "He's a little twisted." But Tristan was snickering a little too.

"White boy humor," said Andrea. "I'll never understand it."

5.

As Dwight Bruno pulled off I-90 onto the Peach Street exit, he was thinking: *This butthole better come across with the item. If he got me to drive my ass all the way over here to Erie and he's already sold it, I'll put my foot up*—Then he slammed on the brakes and slid a little, when he saw that the street was blocked by cops at the base of the exit ramp.

"Are you kidding me?" he roared aloud in the Oldsmobile. "Today, of all days?"

He slowed to a stop, and rolled down his window.

"How do I get to the Mall?"

"Sorry, sir, the Mall's closed today," replied the young Millcreek cop.

"You're kidding me. It's Christmas Eve."

"Some kind of emergency down there, sir. Bad scene."

"Bad scene? I came all the way from Buffalo. I have to..."

"You aren't going to the Mall today, sir. I promise you that. You got to move along now, sir."

"Son of a bitch!" roared Dwight Bruno. He hit the gas and his tires spun, flinging wet clods of dirty brown snow behind him. He rolled across Peach and up the entrance ramp on the opposite side.

He turned on the radio, and fumbled up and down the dial. As he accelerated back onto 90, he heard: "…are dismissing initial reports of extreme violence and even cannibalism in the Mall as exaggerations, but they do acknowledge that the situation is serious, and that no one will be permitted in or out of the Mall area until further notice. It remains unclear whether this situation is connected to…"

Bruno shut off the radio.

"Cannibalism?" he said out loud. "What the fuck?"

He thought for a moment of pressing on, trying his luck at the Mall outside Cleveland. But instead, he turned around at the I-79 interchange and headed back toward the comforts of East Aurora. Screw *Return to Dinosaur Land*, or whatever the fuck it was called. He'd stop off at a convenience store on the way home and buy his kid a present there. A yo-yo or something. Or maybe a lump of coal. That's what he deserved.

Dwight Bruno thought about the ten hundred-dollar bills in his pocket, and thought that maybe he'd stop off on the way home for some sort of Christmas treat of his own.

6.

Then it was Bart McClain's turn:

"I spent one Christmas in a military hospital in Brisbane, Australia," he said. "I was, I don't know, 17 or 18. I'd lied to get in the Army. This was the Big War. For some reason I got sent down to Australia, and they put me with a bunch of these Aussies. Craziest bastards you ever met. We were scouts. They sent us to New Guinea.

"Well, I had almost no combat training. I didn't know what the hell I was doing, barely even knew how to shoot a gun, or even to keep my head down. So of course I got shot pretty bad the first time we come across any Japanese. I don't remember too much about it, but them crazy Aussie bastards got me back as far as the coast, hung me in a hammock in the mangroves, and I was there for, I don't know, weeks I guess. All I remember is crabs and things crawling under my hammock while I hung there.

"Anyway, finally they managed to ship me back to the hospital in Australia, and I got better, and I got released right before Christmas. So them crazy bastards took me to this bar in Brisbane, and they told me look, if you want another drink, turn your glass upside down on the bar. That's how you tell the bartender you want another. But the sons of bitches were playing a joke on me. Turns out that's how tell the whole room that you want to fight."

"Holy crap," said Dipstick.

"So I have a belt, turn my glass over, set it down, you know, firmly, and about ten seconds later I feel a tap on my shoulder, turn around, and the next thing I know I wake up in that same damn hospital, face bandaged up, missing a couple of teeth."

"Those bastards," said Engelsdorf.

"I'll give those guys their due, though," McClain went on. "As soon as I got hit, they all piled in to help. When I woke up, they was all in the beds around me, bruised up, missing teeth of their own. They thought it was just about the funniest damn thing they'd ever seen. We spent Christmas together in the hospital. We had a pretty good time, now that I think about it. I guess it wasn't my worst Christmas after all."

"Well, then, what was?" asked Dipstick.

"Well, when I got out of the war, I was a professional musician for ten years in New York. Played tuba in the pit orchestra of the Radio City Music Hall."

"No way!" said Andrea.

"I really did. And I'll tell you, after the first year or two, I got so sick of Christmas music I wanted to blow the place up. So any one of those years, I guess, could be my worst Christmas."

"I always wanted to be a Rockette," said Andrea.

"My first two wives were Rockettes," said McClain.

"No way," said Andrea again.

"You da man," said Dipstick.

"Well, yeah, but the marriages didn't last too long. They both turned out to be lesbians. I ain't got many regrets in life, but if I had it to do over again I probably wouldn't marry two lesbians in a row."

"Yeah, I think I better jot that life lesson down," said Tristan.

"I don't know how anybody could eat today," said Sherry.

The comment was directed at Dipstick, who was wolfing the remaining Mighty Fine Donuts.

"They're getting stale," he said. "I don't want them to go to waste."

"Your body's not a garbage can," said Sherry.

Everybody looked at her. She hadn't said much up to that point; she just sat, looking at the floor, wrapped in McClain's jacket. But now she was looking earnestly at Dipstick, really wanting him to reevaluate his relationship with food.

"My body's not a garbage can," said Dipstick slowly, staring back at Sherry. "Holy shit, you just blew my mind."

Rick let out a hard snicker at this. Andrea and Tristan exchanged a glance. They'd never seen the third wheel of the Morning Threesome angry before.

"You'll have to let me think about that one for a minute, hot lady," said Dipstick. "After all I'm not too bright. You know, they don't call me Dipstick for nothing."

"Take it easy, Dip," said Andrea.

"Now that you mention it, you're right," said Dipstick. "My body's not a garbage can. It's shaped like one, but it's not…"

"I didn't mean any offense," said Sherry, looking back down.

"Oh, none taken," said Dipstick. "My body's not a garbage can, you're absolutely right. You know what the biggest difference is? A garbage can can't feel pleasure. My body can. Not that anybody thinks it's important for a fat fuck like me to feel pleasure..."

"One of the reasons you remain a fat fuck, perhaps," put in Rick. "A vicious cycle."

"Not helping, asshole" said Tristan.

"Hey, I thought we had an encounter group going here," said Rick.

Dipstick got up. "I'd really enjoy it if my foot had an encounter with your teeth..."

"Dip! Sit the fuck down and shut up!" hissed Tristan.

Dipstick froze. Three or four of The Dead had caught sight of him, and began to shuffle toward the booth. He sat down fast.

"Sorry," he said.

"It's OK, Dip," said Andrea, her eyes shiny. "We're all pissed off about this situation. Let's just try to stay chilled out."

"And as for you, Secret Agent Man," said Brian, "What say you shut the fuck up altogether, and keep the witty remarks to y..."

"George!" said Ellie.

Everybody turned.

Ellie Cotteri was staring up at one of the handful of Dead who had wandered over to the booth in response to Dipstick's outburst.

He was a young man in a tan poplin jacket with wispy light brown hair and a goatee, good-looking in a nondescript way—good-looking except for the right half of his neck, which was missing, cocking his head at a quizzical angle, and for the mindless hunger in his eyes.

"George, what are you doing here?" Ellie said. George came eagerly all the way up to the glass and placed his palms against it.

"Look down, lady," said Engelsdorf. "You're getting him riled up."

Ellie looked down.

"Who is he?" asked Andrea.

"My boyfriend," said Ellie. "Ex-boyfriend, I should say."

"Yeah, I'd call that an ex-boyfriend, at that," said Rick.

"No, I mean he was my ex-boyfriend already. For more than a year. My very ex-boyfriend," said Ellie, and managed to keep *My borderline-stalker, calling me at all hours of the night, I was almost going to get a restraining order against him ex-boyfriend. That kind of ex-boyfriend* from coming out after.

"Nice to meet you, George," said Tristan.

"Jesus, I can't even get away from the fucker here," said Ellie. "What the fuck was he doing here?"

"Buying jewelry," said Sherry.

"What?" said Ellie, looking up again sharply.

"Look at his jacket pocket," said Sherry. "That's a bag from Buster's Jewelry."

There it was, sticking out of his left-hand jacket pocket— the top of small, elegant-looking black bag with fancy gold lettering.

"You bought me a ring, you stupid shit?" said Ellie. "You thought you'd hand me a ring, and I'd melt? And for that you came out here and got torn apart? Shit, you're so dumb I'm embarrassed I ever dated you."

George didn't seem offended by this. He stared at her a few more minutes, slapped feebly a few times at the glass, and then apparently arrived at the conclusion that he couldn't arrive at in life—that he wasn't going to be able to get to her. He stumbled off, and the other Dead followed him.

Another long silence settled over the booth. Then Sherry spoke again.

"I can't help it," she said. "I'd like to see what he picked out for you."

"OK, I have one," said Ellie.

"Your worst Christmas?" asked Dipstick.

"No, not mine. I think mine was going to be this Christmas, thanks to George. I wish he was still around to wreck Christmas for me, the poor guy."

"OK," asked Brian. "Then whose worst Christmas?"

"My great-grandfather's," said Ellie. "You know, I only know this story because of you," she said, looking at Andrea.

"Me?"

"Yeah, I happened to be listening to your show a few weeks ago, and your wacky news item was something about a guy in New York who was decapitated by a subway train."

"I remember that," said Andrea.

"Oh, yeah," said Dipstick, and he chuckled a little.

"Exactly," said Ellie. "You told the story, and these two were making cracks about it, with all the sensitivity that morning radio hosts are so well known for."

"Doesn't seem as funny today, I admit," said Dipstick, but he was smirking anyway.

"Well, I happened to mention the story to my mother," Ellie went on. "And out of nowhere she tells me how her grandfather, my great-grandfather, was decapitated by a train. He was a railyard worker, I guess, and it was Christmas Eve and he was just getting ready to head home, and he's walking across the yard, alongside these tracks, and a piece of metal flew out of one of the cars and took his head right off."

"Oh, shit," said Dipstick, laughing again. "Merry Christmas."

Everybody glared at him.

"Sorry," said Tristan. "If it happened more than a hundred years ago, or to somebody in New York, then it's fair game as far as Dipstick's concerned."

"Well, he's going to love the punchline, then," said Ellie. "Because the thing was, these were poor Italian immigrants, and they didn't have enough to pay an undertaker. So get this. The old lady, my great-great-grandmother, had to sew her son's head back on to his body, to make him presentable for his funeral." And at this, she let out a snort of laughter.

Dipstick, however, looked stricken.

"That's horrible," he said.

"Ahh, that's OK, Dip, laugh it up," Tristan said. "The lady's laughing, and it's her great-gramps."

"Yeah, but just imagine how awful," said Dipstick. "Having to sew your own son's head back on." This time several people laughed, none harder than Ellie.

"Well, you don't want it rolling around loose in the coffin," said Tristan.

"Jesus, you guys say I'm sick," said Dipstick.

"And imagine having to have a funeral at Christmastime," said Andrea.

"Well, I've been to a couple Italian funerals," said Brian. "They're about as lively as Christmas parties."

"Not bad," said Tristan. "Who's next?"

"I'll go," said Engelsdorf. "Except this one is family history, too, it isn't me specifically. Anybody German here? Ever heard of Knecht Ruprecht?"

"Is that like Connect Four?" asked Dipstick. "That's a pretty good game."

"Yeah," said Brian. "Why couldn't my kid have wanted Connect Four for Christmas?"

"No, Knecht. K-N-E-C-H-T. I guess it means, like, 'Farmhand Ruprecht,' or something like that. It's the German Santa Claus. A big dirty SOB with a long beard, dressed in a furry coat and big boots, carrying a big sack of ashes and a big switch."

"Charming," said Tristan.

"My grandfather always told us that back in the old country, on Christmas Eve Ruprecht would come roaring into the house, and he'd ask you if you knew how to pray. If you could come up with a good prayer, he'd give you a present, some candy or something, but if you couldn't, he'd beat you with the switch and the sack of ashes."

"Jesus," said Brian. "This explains a lot about the history of the 20th Century."

"Yeah, no shit," said Engelsdorf. He held up the first, middle and ring finger of his left hand. "My grandfather couldn't move these three fingers. And he told us it was because of Knecht Ruprecht."

"Couldn't pray?" asked Tristan.

"Well, apparently one year when he was like six or seven, he'd been a pretty mischievous little shit all year. Kind of guy he was. So his Mom, my great Great-Granma, arranged

213

with one of her brothers to dress up as Ruprecht, and really put the fear of God into him. So he comes roaring into the house, and all the kids scatter and scream, but he says 'I'm looking for that bad boy! I'm looking for that bad boy!' and he's tearing around the house, and my Gramps knows who he's talking about, no question about it, so he runs into the kitchen and he dives under the kitchen table. He's under the tablecloth, leaning back on his palms, scared shitless of course, and in comes Ruprecht, yelling how he's going to give that bad boy a lesson he'll never forget or whatever, and my great-Granma is pretending like she's giving Ruprecht a bum steer, you know, 'Oh, sir, he's out the back door and into the pasture, he's quick as a rabbit, you'll never find him out there.' So Ruprecht says, 'Well, you tell him that if he knows what's good for him, he'll straighten up and act right,' and so forth. What neither of them know is that Ruprecht's planted one of his big fucking boots right on the poor kid's fingers. Broke three of them right away, and now he's moving around, grinding them up worse."

"Oh my gosh," said Sherry. "Poor guy."

"But my Gramps never makes a peep. Sits there under the table and bites his lip."

"Iron German resolve," said Tristan.

"Nah," said Englesdorf. "Just sheer terror. By the time Ruprecht storms off into the night, my Gramps had fingers like maracas."

"I'm one quarter Dutch," said Andrea. "My Granma used to tell us about Zwarte Piet at Christmas. Heard of him?"

"Nope," said Engelsdorf.

"It means Black Pete. He was a black guy, a Moor, that's what my Gram always called him, who came along with St. Nick. If you were good, St. Nick brought you a present, and if you were bad, you got the crap beat out of you by a black guy."

"Not too politically correct," said Ellie.

"There are all kinds of fucked-up stories like that," said Tristan. "I'm French on one side. My Dad said that his Grampa used to tell him about Pere Fouettard, the Flogging Father."

"Sounds like porn," said Dipstick. ""Like a priest with a hobby on the side."

"No, Dip, no such luck. Pere Fouettard was a guy who murdered his kids, and they hanged him, and as his punishment in the afterlife he had to go along with Santa and beat the naughty little children with a whip."

"As his punishment?" said Dipstick. "Doesn't sound like punishment to me, for that guy. Sounds like heaven. He gets to beat kids, and he only has to work one night a year."

"I know, that always bugged me, too," said Tristan.

"Ah, but Santa found a way for him to use his special skills," said Rick. "The thing that made him different, the thing others cruelly rejected him for, was beating children. But it turned out that Santa saw how this guy could be the Most Special Child-Murderer of All. I think it would make a heartwarming Christmas special."

There was a silence.

"So you're German?" said Dipstick to Engelsdorf.

"What about it?"

"I always wondered something. Those flip lids on those beer steins?"

"What about them?"

"What are they for? I mean, what is it they're supposed to keep out?"

"The fuck do I know?" said Engelsdorf. "Shrapnel, maybe."

"Actually," said Rick, "I know this one."

"Oh Christ," said Brian. "Can't you shut the fuck up?"

"No, no kidding, I really do know this one," said Rick. "It was a public health regulation, because of the plague. The bubonic plague, in the 1300s. A lot of cities and towns in Germany passed ordinances that you couldn't walk around in public with an open beverage. Well, God forbid you keep a kraut separated from his beer that long, so some enterprising Jerry made himself a fortune with the thumb-raised lid."

"Hey, maybe we could go easy on the derogatory terms," said Engelsdorf.

Rick laughed. "Hey, didn't they tell you, Herr Goebbels? You're one of the groups everybody gets a free pass on defaming."

There was a thump. One of the dead, a middle-aged woman whose long hair was clotted with dried blood, had stumbled against the glass. Everyone in the booth automatically sat still and silent as she gaped down at them. After a minute or two she lost interest and wandered off.

"Well, I'll tell you something," said Bart McClain, "Somebody sure as hell left the lid off the beer stein today."

8.

"This one," said Sherry, softly.

"This one what?" asked Tristan.

"This is the worst Christmas ever."

"Well, yeah," said Rick. "You saw your married boss, with whom you were having an affair and who you no doubt thought was this close to leaving his wife for you, get his head ripped from his body, and now you're stuck in a glass closet with a bunch of loser mallrats, in your underwear, surrounded by homicidal dead cannibals. So, yeah, I think that would qualify as almost anybody's worst Christmas, but the rules of the game this dipshit set up were that you tell us about your worst Christmas other than this one. So…"

"Hey, asshole," said Brian. "Didn't we discuss you shutting the fuck up?"

"They didn't know I was alive," said Sherry.

"They didn't know you were alive?" said Andrea. "Who didn't?"

"Those…people out there, or whatever they are. Like I said, when they were in the office, I was sitting on the floor next to the mannequins, and they couldn't tell me apart from them. They didn't know I was alive."

"Thank God for that," said Andrea.

"Yeah, but...That's what I do. Hours in the gym, hours shopping for clothes, hours getting my hair done, the makeup, the shoes. All that money. Never eating anything good. Never eating at all, practically. All so I can look like one of those stupid mannequins, instead of a real living person. And I guess I do."

"Sounds like it saved your life," said Ellie.

"I guess," said Sherry. "But if I get out this, the first thing I'm going to do is go straight to Stefanelli's chocolates."

"You go, girl," said Rick.

"Sorry I didn't save you a Mighty Fine Donut," said Dipstick.

"Yeah," said Tristan. "Step one in Dipstick's Treat Your Body Like a Garbage Can program."

"Hey, they didn't know I was alive, either," said Bart McClain. "I walked right through them, and they didn't even notice me. I'm old, so what else is new? It saved my life, too, but I see what you mean, sweetheart, in a way it's sort of an insult."

"Ok, I'll tell you about my worst Christmas," said Brian. "But first I'll tell you about my best Christmas."

"Is this going to be a Hallmark movie?" asked Dipstick.

"No, the two are related," said Brian. "The best Christmas I can remember is the first Christmas I can remember. I don't remember if I was three, four or five. I'm thinking I was four. My older brother had the Mouse Trap Game, anybody remember the Mouse Trap Game?"

"Sure, that Rube Goldberg thing," said Tristan.

"Exactly," said Brian. "You rolled the ball, and there was a big chain reaction, and if it rolled right, which it almost never did, the trap would fall on your mouse, if you were under it."

"They still make it," said Engelsdorf.

"So like I said, my brother had it, and I was absolutely fascinated by it. So the first Christmas I can remember, I'm up before dawn. I'll never forget that it was still dark in the living room, and my parents gave me my big present, and it was the Mouse Trap Game. There aren't many moments in my whole life that I can remember being quite so excited. It was only years later that I realized that they didn't give me my own Mouse Trap Game, they gave me my brother's Mouse Trap Game. We weren't a rich family, and they talked him into giving it to me, and I was too little to notice there wasn't any plastic wrap on the box."

"Are you sure about this?" asked Ellie.

"Yeah, it occurred to me years later, when I was in college, that that was what they had done, and my Mom confirmed it when I asked her."

"Second hand present," said Engelsdorf. "That sucks."

"It didn't suck at all," said Brian. "It was the best imaginable present at the time, and when I realized it later, it made me realize how hard my parents and all my family had worked to give me a good Christmas when I was little. Best Christmas ever."

"OK, that's nice," said Dipstick. "Now what about the worst?"

"Well, the next few years, when I was five, six, seven, were all great Christmases. I think it was the next year I got Incredible Edibles. Anybody remember them? A little oven in the shape of a clown head. You put this goop in these little molds, and put them in the little clown head oven and it baked them into these jelly candies in the shapes of bugs and snakes and stuff."

"Sounds pretty dangerous," said Andrea.

"It was," said Brian. "You'd burn the shit out of your fingers again and again. Plus, the candy tasted genuinely disgusting. It was great. Then the year after that, I got the Strange Change Time Machine. It was another oven, with this clear-plastic dome in it, and you put these little plastic cubes in it, and they were made out of memory plastic, and as you heated them up they'd unfold into a dinosaur or an alien or something. I guess the idea was that you were sort of grabbing them out of the past or the future or whatever. Something like that. Then there was a little hand-cranked press on the side, and when you were done playing with the monsters, you'd use it to crush them back into cubes."

"Also sounds dangerous," said Andrea.

"It sounds cool," said Engelsdorf.

"It was both," said Brian. "But here's the thing. I look back on all those Christmases when I was a kid, and what occurs to me is that my memories of my family, the food, the singing, going to church, parties at school, the tree, the lights, the stuff on TV…all those memories are dim. But my memory of my big present every year, whatever it was, that's what's crystal-clear."

"That's natural," said Andrea. "You were a kid."

"Maybe," said Brian. "Or maybe I was just a selfish, acquisitive little consumerist prick who happened to be a kid. Maybe now I'm an old prick."

"No maybe about it," said Rick, without looking up from his smartphone.

"So now we come to when I was, I guess, about ten. For some reason I snooped in the cellar, a week or so before Christmas, and I found them. Rock'em Sock'em Robots."

"Right on," said Engelsdorf. "Made by Marx Toys, right here in Erie."

"Yeah," said Brian. "But I was so gleeful at having found them, that I told my Mom that I did. And she yelled at me, and then sat down at the kitchen table and cried. They were broke again that year, and here I'd found the biggest gift they had for me."

"Jesus, why'd you tell her?" asked Engelsdorf.

"I don't fucking know. I guess I thought she'd think I was smart or something. I really don't know. I'm just an asshole, I guess."

"Again, you were a kid," said Andrea.

"By Christmas morning, she'd forgiven me, and I made a big fuss over the game, which really was a cool game, and I guess it was OK. But Christmas was never the same for me after that. And I had that game for years, on the shelf in my room, but just about every time I looked at it, it was like ashes in my mouth. I'd just remember my Mom, crying at the kitchen table."

"Jesus, this is depressing," said Dipstick. "Let's call off the game."

"Presents," said Brian. "Anybody tells you Christmas isn't about presents, they're full of shit. Presents are why all those people are out there in that mall, tearing each other apart, eating each other alive. Fucking Santa Claus."

"Donnie?" said Teddy. He was looking down at the floor. He hadn't spoken in a while.

"Got a story for us, Ted?" asked Engelsdorf.

"No," said Teddy. "I was just wondering. You got two shells left for your shotgun, right?"

He looked up. His face had gone bluish-gray, and there were bags under his eyes.

"No!" said Sherry.

"Jesus God!" said Brian. "What the fuck happened?"

"That woman out there did a Mike Tyson on my ear," he said, and swept back his long dark hair to show it. There was a tiny red spot at the end of his left earlobe. A web of purple-gray streaks had spread from it across the side of his head and down his neck.

"She barely made contact, so I thought maybe I wasn't infected. I guess I was kidding myself. I don't feel so great. I've been sitting here watching my hands turn gray."

"He has to get out." said Rick. "Right now."

"Shut up," said Brian.

"No, Bri, I think he's right," said Teddy. "Donnie? How many shells?"

"Two," said Engelsdorf.

"Teddy. Teddy, hang on, there's got to be something…"

"Chill out, Bri, there isn't," said Teddy. He reached inside his jacket, and drew out a small object, wrapped in plastic bags. He tossed it onto Engelsdorf's lap.

"Since we didn't complete the earlier deal, how about a new one? You get this for one of those shells."

"You're not blowing his brains out in here," said Rick. "Besides, we might need that shell, and we don't need the noise. He just has to leave. Maybe they'll take him apart, or maybe he's too far gone and he just turns, but either way he has to get out of…"

"Motherfucker, if you don't shut up…" said Brian.

"All of you shut up!" barked Teddy. "I'm leaving, asshole, don't worry. But I think you guys can spare one shell. Donnie, I'll step outside, you pull the door shut, leave just a crack for the barrel, I'll stand with my back to you, you put it to my head. OK?"

"Teddy, listen…"

"Shut up, Brian. Donnie?"

There was a long silence. Engelsdorf had picked up the shotgun and was clutching it on his lap.

"I don't know if I can do that," said Engelsdorf.

"You did it back there," said Teddy. His voice was a croak. "It's no different. Come on, man, any minute you guys are going to look like the soup and salad bar at Barbato's to me."

"If you can't do it, I'll do it," said McClain. "I can shoot."

"No," said Engelsdorf. "I'll do it."

"Fuck," said Brian. He slumped his head forward and began to sob.

Engelsdorf picked up the little package Teddy had thrown him. "I don't need this, man."

Teddy managed a smile. "All these years, you sure talked like you needed it," he said. "Anyway, the fuck good is it to me now? You get out of here, and enjoy it in good health."

"You have to do it now, if you're going to do it," said Rick to Englesdorf. "He'll be gone in a minute or so."

"You're very authoritative about this," said Ellie.

Teddy got to his feet.

"Brian," he croaked out. "Brian!"

Brian looked up.

"Do me a favor," Teddy continued. "Tell my mom and my sisters that I loved them. Tell them Merry Christmas for me. I have presents for them in my closet. Just little shit, but see that they get them, OK?"

"OK," said Brian helplessly.

"And give my love to Logan, too, will you?"

"You were a better father to him than I was."

"I think that's bullshit, but if you think so, then be a better father to him. Just spend time with him, that's really all there is to it, I think. He's a good kid."

"OK," said Brian again.

"Like any of us are going to get out of here to do all these wonderful things," muttered Dipstick.

"You sure about this?" said Engelsdorf, getting to his feet.

"There's no choice. Good luck, you guys," said Teddy. "Merry Christmas."

"Fuck you," said Brian, and Teddy smiled. He opened the door, took two steps forward, and stood still, with his back to the booth, angled away.

Some of the Dead noticed the activity, and began to plod toward the booth. In the lead was the scraggly-haired woman in the bulky black coat.

"You again," croaked Teddy.

"Hurry the fuck up," said Rick.

Engelsdorf drew the door to a crack, through which he extended the barrel of the shotgun. He pulled back the hammer, curled his finger around the trigger. Brian lowered his head again. Sherry covered her ears.

But Engelsdorf hesitated.

"Dude," said Tristan.

The scraggly-haired woman hesitated, too, pausing just a few feet in front of Teddy, eyeing him uncertainly. Teddy's head slumped and his shoulders sagged.

"Shoot him now," said Ellie firmly, and Engelsdorf squeezed the trigger, and the shotgun boomed but as it did Teddy toppled forward and landed face-down on the floor. The blast went over his head and caught the scraggly-haired woman in the forehead, tumbling her backward.

"No! Fuck!" yelled Engelsdorf.

"Get inside! Close the door!" yelled Ellie, and Engelsdorf obeyed.

"Idiot," said McClain. "I told you I'd do it if you couldn't."

Once again, the Dead crowded around the booth. Within a few seconds, Teddy Mrozowski had clambered to his feet and joined them, staring down hungrily.

9.

"Mr. Snyderwine? This is Marvin at White Lake."

"Go ahead, Marvin."

"The 12th Street site has been successfully sterilized."

"Good job. What's the media saying?"

"The cloud cover must have hidden the aircraft. They're speculating that it might have been an industrial accident."

"They'll think differently after the Mall gets it. But we'll deal with it. What's our prima donna in the Bahamas say about that?"

"He said he'd have an answer for us within half an hour."

10.

Within five minutes they'd lost interest and wandered off, Teddy among them.

"You stupid shithead," said Brian, as soon as it was safe to talk.

"I'm sorry," said the tearful Engelsdorf. "You can't say anything to me that's worse than what I'm saying to myself."

"Let me give it a try," said Brian.

"No, let it go," said Andrea. "Nothing we can do about it now. Just let it go."

"Guns," said Brian, glaring at Engelsdorf. "You shitheads and your guns. Your bangsticks, your fucking penis extenders. You blasted that fucker in your stockroom like you were playing a video game. Which, as a matter of fact, is why you had the fucking gun with you today. You were prepared to kill people to *defend* a fucking video game. But when it counted, when it could have really meant something..."

"I didn't know the guy in the stockroom," said Engelsdorf quietly.

"No, but you knew Teddy, didn't you?" said Brian. "You knew what he wanted. He wanted to go with dignity. That's all he had left."

"He did go with dignity," said Ellie. "That isn't him out there. Now like she said, let it go, before the rest of us go with considerably less dignity."

"Which we're all going to do anyway," said Dipstick. "Let's face it, the cops aren't coming in here to get us. Nobody's coming, and I don't blame them. We're all going to die today. We're all going to get eaten alive."

"Well ain't you got the Christmas cheer?" said McClain.

"I'm not going to see Christmas this year, Mister."

"What's in the package?" said Brian to Engelsdorf.

"What?"

"What did he give you? What were you willing to trade for your fucking game?"

After a pause, Engelsdorf unwrapped the plastic bag to reveal a padded envelope, from which he drew a .45 record.

"A .45?" said Brian.

"I'm a vinylhead, like Teddy."

"What's the song?" asked Tristan.

"It's called 'Hey Joe,' by Euphoria's Id." Engelsdorf's tone was sheepish. "Garage band out of Saco, Maine. Recorded this in 1967. Hard as shit to find an original pressing."

"You said you had a guy from Buffalo would've paid you a grand for that game. Was this record really worth that much?"

"Well, I bid on one online a few years ago that ended up going for nine hundred bucks. But I had to drop out at a hundred bucks. You hardly ever see it for sale, and I could never pay for it if it was. I envied Teddy this thing for a long time."

"Give it here," said Brian, sticking out his hand.

"Why should I? Teddy gave it to me," said Engelsdorf

"Really?" said Brian. "You're going to argue with me on this? After your performance just now? Give me the fucking .45."

Engelsdorf stared at him for a few seconds, then handed the envelope to Brian.

"Well, thank God we got that cleared up," said Rick. He had been looking down at his smartphone, now he spoke to Ellie. "Alright, listen up. The Oprah marathon is over. In thirty or forty minutes, an hour at most, we'll all be gone."

"What are you talking about?" asked Dipstick.

"What I said. In a very short time, we'll all be gone. And I don't just mean dead. I mean gone. Everybody in here, and those dead fuckers out there, and this whole pathetic mall. In an hour or so at most, we'll all be rubble."

"We'll all be rubble. How do you know this?" asked Tristan.

Rick held up his smartphone. "Because according to news media, including your own radio station, the Micromegas plant as just been wiped out in a massive explosion."

"Micromegas?" said Andrea. "Isn't that the place on 12th street everybody was protesting awhile back?"

"They blew up? Jesus," said Tristan. "OK, so what does that have to do with us?"

"The media are speculating that it might have been some sort of chemical explosion in the plant. It wasn't. The plant was destroyed by a U.S. Air Force bomb called an MOP. Massive Ordnance Penetrator. Nothing Freudian there, right? It's a big-ass non-nuclear contingency plan you drop from a stealth bomber."

"Again, you know this how?" asked Brian, and then he looked at Ellie. "You said he came with you. Who is this asshole?"

"He's from Micromegas," said Ellie. "I'm a helicopter pilot. I got hired to fly him down to the plant on 12ᵗʰ Street. Apparently they found him as charming down there as we have, because when we were leaving, somebody started taking shots at us. We took a hit, and had to do an emergency landing. That's how we ended up here. We came into the mall looking for duct tape."

"So we have this guy to thank for this shit," said Brian. "That makes perfect sense."

"Do you work for the government?" Sherry asked Rick.

"Not at all," said Rick. "I work for the people the government works for. You vote, we pay. The plant was destroyed at the request of my boss. And by now, he'll have heard about the situation here and realized that we didn't contain things at the plant as well as we'd hoped, and he'll advise our friends in the government that this mall needs to be, let's say, sterilized in the same way. In the meantime, he has a corporate subsidiary called White Lake. They call themselves corporate security consultants. White Lake operatives will already have a perimeter set up around the mall, and anybody, alive or dead, who goes out a ground floor exit will be shot before he gets five paces."

"Well, can't you, like, text your boss or whatever?" said Engelsdorf. "Tell him you're alive in here, tell him to call it off?"

Rick laughed. "I'd guess that my boss would be only too delighted to know for sure that I'm in here. That would be dotting the T's and crossing the I's. That's why I neglected to call in and tell him that we had flown away from the plant. At the moment he may be wondering if I'm part of the rubble down there, an idea I'm sure delights him. I'm married to his daughter, and the father of his granddaughter. He hates my guts."

"Why am I not surprised?" asked Andrea.

"OK, so, you've got a helicopter?" Tristan asked Ellie. "Where? Up on the rooftop?"

"Yeah," said Ellie. "But the door to the stairs locked behind us."

"No problem, I have the key," said Tristan, pulling a keyring from his pocket and holding it up. "They gave it to me so we didn't have to use the public johns. Will the helicopter fly?"

"Not very far," said Ellie. "Maybe half a mile. More if we had the duct tape. Then we'll have to hope we can find someplace to set down fast."

"There's a roll of duct tape in the stockroom," said Engelsdorf. "Be a bitch to go get it, though. The stockroom's a dead end."

"We might not need it. Half a mile might be enough," said Tristan. "You said the bomb wasn't a nuke, right?"

"It's worth a try," said Dipstick. "Let's make a run for the roof."

"There's a problem," said Ellie. "The A-Star seats six. After me and this prick, that leaves four seats for seven people."

"I'll stand," said Dipstick.

"Sorry, but no way. It may not take off at all, but it definitely won't if we overload it."

There was a pause in the room.

"OK, we draw lots," said Dipstick.

He reached up and took down a notepad and pen from the counter, and tore off seven sheets. Then he marked an X on four of them, and began folding them in half.

"I ain't drawing no lots," said Bart McClain.

"It's the only fair way, Mister," said Dipstick. "You'll have the same chance as anyone else."

"I ain't getting on no helicopter," said McClain, struggling to his feet, and pulling on his Erie Seawolves cap. "Besides, I've had to take a piss for the last two hours. Merry Christmas, everybody. Your chances all just got better by one. I'm going to go see if I can find that digital camera." He headed for the door.

"You want your jacket back?" asked Sherry.

"No, you keep it, sweetheart. Stay warm." McClain looked around the booth. "All of you. Do the best you can to stay warm." He reached for the door handle.

"Mr. McClain, wait..." began Andrea.

But he didn't. They all watched as Bart McClain opened the door, slipped through, and softly closed it behind him. A few of the nearby Dead glanced listlessly toward the booth at the sound, but when McClain began to walk away from it in an unhurried manner, they lost interest. The group in the booth watched him walk calmly away down the long main concourse, the direction from which he had come.

"That guy rocks," said Tristan.

"Yeah, he does," said Dipstick. "But if this asshole's right, we've got to do this fast." He shuffled the folded slips of paper, and spread them out on the floor. "All right, draw. Don't look until everybody's drawn. I'll go last."

Tristan, Andrea, Dipstick, Engelsdorf, Sherry and Brian each picked up a slip.

"OK, open them up," said Dipstick.

But then there was a click behind them.

They all turned. Rick was standing by the door, his trench coat draped over one arm, pointing a .40 semi-automatic at them with the other.

"I thought I made myself clear," he said. "The bullshit hour is over. This is my company's helicopter, and none of you are invited."

"Fuckhead," said Dipstick.

"Shouldn't that be 'None of you *is* invited?'" asked Andrea.

"Yeah, the sparkling repartee has been a joy," said Rick. "But he travels fastest who travels alone, unless he travels by helicopter, in which case he travels fastest who travels with a helicopter pilot and nobody else. So me and the Bond Girl here are going to say our Merry Christmases right now, and be going." He looked at Tristan. "I will take that key, though."

"You were packing, all this time?" said Ellie.

"One of the perks of using company aircraft."

"Well, look, this is your pilot speaking," said Ellie. "I say we take as many as we can carry."

"I see," said Rick. "OK, let's make this easy. I've already shot somebody today, so why not..." He leveled the gun at Tristan's head.

11.

Teddy heard the shot.

Teddy, or what was left of Teddy, or the rapacious mass of polluted flesh that took Teddy's place, was milling around aimlessly beside a fallen Christmas tree fifty yards from the booth. His head, and the heads of dozens of other Dead nearby, cranked slowly around at the muffled sound of a gunshot.

There was some sort of struggle going on among the Living People over there.

Teddy headed toward the booth, the others stumbling along behind.

12.

"Open the door, dude," said Tristan.

"Let go of me, you stupid fucks," said Rick, writhing.

Tristan and Dipstick held him, one arm each twisted behind his back, and were dragging him toward the door, while he struggled and kicked at them with his one good leg. Engelsdorf reached for the door handle.

"Wait a second," said Andrea. "We can't do this...we can't..."

"No shit, Andrea?" said Tristan. "We can't do this? You saw him point the gun at my head, right?"

They had all seen it. Rick leveled the semiautomatic, and there was a loud bang in the booth, but it was Rick who had barked in pain and fallen, dropping the gun and clutching at his leg. Sherry screamed, and then they all turned, and there was Brian, with a revolver in his hands.

"The cop's gun," Engelsdorf had said. "One bullet left."

So Andrea said nothing, and neither did Ellie or Sherry, and neither did Brian, who sat on the floor, still holding the cop's gun and staring into space.

Engelsdorf opened the door.

"OK pal," said Tristan, as he and Dipstick pulled Rick forward. "The next thirty or forty seconds are really going to suck for you. Hold still if you can, maybe that'll make it go faster. Good news is, there probably won't be enough of you left to become one of them."

"No, no, listen to me you assholes, let me go," Rick babbled. "I just overreacted, OK? We'll all go on the helicopter, everybody we can carry, like she says, no, no, listen, please, my briefcase there, there's a hundred grand in it, in cash, you can have it all..."

"Thanks," said Dipstick, and they flung him headlong out of the booth.

Engelsdorf slammed the door, and Tristan locked it. Outside, Rick got up, drops of bright red blood falling from his pant-leg, and looked at them with the most twisted expression of rage any of them had ever seen. He began to hobble toward the booth, when suddenly Teddy, uncrippled and swift of stride among the Dead, was upon him. He sank his teeth lustily into Rick's throat, more red blood spurted upward, and the two of them fell together to the floor.

A couple of seconds later, from the other direction, a burly Latino man with both legs missing at the knees came scuttling up on strong arms and lunged for Rick's belly, and a few seconds after that dozens of the Dead were clustered upon him, tearing at his joints, his face, his guts, his groin. It went faster than Tristan predicted—in twenty seconds Rick was in twenty pieces, each piece being listlessly fought over by three or four of the Dead.

"An extra seat just opened up on the A-Star," said Ellie.

"Yeah. Let's draw again," said Andrea, and she gathered up the slips of paper, put an X on one more of them, and shuffled them. "This time I'll go last."

They drew again.

13.

"Mr. Snyderwine? This is Marvin at White Lake."

"Go ahead, Marvin."

"Our friend just informed us he's been given authorization for the Millcreek Mall."

"Green light, Marvin."

14.

When it was Brian's turn, he sat there staring until Englesdorf nudged him. Then he drew, and then Andrea drew.
When Brian opened his slip, he saw that it had an X on it.

"Shit," said Engelsdorf. Brian turned, and saw the blank
slip drop from his hand.

"Sorry, dude," said Dipstick.

"It's OK," said Englesdorf, his voice breaking. It didn't
sound like it was OK with him at all. "Getting that fucking
record from Teddy was too much luck for one day, I knew it.
I thought maybe if I gave it back to this guy, I'd get enough
luck back to get out of here, but I guess not..." He pressed
his fists to his eyes, and tears streamed out from under them.

"Would duct tape really help?" Brian found himself
asking Ellie.

"What?"

"You mentioned needing duct tape. Would that really
help?"

"Yeah, I think with a couple of strips to patch the line we
could probably get back to the airpark."

"And you," said Brian to Engelsdorf. He shook him gently. "Hey. You said you have some duct tape back in the stockroom?"

"Yeah," whimpered Engelsdorf. "I'll tell you were to find it."

"No you won't," said Brian. "You'll go get it yourself, and then you'll take my seat. I'll stay here." He tossed him his slip of paper.

"Fuck you," said Engelsdorf.

"You'll take my seat, and I'll stay here," repeated Brian. He took down the notepad, scribbled on it, and tore off the sheet. "Just one thing. While you're in there, grab that fucking game. Take it to my son Logan. Here's the address." He handed Engelsdorf the paper. "Get it to him by tomorrow morning, OK?"

Engelsdorf stared at him.

"Yes, Virginia…" said Andrea, wonder in her voice.

"Here, here's your record," said Brian to Engelsdorf, handing him back the padded envelope. "Like Teddy said, listen to it in good health. Or stick your dick through the middle of it and jerk off, or whatever it is you vinylheads do for fun. That completes our trade, right?"

"Yes it does," said Engelsdorf softly.

"Guys!" said Ellie. "Guys. This is all very nice, but we aren't doing it. We go into that stockroom, those things will follow us, and there's no way out. The back door is chained, right? It's a death trap. We can't go in there, not even for duct tape, let alone for some Christmas present."

"You can if they aren't following you," said Brian, getting to his feet. "Which they won't be, because they'll be following me."

He picked up his baseball bat and stepped toward the door.

"Which way do you have to go get to your helicopter?" he asked.

Ellie pointed down the west concourse.

"OK, I'll head that way," said Brian, pointing up the south concourse. "They'll follow me, which should give you time to get in and out of your stockroom. As soon as you get back out, you can make a break for it."

"Here, here's a present from me," said Engelsdorf. He held out the shotgun. "One shell left. Use it wisely."

"Keep it. You might need it," said Brian.

"Nah, I've got Rick's gun," said Engelsdorf. "Easier to carry, and five bullets in it. Anyway, you've already shown you're better with a gun than I am."

"Yeah, and in case I forgot to mention it, thank you," said Tristan.

"OK," said Brian, taking the shotgun. "Thank you."

"Are you sure you want to do this?" said Ellie.

Brian pointed at the Dead to the left of the door. They were still squabbling over the little that was left of Rick, except for Teddy. Gracious even as a ghoul, he sat a little apart from the crowd, chewing on the fingers of Rick's right hand like they were chicken wings.

"That's my best friend," Brian said. "He came here today so that I could get that stupid game for my kid. That's why this happened to him. Yeah, I'm sure I want to do this."

With that, he opened the door and stepped boldly out of the booth. The Dead looked up and, already losing interest in the remaining scraps of Rick, began to get to their feet.

Brian walked over to his roommate. Teddy looked up at him without recognition.

"Teddy, I'm so sorry," he said, and swung the baseball bat Teddy had handed him a few hours earlier, one-handed, in an arc over his head. It came down with a crunch, caving in Teddy's skull. Teddy flopped backward and lay still.

Brian raised his arms, the bat in his right hand, the shotgun in his left.

"Alright, you fuckers, come and get me," he yelled. "Let's see if you can catch your Christmas dinner."

And off he ran up the south concourse, the Dead following in their dozens and hundreds. Within a few minutes, the people in the booth found their area nearly free of ambulatory corpses.

"OK, folks, he's cleared the way," said Ellie. "Toyman, you're on. Let's go. If there's anything any of you could use as a weapon, grab it."

They all got up. Dipstick was holding Rick's suitcase.

"This is nice and heavy, and it has a handle," he said." "I'll carry this."

"Fine," said Ellie, and managed to keep *But if we get out of here you owe me five thousand* from coming out after.

"Look at this," said Tristan. He was rifling the pockets of Rick's trench coat. "Here's that cell phone he was married to, and here's what looks like a flash drive. Pilot lady?"

"Ellie."

"Ellie, right. Sorry. Listen, I have a suggestion."

"What's that, radio man?"

"Well, if what your late friend Rick said is even a little bit true, doesn't it seem like somebody might be waiting for us, if you go back to where you picked him up?"

"Mm...I guess so."

"I'm thinking if we get off the ground, maybe we should think about landing somewhere else, a parking lot, a high school football field, someplace like that, and seeing if we can't blend in to a populated area. If we can get to a computer

246

and post videos of what we saw, and maybe some of the stuff on this phone or this flash drive, it might improve our chances of still being around for New Years, at least a little.

"That might not be a bad idea, now that you mention it. But first things first, OK? Let's get out of here."

"Solid strategy," said Tristan.

Ellie opened the door, and the six of them headed for JayDee's Toys at a trot, leaving the booth empty.

15.

Brian was thinking, as he ran, of a movie he'd watched recently. It wasn't a Christmas movie. What the hell was it called?

Yul Brynner played a Cossack, and he and his followers were riding somewhere really fast, and as they did more and more Cossacks on horseback kept falling in behind them, with this great music playing, and shouting out Cossack-ish words to each other and generally being very hearty. Brian had found it quite exhilarating.

The Dead were falling in behind him like the Cossacks, except that the Cossacks hadn't wanted to eat Yul Brynner.

And Brian was no Yul Brynner. He was an out-of-shape, underemployed movie theater manager. And he didn't have a horse. He was out of breath, and a hitch was stabbing his side, and he was carrying a shotgun and a baseball bat. He couldn't keep running much longer.

The food court entrance was blocked by another drift of writhing Dead. No way out there. No way out anywhere, if what Rick said was true.

He knew where he wanted to go, anyway. There was something he had to see.

He turned and began to run a wide curve around the far side of the food court. The Horde turned and started toward him.

Brian wanted to head back the way he came, but the Dead blocked the path. He'd have to go around the other way. Three or four of them were closing fast, only a few feet away, reaching. He swung and swung the bat one-handed, cracking skulls, then dodged to the right and jogged down the east concourse.

An enormous collective groan issued from the Horde as they advanced after him. The path ahead of him was clear. He glanced over his shoulder. There were thousands of them. All of them, it seemed like.

He jogged to the left, into the Main Concourse from the other side. As he passed the now-empty radio booth, from up above, he could hear the whirring of the helicopter's rotors.

Well, at least they got airborne, Brian thought.

He felt a wave of envious, terrified rage wash over him. Part of it, he knew, was simple fear of what he knew would soon happen to him. But it was also partly the anger he'd felt as a kid, when his older brothers and sisters got to go somewhere—a Christmas party, say—and he had to stay home.

Then he thought of Teddy, lying on his back just a few yards away, and the feeling passed surprisingly quickly.

He trotted on, really tired now, into the toy store. As he passed the baseball display, he tossed his bat to the floor next to it. Something told him that he wasn't going to be needing it any more.

He paused at the entrance to the stockroom, and looked back. The Horde came toward the store, a moving wall of the Dead, filling the entrance.

Brian pushed through into the outer stockroom, then through hanging plastic strips. He let out a sharp yell of triumph as he saw that *Treasure of Dino-Dragon Island* was gone from the table. Engelsdorf and the others hadn't fucked him over. Logan would get his present.

He turned into the long hallway. The plaid-shirted man that Engelsdorf had shot was still there, just standing there, his head hanging backwards out of sight.

"Hi Buddy," said Brian. As before, the dead man turned to see who had spoken to him, stepped away, and turned again, caught in his pirouetting walk to nowhere.

Brian slipped past him and ran on, to the idiotically chained door.

Then he turned and looked up the hallway. He cracked the shotgun and checked. One shell left.

16.

"Mr. Snyderwine? This is Marvin, at White Lake."

"Go ahead, Marvin."

"Sir, our friend tells us that the airstrike on the mall is about three minutes out. But there's a wrinkle."

"What now?"

"Sir, our ground units reported that your company helicopter just took off from the roof of the mall."

"You're kidding me."

"No sir. It departed about a minute and a half ago."

"So my son-in-law is still alive."

"That's our current theory, sir."

"Slippery little bastard. He's trying to get to the Lear."

"That was our guess too. I took the liberty of sending two operatives to…what's it called…to Grandhill Airpark to intercept him."

"There's a bonus in it for them if they do. And for you, too, Marvin. Have them board the Lear with him, and then give him his severance package once they're airborne. It's a Christmas present I'm giving myself."

"Yes, sir."

"Marvin, I'm sorry you've had to spend your Christmas Eve dealing with this. I'm sure you'd rather be with your family."

"They understand, and I'm happy to help. Merry Christmas, sir."

"Merry Christmas, Marvin."

17.

Around the corner they came, blank eyed, open mouthed, lurching and shuffling and groaning as they advanced, swarming past the plaid-shirted man, Santa at the lead. Brian let out a whimper and backed up a few steps, but he cocked the shotgun.

This is it, he thought. *Like Tristan had said to Rick, the next twenty or thirty seconds are really going to suck. But at least, with this many of the bastards, there shouldn't be enough of me left to join their ranks.*

Two other thoughts gave him a fleeting comfort, if not joy. First, he was done with his Christmas shopping. And second, he had one shell left. Which meant that Santa here, at least, wasn't going to get a bite of him.

He leveled the shotgun.

"God bless us, every fucking one," he said, and then he blew Santa's head to pieces.

NOTE

This story was first published, in a very slightly different form, in 2012. The world scene changes a lot in eight years, so for this reissue I considered trying to update the cultural references, but in the end I decided against it.

There really is a Millcreek Mall, just south of Erie on Peach Street; I misspent a good deal of time and money there myself as a youth. Those who know the place, however, will see that my treatment of its interior geography, and its tenants, is fictional in this story. Likewise, there is no Micromegas plant on West 12ᵗʰ Street, and (I hope) no plant anywhere engaged in that sort of experimental pursuit. Grandhill Aviation, WSER and JayDee's Toys are also made-up. A couple of establishments mentioned in the story—Barbato's Italian Restaurant, Mighty Fine Donuts and Stefanelli's Candies, for instance—are real, and I encourage you to visit Erie and patronize them. But most of the firms here are products of the author's imagination, as are all of the characters.

I owe bottomless gratitude as always to, first, my wife, daughter and dogs, and to all of my family and friends but especially Barry Graham, Ron Strecker, Stan Tuznik, David Gofstein, Elan Head, James Ward, Owen Kerr, Gayle Bass, Lory Varo, Tom Maggio, Deana Sills, Richard Roberts, Mark Tiemeyer, Suzy Newman, Ramin Ackert, Steven Schwartz and Jon Bourke, along with my late and lamented pal Brian Braastad, an enthusiastic early fan of this story.

And to Margaret Alice Warroch for the kind of editing few authors are fortunate enough to receive.

The back cover art is by Vince LaRue.

Lightning Source UK Ltd.
Milton Keynes UK
UKHW010638140122
397142UK00002B/290